THE FUTURE IS SET

A JOSH BRANNON SCI-FI ACTION THRILLER

Nigel Billington

THE FUTURE IS SET by Nigel Billington, 2nd Edition.

ISBN - 978-0-620-93743-6 (e-book)

ISBN - 978-0-6397-2185-9 (paperback)

ISBN - 978-0-6397-2186-6 (hardcover)

Cover Artwork

Cover design: Nigel Billington. Cover photograph: Freida Mcmurtrie. Cover photograph: pixy.org

How can you

break free from a

lie you cannot see?

CHAPTER 1

"Josh! Josh!" came a loud cry. "Get out of bed you lazy bugger!" yelled his mother.

Josh was in his last year at school and had no desire to rise from his warm comfortable bed, especially to push a pen around in subjects he detested. Always he would lie there to the last minute he could squeeze out, before his mother would thump along to his room with heavy footsteps—an early warning to get himself up. She was always ready and very willing to give him a clout. She didn't need excuses for a good thump. "Life moulding" or "character building" she would call it.

"You up yet!" she shouted. "Your breakfast is getting cold!"

Josh knew the different tones of her voice, before she would make that trip to his room for the awakening "life builder" across his head. He knew this was the time to get motivated.

He wasn't scared of his mother, but their relationship was such that if Josh put one foot wrong, she would kick him out of the flat. His earlier childhood years was a routine of waiting for her to return home from work—he was your typical latchkey kid—then getting to bed quickly, before his father would come home from a hard day's drinking.

Josh never saw much of his father in his early childhood years, as he was always one to be avoided. His father's temper had given him an unsavoury reputation around the local towns, especially when drunk, which was most of the time. His life consisted of propping up the bar, coming home and going to bed. He was a registered alcoholic, but was refused more meetings at the local "Alcoholics Anonymous" group because of his persistent trouble-making. The last straw came when he broke the nose of one of the counsellors.

Josh's father left the family home about two years ago after a serious fight, resulting in Josh's mother receiving several broken bones. She had tried to defend Josh from another beating. She was hospitalised for about a month and his father was arrested and charged for the assault. He was remanded in prison and later sentenced to one year. This left Josh to look after himself, but he was used to that anyway; he was just glad to get shot of his dad.

He had last heard that his father had gotten into some very serious trouble with a local drug dealer, and that this drug dealer had connections to some organised crime syndicate. The circulating story on the grapevine was that he ended up with a bullet in the head for shooting his mouth off to the wrong people. Apparently, according to the story, he's now helping to support a motorway structure somewhere, but this has never been proven, although he is still officially reported as missing.

Now, Josh and his mother live alone in an old rundown council block flat. The block of flats was condemned years ago. It was supposed to be knocked down, but in some government budget-saving-scheme all they did was make a few repairs and tart it up with paint and plants. Every morning, Josh had to mop up the damp spots on the walls—his morning chore before going to school.

He got dressed and plodded to the kitchen for his regular morning feast of egg. It was always a surprise to see what form she had turned an egg into. Was it fried, scrambled, poached, or boiled this time? The anticipation was far too much. This was part of their daily routine and Josh hated it, but always managed to hide his feelings well.

"You're going to be bloody late again, and I'm not writing anymore notes to your teacher!" she barked. "They must think I'm a bad mother. And look at the state of you!"

Josh gave the usual nonchalant replies and gestures as he took a seat at the table to eat.

"I need some money," he asked sheepishly, but knowing it was pointless as she was always scrimping and saving what money she could get. She only had a low paid job and relied heavily on government benefits to get by; life was tough.

"What do you need money for?" began his mother's interrogation.

Josh didn't bother to explain, or ask again. He gave up straight away at his mother's stern tone. He could feel a "life changing" warm ear coming on.

"Oh, it doesn't matter," Josh quietly replied.

He had an after-school job at a newsagent but it didn't pay much. He was only fifteen and his employer only paid the minimum amount he was legally obliged to—he was tighter than a duck's arse when it came to money. So, what little money Josh did earn had to go towards the food and bills to help his mum.

"Have you washed?" she carped, looking at him thoroughly from the side.

"Yeah," replied Josh.

WHACK! There it was, first one of the day. Josh felt "enlightened" by the blow across the back of his head whilst stuffing down his scrambled egg.

"Don't lie to me!" she snapped back. "Get and have a wash! You might be getting older but you're not too old for a clip round the ear!"

Josh didn't complain as he knew it would be futile to do so, he just gave his usual agreeable reply. It didn't matter if he had washed or not, he would still do as he was told. He never stood his ground despite being quite strong physically; he bore too many mental scars from times gone by to really care.

He went to the bathroom and splashed some water on the fringe of his hair to make it appear more convincing he had washed. He then waited a minute or so before going back to the kitchen to finish his scrambled egg. He could feel his mum scrutinising his appearance when he reappeared, and when she finished her inspection and walked out of the kitchen, he smiled inwardly to himself, knowing he had fooled her.

One thing Josh was good at was deception. He had to learn it the hard way through the many beatings he endured by his father. He had developed an innate ability to convincingly pull the wool over people's eyes.

"I'm going to school!" shouted Josh, after finishing his meal.

"Have you mopped the water up?" his mum shouted back.

"Yeah, I've just done it!" and he quickly reached for the sponge, wiped it over the damp wall with a single stroke and put it back. "See you later!" His mum gave no reply.

Josh grabbed his coat hanging by the door and put it on. He stepped out of the flat to be faced by fresh graffiti spray-painted on the wall of his neighbour's flat, in bright red capital letters: "PEDOFILE LIVES HEAR". The misspelled words were indicative of the poorly educated residents that lived in the neighbourhood.

The man who lived in the flat, Josh's neighbour, was often taunted by the locals because he was once accused of being a paedophile after trying to help a young girl who looked lost. The mother, in a frantic crazy state, thought he was trying to walk off with her, and so put notices up about him around the estate. The woman was convicted of harassment by the courts, but the fire she started of him being a "paedophile" never went out, and stuck with the community.

Josh knew the guy, and would talk to him now and then. He found out that his wife and two children were killed in a hit-and-run accident, and he had never really recovered. He just shut himself away on his own.

Using an old discarded rag from the floor, and soaking it in water from a balcony plant pot, Josh attempted to smudge the spray-painted letters together so they couldn't be read, but the paint had already dried. He turned to see his neighbour looking out of his kitchen window at him. The man nodded at him for the kind gesture of trying to remove it. Josh returned a smile of disappointment, not because he couldn't remove the graffiti, but because of how people treated each other.

He dropped the rag and continued to school, walking down the concrete stairway belonging to the block of flats. He never used the lift as it always got stuck, and took too long for maintenance to come out to fix it. One time, a drug addict had gotten trapped inside for a week before it was even noticed—having overdosed and died. And the only reason the body was discovered was because of the foul decaying smell. At the bottom of the stairway Josh noticed a newly discarded batch of used needles the junkies had left behind. He began kicking them to one side and down a drain when he was interrupted.

"Oi, come on!"

Josh looked up to see his friend Steve sitting on the wall waiting for him.

"We're gonna be late again because of you!" Steve shouted. "Leave em where they are," he said, referring to the needles Josh was trying to get rid of.

"Some kid might stick emself if I leave em," said Josh quietly.

"That's tough shit then," replied Steve, "they shouldn't live ere then should they!"

That was Steve's typical response. He didn't care about anyone or anything. Josh didn't really know why he hung out with him; he was always aggressive and causing trouble. He wasn't a friend at all. Not that Josh was a saint, far from it—a saint wouldn't last two minutes where he lived—but he had a line he wouldn't cross; Steve had no line.

But Josh knew he didn't have any real friends, he was a loner. He got caught up with the wrong crowd at school and now felt stuck with them as his only "friends". To him, there was no way out, he felt he couldn't change his situation. In fact, Josh's whole problem was that he felt stuck in life somehow, stuck in a routine of living that he couldn't escape. His whole life seemed controlled, but not by him.

Again, Josh did as he was told and walked away with a last-ditch attempt to kick another needle down the drain.

"Have you done your homework?" questioned Steve.

"Yeah, last night in bed," replied Josh.

"Let me see. I need to copy it." Steve reached out his hand.

Josh complied, pulled out a scrappy piece of paper from his pocket and handed it over. Steve took it, quickly scanned through the scrawled words, looked up and gave Josh a wry look of dissatisfaction.

"What the hell is this? I can't copy this, its rubbish," said Steve sneering. "Are you trying to get me into trouble? You know I'm on the edge of getting kicked out of school," he complained, and threw the paper back at Josh.

The problem with Steve was that it was always someone else's fault and never his own. He never took or had any sense of responsibility, except to blag what he felt he deserved to have. His actions, in some form, were always destructive. He would never help anyone unless, in some twisted way, it was to cause someone harm. Secretly Josh hated him, but what could he do? He felt he had to go along with the idiot, as though he was in some kind of hypnotic trance he couldn't escape. Whatever Josh decided or wanted to do, Steve, without fail, was always there to discredit or mock him, so Josh gave up trying; which was what Steve really wanted—to keep control of him. In fact, Steve was like that with the rest of the group he and Josh hung around with.

As they walked to school Josh sensed something. He looked across to a stairwell of another block of flats nearby, and could see someone he thought he knew.

WHOOSH!

Instantly, Josh began to experience an intense feeling of déjà vu come over him. He didn't know why, or really know who this figure was, but certainly felt he knew this stranger from somewhere. Josh had to walk over; he was compelled to do so.

"W—where the hell are you going?" said Steve confusedly.

Josh didn't reply. With the intensity of déjà vu still burning through his mind, coupled with curiosity, he walked towards the unknown figure. It was like he needed an answer to a question, a question he didn't even know.

"Get back here!" yelled Steve.

But Josh, still fixated with a burning desire to know, kept walking towards the figure. But the figure seemed to fade the closer he got, and as soon as he reached the stairwell it was gone. Josh felt confused and astonished. The feeling of déjà vu was so intense it was like he had just woken from a deep dream. He settled down, turned around and walked back to Steve, who for the first time looked worried. Josh could see something different in him, and the difference was the fear of that short moment that Steve had lost control of him. For the first time ever, Josh felt this resurgence of self-determinism, and it felt good.

"What was that about?" Steve was asking in a tone of voice Josh had never heard before, certainly not in him. It was a sense of respect that he was now giving Josh, like an equal, or someone of more importance than himself.

"It doesn't matter. Thought I saw someone I knew."

"Sure. Alright Josh."

The pair silently carried on to school; all the while Josh feeling the sense of déjà vu but never mentioning it, not even the whole day during lessons.

The school day dragged as usual, and made the week seem long.

"Thank god," Josh thought to himself, as the school bell rang at the end of the day. He had been clock-watching for the past hour, counting down each minute to home time.

All he wanted to do was to pack in school altogether. He had no interest or stamina, in learning about subjects that to him were useless, and of no practical value whatsoever. He had no use for the subject matter that was being forced upon him by burnt out teachers, who themselves couldn't even apply what they were lecturing about. All this so he could regurgitate it at exam time, so the school board could decide which schools were better at getting their pupils to memorise pointless facts.

Josh knew what he wanted to do, once he left school, and had already applied to join the army. He had passed his entrance examinations and fitness tests, and was waiting to receive his joining instructions. He couldn't wait. It was a way out of his stagnant existence, and even Steve, with his degrading comments about being too stupid, couldn't dissuade him from joining.

As Josh packed away his school books Steve walked over. "What's up with you? We haven't seen you all day."

"Nothing," replied Josh. But that wasn't entirely true.

"Okay, I'll meet you outside then. Maybe we can go and nick some CDs from the mall before you go to work." Steve was smiling at his "bright" idea.

"No, I'm going on my own. I've got some stuff to do for my mum. I told you that earlier." Josh lied convincingly. He had Steve thinking that he had already been told when in fact he hadn't.

"Alright then," and Steve walked off, joining the rest of the gang who were picking on a boy.

Josh needed some time on his own to think, as the peculiar feelings from earlier that day were still playing on his mind like a burning rod. It had taken up most of his attention during lessons, causing the teachers to single him out with unwanted questioning about their subject matter. He stood up from his desk and walked out of the classroom to head for work. As he walked from school, he felt like he was in a trance, in another world, when suddenly he snapped out of it, realising he was walking home and not to work.

"Shit, what am I doing? I'm supposed to be at work," he told himself. But time had escaped him and he was already twenty minutes late. "What the hell am I doing?"

His mind began automatically working out a plan that would see him safe from getting a roasting from his stingy boss—the newsagent owner. He decided not to turn up for work at all, because, "he had been robbed of his mobile phone on the way". He knew this deception would work well, as his boss had recently had a similar traumatic experience, and would be more sympathetic.

Feeling more with it, and in the here-and-now, Josh continued to walk home, but suddenly there it was again!

WHOOSH!

A sudden surge, a sudden feeling of déjà vu swept over him just as it did earlier in the morning. Josh could feel some kind of presence, someone watching, and he realised he was at the same spot near the block of flats near his home. He felt cold, but intensely curious, as he looked across to the stairwell and could, as earlier, see a figure. It was as though he was looking through translucent glass; the figure was indistinct but familiar in some way.

He instinctively ran towards the figure, and this time, it didn't fade but remained constant, although misty looking. As he approached, Josh's mouth gaped, confusion and fear sweeping over him; the feelings becoming increasingly intense the closer he got. Josh knew the person who now stood before him on the stairs, although it was physically and scientifically impossible. It was an old friend who had died one year past!

Josh stood in front of the "ghost" staring fixatedly at it. Questions were passing through his mind at a rate whereby they were forgotten even before he had time to fully process them. He was too dumbstruck to say or ask anything. Finally, after what felt like hours had passed, it spoke.

"Josh," a faded voice came through. It was a strange sound as though talking through a wall, or an old wireless radio. "Josh, I need to tell you something. Can you hear me?"

Josh was still numb with shock but was slowly coming round. "I don't understand; you are dead," he replied.

"I need to tell you something but haven't got long. Are you listening? I only...." The voice suddenly faded and dropped out, as though the frequency of a transmitter was lost or out of range, taking the ghostly form along with it.

"Wait a minute!" Josh shouted. "Come back!" but his friend had already gone.

CHAPTER 2

THE FOLLOWING DAY STARTED just as every other, with the clanging of Josh's mother in the kitchen preparing a feast of eggs for breakfast, and Josh feeling tired. Feeling tired, not from lack of sleep but the feeling of apathy about the deep rut his life was in. And he was only fifteen.

"Josh, Josh! Get up!" sounded the usual cry of the morning.

"Oh, leave me alone for once," he thought.

Automatically obeying his mother's order, Josh began the effort of slowly moving his body out of bed. He glanced up at the blonde in the pin-up poster sticky taped to the flaky paintwork on the wall above his bed. "I wish," he thought.

He reached down and picked up his school uniform that had been thrown on the floor the previous night, and got dressed. He could smell the sweat on his shirt already and still had two more days to go before the weekend. He always felt embarrassed because he had to wear the same shirt all week; it was the only one he had. To save money, his mother would always knit his school jumpers with a guarantee that something would go wrong. One year the arms were too short and would barely cover his wrists, so had to keep stretching them; the following year it was the neck line that was overly low. He longed for the day to be able to afford his own clothes.

He visited the bathroom to wash his face; looking in the mirror at his reflection, thinking about the unusual happenings of yesterday, and how unreal it all seemed. Although he was trying to deny it, he couldn't, he knew what he had seen.

Leaving the bathroom, he walked to the kitchen and sat down in front of a "soft-boiled" egg. He knew the egg wouldn't be cooked properly; the white all runny as usual. So, he did as he always did; cracked the top open with his spoon, poured out the runny egg-white, and hid it underneath the hollow base of the egg cup so his mother wouldn't see it.

WHACK! Josh received a backhander from his mother across the side of the head. She had walked into the kitchen silently without him realising.

"What the hell did you do that for?" he moaned, wondering if she had seen him hide the egg-white.

"Why didn't you go into work yesterday after school?" she said sternly, "You know we can't afford to lose that money!"

Trying to recover from the sudden "life-builder", Josh adeptly replied, "I got beaten up by some older lads and they took my phone." The lie was in play.

"You get in there after school and make up the time!" she snarled unsympathetically, and left the room.

There was no love between them. Josh felt he was an inconvenience and knew she just wanted him to move out. She was very encouraging for him to join the army as he would be out of her hair. This was the only support he ever really got from her. But he didn't care, not on the surface anyway.

Josh finished his breakfast—what was left of it. He grabbed a sponge from the kitchen top and quickly wiped the damp spots on the walls, then threw it in the sink.

"I'm off!" he shouted, but as always received no reply.

He walked out of the flat, slamming the door shut, and looked at the red smear of paint on the wall of his neighbour's flat. His neighbour had managed to remove some of the graffiti but, although smudged, the wording was still apparent. Josh continued, walking down the concrete stairs, thinking about the day before. The apparition of his friend was etched in his mind like a chiselled groove in a piece of wood.

"What was that?" he thought.

He couldn't reason it out and was stuck in the mystery of not knowing. He thought about telling Steve but common sense had taught him otherwise. No one would believe him and he would most definitely be mocked, especially by Steve.

"Keep it to myself," he decided.

As he reached the bottom of the stairs he anxiously looked around for Steve, but he wasn't there. Usually, he would be waiting but this time there was no sign of him. Josh smiled from a sense of relief and carried on by himself.

While nearing the block of flats where he experienced the "apparition", his senses heightened; he fixated his attention on the spot where he saw the "ghost"—his friend. Nothing; there was no sign of anything. Was it all in his head? Did he really see what he saw, or was it just his mind playing tricks? He felt okay, didn't feel ill. Maybe he had a brain tumour or something? Josh began to doubt himself and deny what he saw. But he wanted it to be true.

Disappointed, he walked on past and began heading for school, but then suddenly he stopped. He knew he shouldn't, but decided not to attend school. For some reason, this felt like a right decision, so turned for the shopping centre instead. Josh never really rebelled in life and felt nervous at doing so; at the same time though he felt excited and alive.

"I'm gonna have to think up some exceptional bullshit for this one," he said to himself with a smile.

He reached the indoor shopping centre. Entering and walking inside, he wondered what to do. "So much for being a rebel," he complained.

He remembered what Steve had said the previous day, about stealing CDs after school, so went to see what he could blag. He walked into a music store and started to look around. He knew the security staff would be busy doing other things as it was early morning still. They wouldn't expect kids to be in there at that time so opportunity was on his side. The store was fairly quiet with only a few staff on the sales floor. They were busy re-filling shelves with stock, so Josh knew they wouldn't pay him much attention.

After approaching a display, Josh selected a couple of CDs he liked. He then surreptitiously moved to a secluded spot in the store, where he could pull off the security tags without being spotted. He knew of a great blind spot he and Steve used many times before, out of view to the CCTV cameras.

Hidden from sight, Josh picked at the security tag that was only stuck on. "Useless," he thought, as he peeled it off and tucked it behind a display. He did the same with the other CD. With a sly look around, to ensure no one was watching, he quickly slipped the items into his jacket pocket. "So easy," he thought.

Josh then pretended to look interested in other CDs, and slowly worked his way towards the exit, for his eventual departure. He knew that he was safe until he left the store, which was when the security staff would make their move. That was always the moment of tension. Josh knew the score; he and Steve had been caught a couple of times for shoplifting in the past. Security would always wait until they would leave the shop before making an arrest. Josh made his move towards the exit. He couldn't see any security staff and felt safe to go.

WHOOSH!

All of a sudden, a feeling hit him, just as though his mother had surprised him with one of her "enlightening wake-up calls". Josh froze for a moment but with all of eternity passing by at once. He hadn't left the shop yet but felt something very wrong. He was pinned like a rabbit being startled at night, with an oncoming car speeding towards it—headlights full on. He just stood motionless, right by the exit.

"What's going on?" he thought. "I can't move."

Frozen to the spot, he recognised the intense feeling, the feeling he had experienced the previous day with the "apparition" of his friend. Déjà vu swept over him, but much stronger than before. Yesterday's feeling was nothing compared to this. But what had caused it? There were no "ghosts" or anything Josh could recognise. So, what had triggered this feeling?

Again, with what seemed like hours had passed on by, the feeling slowly subsided and Josh became more aware of his surroundings again, although his senses were still greatly heightened. He remembered what he was about to do—steal the CDs—but lost his nerve. He quickly walked back to the blind spot where he had removed the security tags, looked around to see if anyone was watching him, took the two CDs from his pocket and dumped them on the shelf. He turned, walked quickly back to the store exit, and left.

Walking about the shopping centre, oblivious to all else, Josh was consumed with trying to make sense of what had just happened to him, and tried to reason it out in his head.

"There must have been someone watching me," he thought. "The security guards were on to me."

This made him feel more at ease with the situation, as he had given himself an answer to what had happened. But despite this rationalisation, somehow, he knew it wasn't the right answer. Something else had triggered that feeling, just as it did the day before with the sighting of his "dead" friend. But Josh hadn't seen anymore "apparitions" or "ghosts".

He decided to go to a café, get a drink and calm down. On his own, sitting at a table and sipping his drink, he watched the people in the mall wandering around shopping. He couldn't help but think to himself, how unhappy everyone really looked; how they were trying to supplant their unhappiness by buying things that would only interest them for a few days. Then, to rekindle their lost happiness, would buy more things. It was a materialistic mess we had gotten ourselves into. Genuine happiness seemed out of reach, and people had to pretend they were happy. Josh hated the bullshit. He knew there had to be more meaning to his life, but felt trapped and controlled in a way he couldn't understand.

"Hey," a sudden voice interrupted Josh's thoughts, causing him to instantly turn around.

WHOOSH!

Josh was hit square on, with the full intensity of déjà vu, similar to what had swept over him in the music store. He was staring at some human figure; a vacant look on his face and the dramatic feeling of knowing this person. It was all too surreal. His attention was fixated on the feeling, more so than the person who now stood in front of him.

"Hey," the voice repeated.

Josh could barely discern that it was a man's voice, and as his trance lessened, the vague figure focused into view and became more real. A man, standing by the table, was looking down at him with a stare that felt like he was drilling holes through Josh's head.

"Oh shit; security from the music store," thought Josh, but saw he had no uniform on. "Maybe he's a store detective?" But knew he had dumped the CDs in the store and left with nothing. Dozens of thoughts flicked through his mind as to who he was, but none were making sense.

"What do you want?" Josh finally replied.

"The sugar!" asserted the man. His voice came across with a direct intensity that made Josh feel as though the man had twisted his insides around.

"Oh—okay, yeah—take it," and Josh slid it across the table to him.

"Thanks!" The man walked away, to sit at another table within eyeshot.

Josh was feeling extremely uncomfortable, with a certainty that he somehow knew the man, but not recognising him at all. He watched the man sitting at his table with his head down hiding his face, stirring a hot drink. Looking at the table, Josh noticed it already had a jar of sugar on it.

"Why did he ask for my sugar if he's already got some?" he thought. He started another instantaneous lengthy list of possibilities flooding through his head, as to who this stranger was.

Anxiously, Josh rose from his seat, leaving his drink half-finished, and left the café. "I should have gone to school," he thought.

He walked amongst the shoppers, still thinking intensely about the stranger, but then decided to put the whole thing down to his nerves from when he tried to steal the CDs. His senses, still alert, had him feeling paranoid and constantly looking over his shoulder. It was all too much, and so he decided to go to school after all.

As he walked towards the shopping centre exit, he caught a glimpse of someone staring at him. It was the stranger from the café. Was it just a coincidence or something more? Josh couldn't tell. He quickened his pace and his heart thumped through his chest from nerves. He opened the exit and started to walk fast. He walked a few blocks, stopped and turned around, no one was following him. He turned again and carried on walking.

"It's all in my head," he thought. Then suddenly he was grabbed from the side. A hand came from nowhere and grabbed Josh's jacket. It was the stranger again.

"What do you want!" screamed Josh, "I haven't done anything!"

"Shut up, you're drawing attention!" a deep voice snapped as the stranger dragged Josh down into a side alley.

Josh was pushed hard up against a wall. He started to shout for help but was suddenly struck with a blow to his stomach which took the wind out of him, preventing him from shouting further. He had been in fights before and had received many punches, but this was a blow that put him out of action, nearly crippling him to the floor. As he was trying to catch his breath, he saw the stranger looking up the alleyway where they had just come from. He then turned his attention back to Josh.

"Come on, follow me!" he commanded.

The stranger started walking away down the alley. Josh didn't understand, the man wasn't forcing him but seemed to take it for granted he would obey. He was right. Although Josh was scared and confused, he suddenly felt the stranger wasn't a threat anymore and felt compelled to follow.

Looking at the man from behind, Josh could see he was physically well built. He had a fast deliberate pace that was difficult to keep up with. He didn't even look back to see if Josh was following; it was as if he knew he would be.

"Where are we going? What the hell is going on?" Josh yelled as he quick-stepped behind to keep up. There came no reply. "Look if you don't stop and tell me what's going on I'm leaving!"

This prompted the stranger to look behind at Josh, although not pleasantly. He turned, grabbed Josh's jacket and force marched him against his will. The man didn't say a word, he didn't have to. Josh knew, no matter what, that if he didn't comply, he would be worse off.

As the man marched him out of the alley and down another street, Josh could see him continually scanning the area as though looking for someone, or something. He appeared wired, and on the alert.

A minute or so later, they came to a parked car in a quiet street. The man used a key remote to unlock the doors. He opened the passenger door, pushed Josh into the seat and closed it. He walked around and got into the driver's seat; not saying a word the whole time.

As he got in, Josh noticed a dark object under the man's jacket as it flapped open slightly. He caught a glimpse of what looked like the handle of a gun hanging down the side of his body. Josh started to worry even more. He had no idea what he had gotten into, or why he didn't try to run.

The man started the engine and pulled off fast. Driving along, at a fast speed, he kept looking in the rear-view mirror. He drove down one road, U-turned and drove back up the same road again. After a few odd manoeuvres he slowed his speed and appeared to calm down a little.

"Look I don't know what's going on, but people will be worried about me. What's going on?" Josh took the opportunity to ask again.

"Don't worry Josh, your mother won't be concerned, she never was."

Josh was shocked that he knew his name and appeared to know about his life.

"Who are you and how do you know my name?" Josh questioned.

"I know more than that Josh. I know where you live, who your friends are, your parents, about your father who used to beat you, that you are to join the army soon and more. There is nothing about you I don't know."

"But how do you know, and who are you?" Josh anxiously replied. He was desperate to know.

"More of that later, but in the meantime, I need your help," said the man, "I need you to come with me; I have something to show you."

And without question, just blind obedience, Josh agreed.

CHAPTER 3

AFTER A SHORT SILENT journey, the car pulled up outside an old industrial estate on the outskirts of a nearby town. Josh knew the town as it was one of his father's favourite watering holes for a night out drinking, where Josh was taken as a kid before his father became completely lost to drink.

"That's how he knows me, he knew my dad. Maybe he's a drug dealer, or one of the gang that killed him," he thought.

Josh was trying to fill in what he didn't know with anything he could come up with. He was still desperate for answers. Faced with an absence of facts he simply made up his own in a fool's attempt to complete the puzzle. He had no real facts however, about who this man was and what he wanted Josh for, so his mind worked overtime, filling in the empty spaces with all sorts of "what ifs" and "maybes".

The man got out of the car, walked round to the opposite side and opened the passenger door.

"Get out and follow me," he ordered.

Josh immediately responded without question. He felt like a robot—programmed with instructions and obeying without thinking.

The man headed for a door to what appeared to be a derelict building. The windows were dirty, some broken, and there was no sign of occupation in any of the nearby buildings. They entered through the door.

Inside the building Josh could smell the stench of dampness just like at home, but stronger. It was dim, with minimal light coming through the windows and skylights. The further Josh walked inside the more serious he felt. A fleeting thought passed through his mind to run, but he couldn't find the will-power to break the stranger's control over him. Josh followed the stranger across a somewhat empty warehouse to another door.

"In here and shut the door behind you," the man commanded, as he pushed a security code into an electronic keypad by the closed door. The door opened and they entered an inner room that was unlike the rest of the building. It was clean and orderly.

WHOOSH!

Josh was suddenly struck with another intense feeling of déjà vu. "I feel like I know this place," he said. "I feel like I've been here before." The man said nothing.

In the room were a couple of tables with computer terminals set up alongside each other. On the walls were maps and other documentation, along with photographs. It was like something out of a spy movie. It looked militaristic, like a command centre but on a much smaller scale. Josh knew, from looking at the room, this had nothing to do with his father, and certainly no drug dealer.

"What's going on? What is this stuff?" Josh asked.

"Sit down," the man pointed to a chair. Josh sat without thinking. The man didn't say anything, just stared at Josh. It was as if he had found his missing son or something, and was struck dumb by the encounter.

Finally, the man spoke up. "I need your help."

"But why do you want my help?" Josh replied.

"You've had some unusual experiences lately; things you can't explain."

Josh suddenly froze. "Yes, but how do you know any of that?"

The man continued, "I can give you some but not all of the answers. First, you must tell me precisely what occurred. I mean precisely!"

Josh explained everything about what had happened over the last couple of days; the encounters with his "dead" friend, and the déjà vu feelings he's been experiencing. The man made him go over it and over it in detail until he had recalled every aspect. Josh felt exhausted, like he had been through an interrogation for hours.

"Good," the man said, and walked over to one of the tables, taking a seat by the computer terminals.

He reached for some papers and started making notes. He then logged on to one of the computers and Josh, straining to get a look, caught a glimpse of what appeared to be a personnel file. He could vaguely make out a profile photograph along with accompanying information, but from that distance it was too far for him to read.

The man stood up and walked away from the table. He stood in thought for a couple of minutes.

"Stay there," he said, and the man walked out of the room, closing the door.

Josh remained sitting, but his inquisitive nature pushed him to go and look at what was on the computer. Worried about getting caught, he tentatively walked across the room to the terminal the man had used just moments before. The screen was still on and as Josh reached it to take a quick look, he suddenly heard the door's keypad being pressed on the opposite side of the door. He immediately bolted for his seat but not without first reading one main word on the screen: "View Corp".

The man re-entered the room and looked straight at Josh, staring as though he knew he had been at the computer.

"So, what did you read?" he said.

"Read? W—what do you mean?" Josh wriggled around in his seat from the uncomfortable feeling of being found out.

The man gave a slight grin. He pulled out what appeared to be a large mobile phone or small handheld computer device from his jacket, then connected it up to the main computer he had just used. After a minute or so of working at the computer—tapping on the keyboard, he disconnected the device, put it inside his jacket pocket and logged off the computer he was using.

"I said, what did you read?" the man repeated.

"Nothing; I wanted to but thought that I shouldn't," Josh replied. He thought it would be more convincing to admit some, but not all of the truth, as this man seemed no fool.

"I said, what did you read?" the man questioned further.

Josh was surprised that he wasn't convinced by his half-truth. "View Corp. View Corp was all that I saw, nothing more."

The man grinned as if he already knew but just wanted to see Josh sweat a little. "Does that mean anything to you?" he asked.

"No," replied Josh. "Is this about my dad?"

"Your dad! No. This has nothing to do with him. But it has everything to do with what you've just read."

"What, 'View Corp'?" Josh asked curiously. He perked up wanting to know more.

"Yeah. I work for the government, an agency," the man revealed, "that's all you need to know about me."

"But what do you want with me?" asked Josh.

"I already said. I need your help." The man answered but without being specific.

"But what can I do?" Josh felt like he was a dog chasing its own tail and never reaching it. The man was a closed book, a continuous enigma, and Josh felt he knew even less the more he asked.

"Plenty, more than you are yet to realise," the man replied.

Josh was ever more confused at the cryptic conversation. Time had passed quicker than he had realised. "Look I better go now. It was good talking but I've got to get to school."

The man, staring at Josh, reached into the inside of his jacket. Josh knew what he had concealed there. The man pulled out an automatic pistol, gripped hold of the top slide and cocked it sharply. The noise was unmistakable; Josh had seen many action movies on T.V. before but this was real life. He began to get scared and his body stiffened from fear. The man suddenly looked like he did earlier—fully alert and deadly serious. He looked at a panel on the wall with flashing lights then suddenly switched into action. The man flicked a switch next to the computer terminals to activate a hard drive wipe. Josh knew something was wrong but not knowing what to do did nothing—sitting semi-frozen in his seat.

"Get up and do as I say, exactly as I say!" the man dictated. Josh was fed a new command and immediately stood up without thinking.

"Stand over by that wall!" The man pointed and Josh franticly moved to the wall. The man was facing and pointing his weapon at the door they had come through.

"See that lever, pull it towards you!" the man gestured with a single nod of the head at a lever.

Josh pulled down on a lever that was halfway up the wall and heard a sharp clang. A second doorway opened on the opposite side of the room. The man moved fast to the doorway, quickly looked through and stepped into another room. Josh followed. The man instantly pushed the door shut behind them.

"Follow me and don't make a noise."

This was getting all too much for Josh, he had no idea what he had gotten into, and certainly had no idea of the danger he was now facing.

The pair moved quickly through the room to another doorway that had a small window at face level. The man stopped and briefly looked through. As he opened the door, a burst of bullets ricocheted off the walls and door frame causing the man to jump back into the room for cover. Josh fell to the floor in terror.

"What the fuck is going on!" Josh screamed, while trying to push his body down flat.

The man grabbed Josh's jacket and lifted him off the floor like he was a rag doll. He was much stronger than Josh first thought.

The man crouched by the door, still holding Josh firmly. "Keep your body low and when I say "move", you MOVE!"

Josh felt his bowels opening up from fear but was suddenly jerked away as he heard "MOVE!"

They both exited the room, and sharply turned left, as another volley of bullets was fired in their direction. In the commotion, Josh saw a piece of flesh being torn from the man's left arm; blood splattered in Josh's face. He was dragged by the man to a piece of nearby broken machinery, for cover.

Ripping open the sleeve of his jacket, the man briefly inspected his wound where he had been grazed by a bullet. Josh could see a bloodied groove in the man's arm where the flesh had come from. There was no time to patch it up. There were darkened figures swiftly moving in to their location and the man suddenly snapped into action again. He pointed and double tapped his pistol—firing two shots—in the direction of one figure, and instantly it dropped to the ground. Josh could see the body of a man still clutching a weapon, two bullet wounds to the chest, only inches apart.

Again, the man shouted, "MOVE!" and pulled Josh with him.

More gunfire was heard and bullets ricocheted all around them, but less accurately than before. Sprinting to an exit, the man discharged his pistol at another figure standing out in front of them. He too dropped to the floor with two bullet wounds centre of the chest. As they ran outside the man stopped, turned around and took up a defensive stance. Another figure came through the same exit but was suddenly stopped short by a double tap of the man's gun; the figure meeting the same fate as the others. Without hesitation the man turned, grabbed Josh and dragged him off again; running hard.

After running for a mile or so, away from the industrial estate, they stopped.

Out of breath and adrenalin pumping hard, Josh started to freak out; shock was starting to affect him. "I can't believe what just happened! What just happened? They tried to kill us! They shot you!" Josh was becoming hysterical.

WHACK! The man soft-punched Josh in the side of the body, enough to make him wince in pain.

"Why the hell did you do that?" screamed Josh.

"You're losing it, you need to stay focused," said the man calmly, as though getting shot and killing three people was an everyday occurrence. "I think we're okay now but we have to keep moving, they know where we are."

"Who are they? You haven't told me a bloody thing!" Josh's hostile emotion made him more focused, which was what the man needed him to be.

"They are 'View Corp'," the man stated in a matter-of-fact tone. "Now let's get going."

The man holstered his weapon under his jacket, pulled out the handheld computer from his pocket, and started walking. Josh followed. Holding his wounded arm, the man approached a line of parked cars. Using his elbow, he smashed the passenger side window of one of them, reached in, opened the door and climbed inside. Josh watched as the man reached over and speedily removed the steering column cover, stripped and re-connected the wiring—starting the engine, and with a forceful jerk and turning motion of the steering wheel, broke the steering lock.

"I need you to drive," he said.

"But I can't drive," Josh replied.

"You got into trouble with your friend Steve for driving without a licence, so don't tell me you can't drive. Now get in and drive!"

Josh was taken aback by what he knew about him but immediately complied. He jumped in, put it in gear and drove off. "Where are we going?"

"Wait a minute." The man began tapping on the computer device. "This will show you where to go," and he placed it on the dash board. Josh began following the instructions on the device – similar to that of a sat-nav.

While tending to his bullet wound, Josh could see the man was in pain by the severe look on his face.

"How did you know about me and Steve; the police never caught us?"

"No, but your dad found out didn't he, gave you a right belting; nearly put you in hospital."

"How do you know any of that?" asked Josh.

"Like I said before, I know all about you. Now shut up and drive."

The instructions from the device had Josh driving for half an hour. He looked across at the stranger who was sitting quietly; his eyes were shut and he was clutching his arm. There was blood seeping through a makeshift dressing he had applied to his wound, but it needed further medical attention. They turned off the main road and into a housing estate, as instructed by the device, and then pulled up outside a house in a cul-de-sac. The man opened his eyes and grabbed the computer device.

"Get out," he said.

Both he and Josh got out of the car and the man started walking away. Josh followed without hesitation. They walked a mile or so into a residential area. The man led Josh to a house, and for some reason it, or the area, seemed familiar to him. The house was just the same as any ordinary house by the usual standards, but after experiencing what had just happened to him, Josh was not being complacent about what was "normal" anymore.

Walking up to the front door, the man looked around and approached a small panel. He opened the panel to reveal an electronic keypad. He tapped on some numbers and a whirring sound could be heard from behind the door. As they stepped inside, Josh was half expecting to see an array of weapons and equipment or computers like before, but no; it seemed an ordinary house. As the man closed the door behind them, an automatic locking system whirred in place, securing the door.

"Who lives here?" asked Josh.

"Me," the man replied, with a strain. "Sit over there and do nothing," and he pointed to a comfy chair.

Josh sat down as the man left the room. Looking around, Josh was beginning to notice oddities about the room. Although on the surface the house looked normal, there were things that didn't quite add up to what you would expect of a "normal" house. There were no photographs or pictures of anyone, anyone at all. It also looked very clinical, as though it was never really lived in. The cracks of normality started to show the more Josh looked, and it started to reveal a more sinister undertone. What was this house?

After twenty minutes or so the stranger re-entered the room, naked from the waist up. Josh's attention went straight to the man's arm where he had been shot. The gape of the wound had been crudely stitched and looked a mess, but the bleeding had stopped. The man reached into a cupboard and pulled out a military-style field dressing, tore the wrapping with his teeth, pulled out the bandage and wrapped it around his wound. He winced as he did so. Josh couldn't help but noticed the man's physique, which showed he was in perfect physical shape, and explained how he was able to jostle him around so easily.

"What is this place?" asked Josh.

"What does it look like?" Again, no discerning answer just counter-question.

"It looks like a home. But it's not. There are no pictures, family photos, nothing personal."

"Well, there you have it then," smirked the man, "you already know."

"What is that supposed to mean 'I already know' know what? You haven't told me a bloody thing, just leaving me to make guesses. You're really pissing me off!" Josh voiced his frustration.

The man stared hard at Josh with an unpleasant look, a look Josh was familiar with, like the one that preceded the body blow he was given in the alleyway earlier. He knew it was time for him to shut his mouth.

Breaking the stare, the man turned and opened another cupboard. He pulled out a silver foil pouch, opened it, picked up a spoon and started eating from it.

"You hungry?" he asked.

"Yeah," replied Josh, still feeling annoyed.

The man pulled out another foil pouch and threw it at him. Josh caught it, pulled it open and looked at the mushy content inside.

"What's this?"

"Army rations. Get used to it."

"So, you're in the army?" Josh asked. But with a lack of response, he may as well have directed the question to the wall. "So, what is View Corp?"

The man looked at Josh then rested himself in a chair. "View Corp is an organisation protected by those who would... well you know, you've already experienced what they're capable of. I only found out about them through my investigations and have had little to go on. But they have sweeping powers, and every time I make progress in my discoveries, they seem to be one step ahead."

"But what has this to do with me?" Josh asked worryingly. The man said nothing.

"So how did you find out about View Corp, and what do they want?" Josh continued.

"Through a file I wasn't supposed to see. I found it whilst working another assignment I had been tasked with, and found a lead which crossed over and led me to View Corp. I discovered some kind of experimentation was taking place, something very serious but no mention of what exactly. There was also mention of...," and the man stopped.

"Mention of what?" quizzed Josh, and waiting desperately for an answer.

The man knew exactly what he was doing. He knew more than he was letting on, and fed Josh only enough information to keep him dangling and wanting more. That was his game. The man had him hooked. Josh was so eager to find out more that he didn't realise the danger he was being led into.

"I need you to help me. I may have found a location, a place where View Corp could be situated. And I need you to come."

The man was testing Josh's willingness to participate, by asking and not forcing him. He had fed him enough information to see if he had been hooked. He knew that a person was of more use to him who was a willing, not an unwilling participant. A person who had to be forced needed more control and babysitting, and the man knew he didn't have the time for that. He needed Josh's full co-operation.

"Okay, so where are we going?" Josh eagerly replied.

The man smiled inwardly at his success. "Follow me."

CHAPTER 4

LEAVING THE HOUSE, THE man took Josh back to the industrial estate, using another old "borrowed" car he had picked up along the way. This time the man drove. Once they reached the estate, he pulled over into a quiet side road.

"Wait here. I'll be back shortly," said the man, and walked off, leaving Josh alone in the car.

Josh waited, feeling nervous and worrying that the man might be killed. Time ticked by. Minutes passed that seemed like hours and still no sign of him. Staring hard through the car window, Josh waited, hoping the next car that drove by was the stranger; but no sign. The wait was becoming too stressful.

"I have to get out of here. I need to go," Josh said to himself, but feeling compelled to stay as though he wasn't allowed to leave. As he started to force himself to open the car door, in a weak attempt to escape, the stranger drove fast around the corner, this time in his own car.

The car pulled up next to Josh and the man shouted through the window, "Get in!"

With hidden reluctance, Josh did as he was told and swapped cars—getting into the stranger's. Just as soon as he was in, the man quickly pulled off, driving away from the industrial site. Looking in the wing mirror, Josh was happy to see the site disappearing into the distance. His stress subsided and he could feel the instant relief in the whole of his body. He hadn't realised how tense his body had been, until now.

Mostly in silence, they had driven for almost an hour with the guidance of the handheld computer device. The coordinates of the suspected whereabouts of View Corp pinpointed an isolated area with no buildings or main roads. In fact, after checking satellite imagery, the picture showed the area was made up of just fields and patches of densely covered wooded areas.

The device indicated a turning off the main road, taking them onto a dirt track, and Josh sensed the man becoming very wary as they continued.

"These tracks are fresh."

"It could be a tractor, a farmer or something," Josh replied.

Josh started to get nervous knots in his stomach and his mouth became dry. His body seemed to be preparing itself for something that he was hoping wouldn't take place. Regardless, he was caught by the intrigue of it all and he wanted answers.

Pulling the car off the track, the man stopped in a slightly wooded area. "We walk from here," he said, and got out.

Following his lead, Josh got out and watched as the man walked to the rear of the car and open the boot. He took off his jacket and reached inside the boot space. He lifted out a semi-automatic rifle and hung it across the front of his body, using a rifle sling. He put on his jacket and pushed the weapon underneath to conceal it. Josh knew he was in danger and his body was reacting accordingly—heart beating hard and fast and feeling nervous, but strangely, he also felt the excitement of it all. This was a new experience for him, it was taking him out of the rut he was stuck in, and he liked it. It felt like a game. He felt like he was in a computer program acting out in the game, but then he remembered earlier, the man's gaping wound—that was no game!

"This way," said the man, and he started walking in the direction of a small wooded area on the edge of some fields.

The man led Josh along the edge of a field, along a hedgerow. As they drew closer the man stopped, crouched down in a ditch and pulled out his weapon from under his jacket. He raised it into his shoulder and looked through a mounted telescopic sight. Josh could see the pain in his face as he used his wounded arm to steady the weapon. The man scanned the area around the location but saw nothing unusual at that distance, so stood up and moved forward. They continued this tactic every hundred metres or so: crouching down and the man scanning the area for danger, until they reached the wooded area.

Looking around the immediate area of the location revealed nothing at first, and Josh was both relieved and disappointed, then the man beckoned Josh with a serious look and a nod. Josh moved in closer and watched the man staring intensely at what appeared to be undergrowth.

"What is it?" asked Josh.

"An opening, through there," and the man indicated with the barrel of his weapon.

"I can't see anything," said Josh staring hard.

"Look through the undergrowth and not at it," replied the man, and he pulled aside some bushes that had been purposely placed to conceal the opening.

WHOOSH!

A strong feeling of déjà vu swept over Josh, forcing his attention elsewhere. For a brief moment or two he was stuck in his head, causing him to delay. A feeling of danger awakened his senses. "We shouldn't go in!" Josh said loudly, but the man had already gone through.

Josh tentatively followed with the burning feeling of déjà vu clawing at his senses to not go further. As he caught up with the man, Josh could see what appeared to be an old out-building. This was not visible from beyond the concealment of the bushes and trees, even from an aerial viewpoint. The building was a dirty grey colour with plant-life creeping up the walls; a concrete looking box unnaturally poking up from the ground bearing a heavy looking door. Apart from the doorway, the structure was surrounded by a gentle embankment of earth that partially concealed the structure.

As the man approached the door, Josh shouted: "Wait!" The man immediately turned, and for the first time seemed to listen to Josh's direction.

"What's wrong?" he asked.

"I'm not sure. We just shouldn't go that way, go round the back."

The man heeded Josh's words and stealthily moved up the embankment and around the rear of the building. There was a small partially concealed opening, low down, just above surface level of the embankment, covered with brambles. Trying to avoid the thorns, the man carefully pulled and pushed the brambles to one side, revealing a small window—a window that wasn't ordinary but made of dense glass.

The man crouched and looked through it. There was no way to break the thick glass to get in, even from the force of a bullet—which was not even an option unless they wanted their presence to be known. So, in order to gain access, the man had to find and exploit its weakness. The building was old, and although the glass was able to withstand the pressure of time and the elements, the surrounding brickwork and concrete couldn't.

He pulled out a knife from his waist belt. With it, he scraped and picked at the degraded brickwork around the window's edge, until enough had been removed. He put his knife away and lay on his back, placing the soles of his boots on each side of the glass window. Repeatedly pushing in turn, on both sides of the window, with his feet, finally forced the remaining crumbling brickwork to give up, releasing its grip on the window, and allowing access.

The man pushed himself through the opening, feet first, and dropped down to floor level, followed by Josh. Once inside, they stood looking at the inside of the door they were about to go through; an explosive charge had been set as a booby trap for anyone coming through.

"I sensed something was wrong and I was right, but how?" said Josh.

The man looked with a smirk, like he knew something Josh didn't, but never said a word.

"We can use this."

The man looked at the booby trap and started to carefully disarm it; pushing a piece of wire he found on the floor into the hole of the safety pin mechanism. He pulled off a small strip of tape from the field dressing that covered his wound, and pressed it around the wire to hold it securely in place. The device was made safe and he placed it inside his jacket.

A concrete stairway led downwards for approximately thirty metres or so to another door. Both walked down the stairs, the man alert, with his rifle butt pressed into his shoulder, and Josh following along nervously. Standing at the bottom, they faced a door made of heavy metal. The man pushed on it to see if indeed it was locked and to gauge its strength; it held fast.

"It's locked. What shall we do?" asked Josh.

The man stood looking at the door. He had one solution in his jacket, the explosive device he had just disarmed, but didn't want to attract attention. He needed an alternative method of entry.

"There must be another way in," said Josh, but the man said nothing.

Josh watched the man analysing the door and walls. He pulled out his knife again and started to scrape at the wall, half way up near one edge of the door. The wall was weak, and crumbled fairly easily with enough pressure. He kept at it for around half an hour, whilst Josh sat on the floor looking at the wall; bored.

CLANG! Suddenly, Josh was jolted from his boredom by a loud metallic noise. The man had managed to release the door by sliding the locking bolts out of the wall he had stripped away. Josh immediately stood up, watching the man make his next move; pulling the door ajar. He peered through the gap, pulled it open wide enough to slip through and gestured to Josh to follow.

Josh came through to the other side of the doorway. "What is this place?" he asked, while looking around.

On the other side were closed doors along a corridor and an open space at the end. There were no lights on, except for some sort of emergency lighting which half lit the space around. The man, pointing his weapon, tactically moved along the corridor trying the doors as he went, but they were locked. As he and Josh reached the end of the corridor, to the open space, it suddenly became clear where they were. The walls were pasted with warning signs and emergency procedures: "Early Warning Alarm", "Contamination and Decontamination Procedure", "Power Failure Emergency", and so on.

Despite the old Cold War notices, there was evidence that the old fallout bunker they were in, was still in, or had been in use recently. With a week-old newspaper, a take-away food container, and discarded wrappers strewn across a desk, it was highly probable the bunker was occupied.

"Josh, check over on that desk," and the man pointed.

"What am I looking for?" Josh asked.

"Anything in relation to View Corp—files, documents."

Josh started his search, and as he was looking around, noticed the man searching through a filing cabinet. Paused, looking intently inside a drawer, Josh watched the man pull out a file, quickly stuff it inside his jacket, and close the cabinet drawer.

"Come on, let's go. There's nothing here," insisted the man.

Josh became suspicious, "Have you found anything?" he asked.

"No," replied the man. "Let's go!"

The man started to walk back down the corridor the way they had come, but froze suddenly.

"What is it?" whispered Josh.

The man raised his hand with a firm palm facing Josh, gesturing him to be silent. Josh started to worry and immediately backed up against the wall, trying to be as small as possible, to go unnoticed. He watched the man pull his knife out, and push his body into a shallow recess, slightly out of view.

The only thing Josh could hear was the strong thump of heart beats banging on the inside of his chest cavity, but he soon became aware of the sound of voices. There were two voices coming from down the corridor, seemingly chatting like nothing was wrong. He noticed the stranger poised; fixated towards the sound and ready for attack. As the voices grew louder and clearer, Josh watched the man swiftly spring from his hiding place, leaping into action, going about his business—his product: death.

He was fast and decisive when he attacked the closest target—a man; a man who had no chance when the knife was swiftly inserted into the back of his neck, at the base of the skull. A quick stab, and sideways jerk of the blade, cut his spinal cord, causing him to instantly flop to the floor. The second target, another man, had already begun to run, but only made it a few feet before he too was set upon and taken out in the same way. No screams, no cries for help, ever made it past their lips.

Josh was shocked and said nothing, it was over in seconds. There was no hesitation from the stranger and no hint of any remorse, just as though it were an everyday occurrence for him, and all part of the job.

"Josh, come here!" the man commanded.

Again, like a puppet, Josh did as he was told. As he walked shakily towards the man, he stared downwards at the two bodies prostrate on the floor, blood flowing from their gashes. He could see one man's spinal cord protruding slightly from the neck.

BLAARGH...SPLASH! Josh threw up over the floor.

"Hey!" responded the man quietly but firmly; "Sort yourself out, there could be more."

The man crouched to quickly search through the pockets of the dead bodies; both wore white coats as though they were doctors at a hospital. He grabbed and pulled off a tag that was clipped onto the pocket of one of the white coats. Josh read the wording printed on it: "Dosimeter". The other corpse also had a similar tag pinned to its jacket.

"What is that?" asked Josh, as he spat and wiped vomit from his mouth.

"It's for monitoring radiation levels," answered the man and he stood up. "Come on!" The man walked back down the corridor. One of the doors he had tried earlier was now open. He walked through the doorway.

After a partial recovery and looking extremely pale, Josh followed him in. "What is it?" he said, looking at the man.

The room was a laboratory with a glass panel dividing it into two. The man was standing looking through the glass. Josh joined him. On the other side was a device—similar in size to a car engine—positioned on a table. It was constructed out of metal, with various wires and dials, and some kind of glass lens at one end.

"It appears that View Corp is a terrorist organisation, building a weapon. And based on the badges those two in the corridor were wearing, probably nuclear," revealed the man. "But what the target and motive is I don't know. And the other problem is that there is no one else here: no protection, no security."

"But that's a good thing, right?" replied Josh.

"No, it's not. They left no protection for two reasons. Either this place is no longer seen as a top priority or...," and the man stopped.

"Or what?" asked Josh.

"Or they knew we were coming, and have set an ambush for us."

The man put his hand inside his jacket and pulled out the explosive charge he defused earlier. He opened a door, separating the two sides of the glass panel, and stepped through to the other side. He positioned the explosive charge close to the nuclear device.

"What are you doing?" asked Josh from the doorway.

"I'm going to destroy this device," said the man casually.

"But you'll kill everyone with a nuclear explosion!" Josh protested at the lunacy of it.

"It doesn't work like that. For the device to trigger a nuclear explosion it requires a particular detonation. This device will only destroy the nuclear weapon itself, without causing a nuclear reaction. It's simple."

He carried on setting the device up; priming it with a makeshift timer device he constructed himself out of electrical parts found in the room. The man was expertly casual about what he was doing.

"Right, we've got ten minutes to get out of here or we go up with it."

The man pulled Josh out of the room and started back down the corridor the way they came in. Moving quickly up the stairs, back to the small window they had climbed through, Josh noticed how dark it was getting, with daylight fading. With all that had happened, he hadn't realised the day had passed by so quickly.

"Shall I climb through first?" Josh asked, looking at the small window.

"No, we haven't got time for that, we'll use the main door," said the man.

WHOOSH!

Josh had another rush of déjà vu sweep over him, but before he could say anything or give warning, the man had already opened the door.

CRACK-CRACK-CRACK! CRACK-CRACK-CRACK!

No sooner had the stranger stepped through the door than the man was struck in the chest by a volley of bullets. His body was pushed backwards with great force and he landed on the floor—sitting with his back resting against the wall. Josh wet himself. He could feel his whole body loosen with fear, and felt the flush of warm urine flow down his school trousers. He had never been so scared in all of his life.

"J−o−s−h," croaked the man, with bloodied saliva bubbling from his mouth. He was barely alive. Josh looked at him, saw the wounds to his body and started to panic. The man took three bullets to the chest and one in the gut. He was pumping out blood. It was surprising he was still alive, let alone able to talk.

"J−o−s−h," he repeated. Josh knelt beside the man. "You−need−to−continue−this, you−need−to−continue−this," he said weakly.

"Continue what?"

"My−jacket; inside−my−jacket," the man was slipping away.

Josh opened the man's jacket, revealing the file he had pulled from the filing cabinet earlier−the file he denied as having. It had a bullet hole through it, and was covered in the man's blood. The man was turning pale and Josh knew he was going to die.

"What's your name?" Josh asked. "You never told me your name." The man slipped away.

Josh felt under immense pressure. He was alone now and in extreme danger, and all he could think about was wishing he had never skipped school.

"Come on Josh, pull it together, you gotta go, you gotta get out of here," he told himself. And without further hesitation—using the stranger's body as a step—climbed up, and pushed himself through the small window they originally came through. He was outside.

Looking around he couldn't see anyone. The fading light and night were on his side. He remembered where the car was hidden, but thought if View Corp knew they were there, then they probably saw them arrive, and would know the car's whereabouts. He decided to make a break for it and make his own way back.

He scarpered hard and fast from the bunker, through the trees and across the fields. No one seemed to have followed him within the distance that he covered. And in that short space of time, he suddenly heard a loud but distant bang through the evening air. It was the explosive device the stranger had set to destroy View Corp's nuclear device.

Josh was extremely relieved he was out of the way and felt a little safer, but was by no means out of danger. He started to head back for the road and home. What was he going to tell his mum? What was he going to tell Steve? What was he going to tell the police? It was all too fantastic! He couldn't have made this stuff up, even to lie his way out of a corner. It was unbelievable!

Then Josh suddenly realised: "The file." With all the tension of getting away, he had forgotten about the file. He reached in and pulled it out from his trousers where he had stuffed it in a hurry to escape. It smelt of a mixture of blood from the stranger and of his own urine, and was partially glued closed with the bodily fluids. He slowly peeled open the cover to look inside; it contained nothing apart from one solitary page. The page was about him!

CHAPTER 5

Seventeen years had passed since the day Josh helped the stranger. No real explanation as to who, or what he was, had ever been revealed, and Josh had all but forgotten the incident. Slowly, over the years, it had faded into an occluded memory, of which he had never disclosed to anyone. With no mention of the incident on the news channels, Josh kept it a closely guarded secret.

Now, at the age of thirty-two, Josh had established himself well in the military. He had reached his goal and moved out of his home town when he joined up at the early age of sixteen, and hasn't returned since. He lost contact with his mother, and had no intention of staying in touch with Steve, or the group he kicked around with at school. As far as he was concerned, that life never existed.

Josh did his basic training at an old military camp in the middle of nowhere, with only a small village situated nearby. It was desolate; an ideal training ground for teaching new recruits how to fight. Josh spent some of this time on military exercises, marching long distances with extremely weighty equipment, and having to conduct live-firing exercises whilst exhausted. Most recruits loathed this part of training, but for him, it was exciting.

Many recruits had dropped out in the first few months with all sorts of excuses, but Josh knew he couldn't go back to his old life, so pushed himself to succeed. He got noticed by the instructors for his physical fitness and stamina right from the start of training, so was given a temporary promotion. This was the first time Josh had received any kind of recognition, and for the first time he felt proud of himself. Being in the army had forced him to stand up in life, and to his surprise, pushed him to stick up for his beliefs.

Upon completion of his training, Josh joined his regiment. He served in different countries and war zones, and had proved himself a worthy soldier. He had made the rank of sergeant and gained great respect from his fellow comrades. But what he didn't know, was that someone had been watching his career, with great interest.

Josh was pulled in to see his regimental commanding officer.

"Sit down sergeant Brannon," said the C.O.

It wasn't often the lower ranks would get called in to see the C.O. unless they were on a disciplinary, so this was a unique experience for Josh.

"Sergeant Brannon, these two gentlemen are here to speak to you. I've already been apprised of the content of the discussion, so will let them get on with it," and the C.O. promptly left the room.

Standing at the back of the office were two men dressed in suits who, despite their civvy attire and non-standard haircuts, were military. After the C.O. had walked out, the pair walked to the front of the office and seated themselves at the C.O.'s desk.

Josh knew special forces types, and these were special forces. He had been seconded to an SF unit whilst on active duty, making a remarkable impression by means of quick judgement and selflessness during an enemy engagement. He had saved the lives of several comrades and as a result was awarded a military medal.

Josh looked straight at the pair with full eye contact; he didn't care who they were. The army had grown Josh a pair of balls any man would be proud of. One of the men began the conversation.

"Sergeant Joshua Brannon. Comes from a broken home, bit of trouble with the law—nothing major—left home at sixteen to join the army, been on active duty—a few times—won a military medal, worked with special forces, single, and no attachments." The man listed out Josh's life-history from memory.

"Josh, do you like your country?" he asked.

Josh hesitated with an answer, thinking, "What the hell?" It was the sort of dumb question an actor would say in one of those pathetic patriotic films that would make you cringe. Josh was no patriot; he only joined the army to escape his former life.

"Oh, love it," Josh replied with subtle sarcasm.

The man stared. "What would you do for your country if it were in danger? How far would you go to protect it?"

"Will you cut the crap, stop talking in riddles and explain yourself!" Josh snapped. He had no patience for these types of questions.

"Your file says you can have a bit of a short fuse. Is that a problem? Are you able to control it when needed?" the man continued.

"The only time it's a problem is when I don't get straight answers, or get the run around by people asking dumb questions." Josh was getting wound up. He preferred straight talkers and no bullshit. Army life had pulled him out of his former restrained self. His mouth and ability to say exactly what he thought had gotten him into much trouble on occasion.

The man looked at his counterpart and nodded. They obviously had agreed something before the meeting, and of which they now had their answer.

"Look, what's going on? What's this all about? Why am I here?" countered Josh, with his own set of questions.

"We're looking for talented individuals with the capability of working alone under pressure for long periods, in different environments. Is that you?"

"You clearly have a file on me so you must know my abilities. And it's obvious you wouldn't have come all this way, from wherever you've come from, just to play bat 'n' ball with questions. So, like I said, let's cut the bull, and tell me why you're here, and what you want?"

The man smirked, and Josh knew he had achieved a good impression.

"We want you to work for us, subject to passing the training programme of course, but that shouldn't be a problem for a man of your calibre, should it?"

"Well, that would depend on what training programme and in what capacity the work would be," replied Josh.

"Yes... well let's not get into too much unnecessary rubbish at this stage sergeant Brannon, but suffice to say, we work for the government under the direction of the Joint Intelligence Committee."

"Hmm, Military Intelligence," thought Josh. He was thinking how odd it was to recruit straight from a military regiment, and was trying to understand why they specifically came to see and interview him. "How long have I got to think about it?" he told them.

The man looked at his watch, "One minute, then we're leaving."

Josh pondered briefly, thinking about his life, where he had come from and what he had achieved so far. It was a quick thought process and he didn't take long to come to a decision.

"Okay, I'm in." Josh decided he wanted more. He felt he had reached his limit serving in the regiment and needed a new challenge, but what exactly that new challenge would be, was unclear.

Both men stood up and congratulated Josh on his quick decision.

"We'll be in touch with further details and will make the necessary arrangements for your pending transfer. You've made a good decision Josh; you won't regret it."

The man Josh was talking with picked up a file that was tucked down between the side of the desk and a briefcase. He placed it on the desk, then reached down again to pick up the case. As he reached for it his suit jacket accidentally brushed the file, pushing it over the edge of the desk, onto the floor. Making it appear natural, Josh quickly took the opportunity, bent down, picked up the file and purposely opened it.

WHOOSH!

Josh suddenly began experiencing an intensity of déjà vu sweep through him. He hadn't experienced this feeling since he was fifteen, when involved with the stranger and the incident with View Corp. This time however, the feeling was justified. In the past, Josh was unaware of exactly what had triggered the déjà vu; generally, it was just the idea of something having occurred before in some way. This time it was different, he knew without a doubt what was triggering it, and it unnerved him.

"The file!" he thought.

As soon as he opened the file, he suddenly became aware of its content. It was a solitary page; one he recognised and had had in his possession before. The page was the same one in the file that was given to him by the stranger some twenty years ago—the stranger that had been killed by View Corp.

"It must be a copy," he thought, but couldn't understand it. "Where did they get it from?"

"I'll take that," said the man, reaching out his hand.

Josh passed the file over. The man took it and stuffed it into the briefcase.

"We'll be in touch with your C.O. about the transfer," and both men promptly left the office.

Still a little dazed, Josh watched as they walked past the adjutant's desk on their way out. All he could think about was the file. He knew his past, in some way, was catching up with him, but was unsure how and needed to find out. He decided to follow, giving them several seconds head start before setting off himself. He watched from the window as the two men got into a black saloon with slightly tinted windows. A small puff of smoke from the exhaust indicated they had just started the engine. Seeing the car begin to move, Josh ran at full speed out of the C.O.'s office, down the stairs and out of the building to get to his own car—parked across from the barrack rooms. As he reached it, he turned to see the direction the two men were taking as they passed through the gate by the guardroom—left turn. He quickly jumped into his car, started it up, and pulled off to follow.

After driving fast to catch up, Josh began following the two men in the black saloon. He knew he had to be extra careful in using his own surveillance methods, as these guys were professionals and would most certainly be surveillance aware. Josh couldn't afford to be seen. He kept at least one car between him and the two men as cover—to prevent from being spotted, and so was able to follow the vehicle in close proximity through the busy streets. The car eventually pulled up outside a large official looking building, where one of the men got out. It was the main one of the pair, the man who had done all of the talking. He walked into the building through the front door, and the car pulled away.

"Who to follow?" thought Josh. He decided upon the main one of the two.

Josh parked his car in a restricted zone but didn't care; he needed answers. He got out and walked to the building he saw the man go into. Trying not to make himself stand out, he slowly walked past making mental notes of what he could see. As he looked through the glass front doors, Josh could see a reception area opposite the doorway with two security guards. There were security cameras affixed externally on the wall facing the door. He also noticed there were no windows at street level but started from the first floor upwards. From the front, Josh determined the building was highly secure.

He decided to do a quick check of the building's rear to see if, like the front, it was just as secure. He walked around the back; noting several strategically positioned security cameras covering the external aspect. The building had an underground parking facility that was closed off by a metal grid shutter. Walking past the metal shutter, Josh could partially see inside. A figure appeared behind a glass window in a security office, which he assumed to be another security guard. Seeing this, he realised it was too risky to attempt to go inside without compromising himself, and so decided to carry on his surveillance from his car.

Josh returned to his car. It had already been given a parking ticket—stuck to the windscreen, tucked in a plastic bag. "Bloody traffic wardens," he complained, and pulled it off.

He opened the door, got in and threw the ticket on the passenger seat. After starting the engine, he drove to a spot more suitable for watching the front entrance of the building. He parked between two other cars—giving him some cover—and shifted himself into the back seat, to make him less conspicuous. He had a clear line of sight of the front door, and now it was just a case of waiting to see who came and went.

Josh had done surveillance many times before, and knew it could be long and drawn out. Usually though, he would have been prepared, and taken with him some food and a means of relieving himself without having to leave his post. He could already start to feel a build-up of pressure in his bladder, but was able to suppress the discomfort.

Sitting for some hours, Josh watched intensely the people that came and went from the building; mostly clerks and office types in suits. He could spot the military types a mile away. It was just beginning to get dark and his attention was diminishing through lack of food; but suddenly he noticed the man who had interviewed him earlier that day leave the building. Josh's alertness perked up, causing the pangs of hunger in his stomach to vanish from his attention.

He watched closely as the man, still carrying his briefcase, walk across the street away from the building. Josh casually exited his car and followed on foot. Keeping his distance, he followed from the opposite side of the road, using other pedestrians as cover to keep out of sight. Josh watched him go into a pub, not far from the building, and so waited outside in a doorway across the street.

Through the pub window, Josh could clearly see the man sit at a table. He was sitting on his own for a few minutes until another man joined him, and started making conversation. The second man had the character of a politician or lawyer. Also carrying a briefcase and dressed in a dark suit, he looked haughty and arrogant.

Josh was eager to know what they were talking about but couldn't expose himself. It was better to just see and not hear what was going on than be caught. He watched the man who had conducted his earlier interview reach down into his briefcase. He pulled out a file, the same looking file that contained Josh's profile, and handed it to the second man.

"What the hell!" Surprised, Josh continued to watch with burning curiosity. He had to find out who the other man was.

Both men stood up. The second man, the arrogant looking "politician" type, left the pub first, carrying his briefcase with the file inside. The first man Josh had followed also left, heading back in the direction he came. Josh lowered his head to avoid being spotted as the man passed by on the opposite side. As soon as he had passed, Josh looked up for the second man—he was now the fresh target.

His new target hadn't gone far and was walking away in the opposite direction. Josh kept his distance and, as before, observed from the opposite side of the road. They walked no further than a few streets when a car raced past Josh, braking with sudden force, parallel to the "politician". Right away Josh knew something was wrong. He saw a quick flash of light shine through the rear windscreen, from inside the car, coupled with a sharp suppressed smacking sound. After which, the car door immediately opened with a figure jumping out and jumping back in again. The car immediately raced off down the street, car door closing as it went. It was over in a matter of seconds.

Josh sprinted to the man, who was now lying face down on the concrete—blood flowing from a bullet wound in the side of his body. A crowd started to gather round and Josh directed a young man to phone for emergency services. Josh, knowing battlefield first aid, immediately checked if the man was still breathing—he was barely, with shallow breaths. Josh applied direct pressure to the bullet's entry wound to stem the flow of blood, but looking at the man's face, he could see he wasn't in good shape. He had dealt with bullet wounds before and knew the signs of imminent death. Josh checked the opposite side of the body. There was no exit wound, so he knew the bullet was lodged inside.

"Can you hear me?" Josh called to the man. No response. He was unconscious with a pulse that was barely recognisable.

Josh looked for the briefcase the man was carrying, but it was gone. He instinctively knew the dark figure, that had just carried out the hit, had taken it, along with the file about him.

"Can you hear me?" Josh repeated, as he ripped a piece of the man's suit off, pushing it firmly onto the wound, and taping it in place with duct tape borrowed from an electrician in the crowd. Although breathing shallowly, the man's level of response was non-existent.

Hearing the sirens of emergency vehicles in the distance, Josh knew they were heading in his direction. He couldn't get caught up in the shooting and needed to make a break for it; but he still needed some answers. He rapidly frisked the man and searched through his pockets finding his wallet. Opening it, he found the usual items: money, credit cards and something he least expected; an identity card bearing the title: "Central Intelligence Agency".

Surprised, Josh removed the card, keeping it in his hand. He placed the wallet back, released his hold of the man and stood up. Knowing the crowd were watching him, Josh stood with them—watching the man until he could see the crowd's attention had switched from him, to what was now a corpse lying in the street. Feeling safe to do so, Josh slowly stepped back into the crowd to cover himself. He stepped back further, right to the back, and made a quiet departure.

Walking away from the incident, he briefly turned his head to see the emergency services now arriving at the scene. He quickly picked up his pace, and without stopping, returned to his car.

Sitting in his car, Josh contemplated for a moment or two, recollecting and processing what had just happened. He reached into his pocket and pulled out the identity card he took. With blood smeared over the photo, Josh took a better look of the dead man—William Byrnes.

"What does the C.I.A. want with my file? What the hell is going on?" Josh was flooded with questions surrounding the file—the file on him. He had no answers. All he could do was to sit on what he knew, at least for the time being. He started his car, pulled away and headed home.

CHAPTER 6

THE FOLLOWING MORNING, JOSH woke up early as usual. He turned on the T.V. for news of what had happened the previous evening, concerning the shooting. So far, nothing was being mentioned. He left the T.V. on, to follow along, just in case a special report was broadcast while he readied himself for work.

Being a sergeant and a single man, he had plenty of spare cash, so rented an apartment in a block of flats not far from the barracks. Although he worked with a bunch of mostly sound guys, he was still a loner, and liked the idea of getting away from the barracks to be on his own.

As he ironed his uniform, he heard the hourly news broadcast begin, so dropped what he was doing to watch. The main headlines were reported first, but oddly, no mention of the incident.

"Hmm—that's strange; nothing," he thought. He knew the media liked to report bad news, to push their sales up or promote some agenda, so the shooting must be near the top of the editor's pile somewhere. "Maybe it hasn't hit the national headlines yet. I'll check the local rag."

With that in mind, Josh continued to get ready, pressing and starching his uniform. One thing he disliked about being in the army, was the barrack room bullshit of dressing smart, doing parades, and looking nice for the public. All he wanted was to be operational in the field—getting his hands dirty.

Josh had applied for a transfer to another regiment that was due to go on operations, but was flatly refused. He never received an adequate answer for the refusal, but was simply told he was needed in his own regiment. To him this was just a lame answer and in fact no real answer at all. He knew of a couple of guys from C Company, that hopped from regiment to regiment, just so they could get into the action; they had no problem with multiple transfers.

He had proven himself to be of great value to other agencies, whilst serving abroad with his own regiment, and could think of no genuine reason that would prevent him from serving with another regiment. He wondered if it had anything to do with him sleeping with his platoon commander's wife. For that mistake, he had received an informal reprimand by his commander; informal and unofficial, as his boss wanted to keep it hush-hush. There was a possibility that his commander had stirred up trouble for the transfer, but he would more than likely want to see Josh gone, with the hope of being killed in action.

Josh pulled back his curtains to let the early morning light in; it was raining again. He looked out of the window and down across the street, with the hope of glimpsing his neighbour. With curtains open and lights on, she could sometimes be seen through her front living room window. She would always smile when she saw him, which was often, and particularly when he was dressed in uniform. So, he would always make an extra effort to look smart in case he bumped into her.

Finishing his ironing, he hung his uniform on a hanger to inspect it as though it were on parade. With no wild creases, pressed flat, and looking crisp, he passed his own uniform's inspection, and went on to make breakfast—eggs; a stuck habit from the past. He sometimes caught himself thinking about the breakfasts his mother had made—had he become her in some way? He sat down and ate fast; eating was something he had to do to keep the body alive—it was a chore. He cleaned up and put on his uniform, checking himself in the tall mirror for imperfections he needed to correct, there were none.

Fed, dressed, and ready for work, Josh left his flat. He always used the stairs instead of the lift; another habit left over from his past. It was a habit he couldn't seem to shake off or change. Life was like that—full of habits and routines that kept him "safe", but feeling stuck. Despite being in the army, his thoughts and actions were often bent on comfort and safety, but he longed for challenge, risk, and freedom of choice.

Walking out of the building's main door and into the street, he noticed a white van parked across the way. Usually, he wouldn't have paid it much attention except for the fact the windows were slightly steamed up, as though someone was inside. He immediately rationalised it to himself and thought no more of it. He had more important things to concern himself with right now. Looking across the road, on time as usual, there she was, standing outside—the woman he watched nearly every morning from his flat window. She looked over at Josh and smiled.

"Good morning!" she said out loud.

"Hello," replied Josh.

He smiled, and continued walking to his car. That was the extent of their morning ritual—social pleasantries. He liked her, but despite being a highly skilled soldier, he had no skills with women; particularly with ones he really liked. He had never had a serious and meaningful relationship. A meaningful relationship to him, was a drunken one-night affair; no complications, no fuss. Again, he played it "safe", but in truth, he was a retard at building relationships and friendships—a social misfit.

"Sofia!" she shouted to him.

Josh turned. "Sorry?"

"My name, if you were wondering. It's Sofia."

"Oh—right," Josh hesitated, not knowing what to say or do. His social defence was suddenly shattered by a few words from a pretty woman; his social wall, now broken to pieces, made him feel uncomfortably exposed.

"And you are?" she continued. "It's polite to return a name."

"Yeah—sure, Josh—my name is Josh."

"Well nice to meet you Josh."

"You too," he replied.

They both smiled at each other and went their separate ways.

Josh got into his car, closed the door, and pushed the key into the ignition switch. He stopped to contemplate, while staring at the wet windscreen—his attention not on the rain, but on the memory of the moment he had just experienced with the woman he now knew by name. "Sofia," he thought, and smiled.

Whilst coming to the end of the recollection, his attention became distracted, causing him to focus outwardly. As he looked out through the wet of the windscreen, he caught a glimpse of movement coming from inside the back of the white van. It was too indistinct to know exactly what made the movement, but he knew there was someone or something in the back of it.

Not really knowing why—perhaps his recent experiences or just plain curiosity—his instinct kept him interested and so he waited, focusing his attention on the van. But because he didn't see anything else, no further movement inside for a minute or so, he started to wonder if he'd imagined it whilst thinking about Sofia.

The car engine turned over as Josh turned the ignition key. He flicked the switch to operate the wipers, to clear away the rain, which also made it easier to see the van. There it was again, a slight movement of something shiny.

"Hmm—definitely someone or something in there," he thought.

Josh pulled off, driving down the street, passing the van. As he drove past, he kept looking forward, pretending he wasn't interested or that he hadn't seen anything. He didn't want to make it obvious he was suspicious of it. He turned the corner at the end of the road, out of sight to the van, and parked up. He got out of his car and doubled back on foot. Standing on the corner and making sure he didn't expose himself; he watched the van from a distance, wondering if whoever was in there knew he was there.

Time was ticking by, with nothing happening, and so he decided to leave, at which point the back door of the van opened and a man clutching a black holdall stepped out. As he got out, the man looked around, up and down the road. Josh instinctively knew this guy was up to no good, he knew the signs of a crook. He had been involved in a number of questionable activities as a teen to know the signs. The man crossed the road and entered Josh's apartment block. Josh raced back on foot to follow him. Entering the block into the lobby area, there was no sign of the crook. The man was taking the lift. Josh watched the lift floor indicator stop at his floor, so using the stairs, made his way upwards. He knew where the man was heading, he didn't know why but had this instinctive feeling it was his flat.

When Josh reached his floor, he opened the stairwell door slightly. From there, he could see his flat door and the man standing, facing it, with the black holdall at his feet. The man reached down and pulled something from it, put it up to the lock and firmly jiggled until the door opened. He had picked the lock and entered the flat.

"Steal from my place will ya," thought Josh. He could feel his anger boil up, and the need to sort this bloke out.

Josh walked quietly up to his door, opened it slowly and sneaked inside. He could hear, but not see the intruder inside, who was making some, but little noise. As Josh crept towards the noise source, the man came into view. He was standing partially inside one of the cupboards, with his back to Josh.

"What the hell are you doing!" shouted Josh aggressively. The man immediately turned to face him.

WHOOSH!

Josh was suddenly overcome by another extreme déjà vu experience. Sudden memories began flashing through his mind and within seconds they were gone. He was hesitant and startled, allowing the man to suddenly make a break for it. Josh was slow to react, still feeling the effects of remembering this person or situation somehow. Reaching out, Josh made a failed attempt to grab the intruder, and all he could see was the blur of a fast-moving arm being thrust toward his face. The man struck Josh hard. He felt a sudden heavy blow followed fast by pain to his face; he was pushed back from the force and fell backwards over a chair. Looking up, half dazed, Josh could see the back of the assailant running from his apartment. Josh clambered up the furniture, getting to his feet and gave chase, but the intruder already had a good head start.

"The van!" Josh thought suddenly—knowing the man would be heading for it—and went to intercept him.

He ran down the stairs and out of the apartment block. Looking across at the van, the assailant was already inside; engine revving fast and manoeuvring hard to get out. He clipped the rear wing of the car in front and sped off up the road. Josh attempted to get a licence plate number, but was too dazed to even see it clearly let alone remember it; his head still fuzzy with a combination of pain from the blow, and the feeling of déjà vu.

"Are you okay?" It was Sofia.

"Hi, yeah... I'm fine," Josh replied, thinking about his sore face.

"No, you're not, you're bleeding. Come in and I'll fix you up."

Josh agreed and followed her home. Despite what had just happened he couldn't help but admire her; she just seemed to take his attention away from the pain. She was his ideal, and he wanted her to know, but felt too awkward to say.

"Sit down there Josh," she spoke in a soft voice, "I'll get some ice."

He sat down, looking around the room. There were a few framed photographs of what appeared to be family, probably Sofia's parents and siblings. He knew she was single from the lack of a ring on her finger, and the absence of any man in her home. Josh had been secretly watching her since the first time he saw her. He continued looking around, noticing a collection of romantic CDs stored on a wooden stand. He smiled. Being romantic wasn't something he would allow others to see in him, particularly in his line of work.

Sofia re-entered the room carrying a bowl of water, bag of ice, and cotton wool. "You'd better take your coat off; saves you from getting more blood on it."

Josh felt like a child again, when his mother used to dress his bumps and bruises—she was never so caring though. He removed his coat and placed it on a chair beside him.

"Nice photos," he said, trying to make small talk but also leading on to other questions he wanted to ask.

"Thanks, they're family; my mum and dad, brother and sister," she replied, as she set the bowl down on a table next to him.

Josh smirked to himself; he had already figured that out.

"So, what's all this about?" she quizzed, asking about the fight, while pulling out a piece of cotton wool from the bag.

"Oh, just someone trying to burgle my flat, and I caught him at it."

He knew that was a lie and there was more to it, but he wasn't exactly sure who he could really trust, and what was going on. His instincts were telling him it was somehow connected with the two men who had visited him at the barracks the previous day, and the C.I.A. officer who had been shot.

"Put you head back," said Sofia, and with the palm of her hand on Josh's forehead, she pushed gently back.

He was looking up, straight into Sofia's eyes, as she soaked the piece of cotton wool and gently dabbed it on his face. Although her physical beauty captivated him, he could now see the person behind the eyes—a caring soul. And as Sofia wiped the blood on his face their eyes connected; Sofia now looking directly at him, through his eyes. He felt an awkwardness well up inside of him. He had too many scars, too many sins he didn't want her to see. To him, she was an angel, and he was a demon.

"Don't worry too much, I'll be okay."

Josh was trying to play down how he felt about her. He couldn't handle these situations. For him, commanding a platoon of soldiers, under heavy enemy fire, was significantly easier than facing how he felt about this one woman.

"Don't be silly. You soldiers think you're tough, but I can see through you Josh. Now sit still."

Josh did as he was told. Usually though, if a stranger told him what to do, he would feel resentful and build up a strong resistance inside of him, but it was different with Sofia; she was different.

After wiping the blood away, she reached for some soothing cream. She squeezed the ointment onto another ball of cotton wool, and gently massaged it into the cut on his face. Josh continued watching her; catching Sofia's eyes as they looked at each other. He could sense a build-up of strong feelings between them, but nothing was said.

"There, that's all done," she said, and nervously moved away.

"Er—thanks," said Josh, sitting upright.

There was an awkward tension between them that made them both feel vulnerable; accompanied by a heavy silence. The lack of conversation seemed to stretch time, as well as the awkwardness. In his head, Josh was frantically searching for something to say but failing miserably; his complete clumsiness becoming more apparent to him.

"Would you like a drink?" Sofia broke the stiff silence with the tradition of offering drinks to a guest.

Josh stared at her standing in the doorway; her face, her form and flowing hair was a picture of perfection. Hypnotised by her beauty, his unbroken stare and lack of answering was giving him away. He could feel his self-made veneer that "protected" him was being stripped, stripped to reveal how he felt for her.

"Josh, would you like a cup of tea?" she repeated.

"Um—yeah, that would be great, sorry, uh I think I'm still a little dazed from the thump." Josh was rambling a little, trying to hide his true feelings, but Sofia just gave a slight smile. She knew!

She went into the kitchen to make tea, leaving Josh to sit quietly alone, thinking about his rambling moment. "You idiot," he thought, criticising himself. "What the hell was I doing?" He wanted to impress her, not make her think he was a blathering fool.

She returned with two mugs of tea and passed one to Josh, "Here you go."

"Thanks." Josh took the offering. "Look I'm sorry about the rambling a minute ago, I'm not normally like that I can assure you. I'm usually quite decisive and direct and it was just the knock to my face that has made me a little uncertain. I don't usually stare and say stupid things."

Josh was doing it again. He was trying to convince himself he had no feelings for her, and tried to cover it up with more rambling, but he was making it worse. He was usually good at lying, and very convincingly at that, but with her, he felt like an open book. She smiled at him, without any judgement. She was smarter than him.

"Do you need to call your work?" she asked.

"No that's fine, I won't stay long. I'm in charge today as my platoon commander is on a training course, so I have no one to report to."

"I see," said Sofia, "what about the police?"

Josh paused for a moment, sipping his tea slowly so he could gain more time to think of an answer. He didn't want the police involved and he didn't want Sofia to know why.

"So, are you going to call the police?" she asked again.

Josh knew she was no fool and had to give her an acceptable answer.

"He didn't get away with anything, and I didn't even get his licence number, so the police won't have anything to go on. It would be a waste of time to get them involved."

Josh knew that wasn't the real reason. He didn't want anything coming back to him regarding the shooting of the C.I.A. officer, as he still had the man's I.D. in his possession. He also hadn't dealt with his clothes he wore which were stained with the man's blood. He would certainly have some explaining to do if these were discovered in his apartment. But the main reason, was that he also knew this was in some way connected to the incident when he was fifteen, and the stranger that was killed in front of him. This, he instinctively knew, involved View Corp.

Josh finished his tea and stood up. "I better go."

"Sure, let me show you to the door." Sofia stood up and walked ahead of Josh.

As Josh stepped out of the house, he could feel himself linger, as he wanted to ask her out on a date.

"Is anything wrong Josh?" she asked.

"Er—no. See you around," and he walked off heading back to his flat.

Sofia smiled, and watched as he walked away, knowing this wouldn't be the last time they would see each other. She stepped back inside the house and closed the door.

CHAPTER 7

JOSH RETURNED TO HIS flat; his front door was still wide open. Inside, he looked resentfully at the chair he had fallen over, after being struck in the face. He was annoyed at the damage done to his pride but was consoled by the fact that, had the situation turned out differently—in his favour—he wouldn't have spent time with Sofia. He was willing to have his pride dented for such a prize.

Almost certainly, at any other time, Josh would have gotten the upper hand; he was physically very strong, due to the intense workouts he put himself through. He always felt he needed to set a good example for the troops under his command. And he despised the N.C.O.s and officers who were themselves unfit, but still expecting their own troops to be in good physical shape. To him, they were the worst hypocrites.

He thought that of his own platoon commander who, for an officer, was himself not very fit—physically and mentally. Josh had decided he wouldn't think twice about putting a bullet in him if he put the lives of his men under unnecessary risk, because of his inability to cope in war zone situations. And it wasn't because of the fact that Josh had slept with his wife, it was just the simple fact of survival, and that he was a huge liability.

His platoon commander was given his position only as a temporary stepping stone toward some higher post in the army. He had been earmarked for some office job in main army headquarters somewhere, but was ordered to first get some on-the-ground experience in an infantry battalion. Unfortunately for Josh, he got the short straw to babysit the man, simply because he was the most proficient sergeant in the regiment. It sucked that being good at something got him penalised.

Putting the upturned chair back in its rightful place, Josh remembered the man was looking inside one of the cupboards when he disturbed him. Walking into the room, the cupboard door was wide open. He knew there was nothing of value inside, just some old boxes he used for packing when he first moved in, of which he had decided to keep. The boxes however had been moved to one side, allowing Josh to notice something wrong with the flat's electrical box. On closer inspection he noticed the cover of the junction box was loose, with only one screw still in place but partially undone.

"Why was he messing with that?" Josh whispered to himself.

He removed the last screw and took the cover off. Looking further, he inspected the wiring—all of the wiring into the flat, including phone line. He was no electrician but knew when something wasn't right. Attached to the phone line was a small black object that appeared very much out of place to the rest of the wiring. He had an inkling of what it was; a listening device. The intruder had tapped his phone line.

Josh stood back looking at his discovery, puzzled as to why, but knowing it had to be related to everything that had been happening to him. The only thing that made sense to him was the pattern of unusual occurrences.

"What now?" he thought, and then remembered an old army buddy who had left the army and started his own private investigation company. "This will be right up his alley."

He pulled his mobile phone out of his pocket and fingered through his contacts list: H, I, J, K, L, M "Mac." Finding his name, Josh tapped on the profile and pressed "CALL". With just three rings he answered.

"Hello can I help?" answered Mac in a formal voice.

"Hi Mac it's Josh here, Josh Brannon."

"Josh! How ya doing mate? You still in the army?" His tone changed as soon as he recognised Josh, and the familiarity they once had popped back instantly.

Josh usually hated getting in touch with old army comrades as all they would talk about were the "good old days", which bored him senseless. He always looked at the present—the here-and-now—or the future, and always wanted to leave the past where it was—behind him. He hated digging it up, particularly his own troubled history. It was odd to him, with soldiers that had left the army because they wanted to move on or because they disliked it, how they would always talk about it; even join military associations. It was as though they were stuck in the past and hanging on to it. But Mac was different. He was a "go-getter" type person and Josh always liked that about him, and respected him for it.

"Yeah... I am," Josh replied monotonously to the trite question. "Look Mac, I've got a problem and need your help. Are you still doing your private investigation work?" Josh jumped straight to the point rather than go down memory lane.

"Yeah, doing really well as it happens. Just been to Saudi on a lucrative job, and got a great bonus as well. I can't talk about the case but just to say it was high profile and heads will roll, if you pardon the pun," Mac bragged. "So, what's up, what do you need Josh?"

"I had a break-in this morning and found something on my phone line. I need you to check out my place for bugs. Do you still do that?"

"Right, stop there!" Mac ordered. "Don't say anymore. Just say yes or no, okay?"

"Yeah sure," Josh replied, with a hint of resentment at being told what to do. He was the one normally giving orders, not so much taking them.

Mac became serious and less friendly, as the knowledge and training of his trade kicked in. He knew, if a listening device had been planted in Josh's flat, the eavesdropper would more than likely be a party to the conversation they were now having.

"I'll meet you in half an hour, at our old drinking spot, okay?" said Mac.

Josh thought for a second about needing to get to work, but decided that finding out what the hell was going on was more important, so would phone his next in command to take over the morning's training.

"Alright Mac, thanks mate, see you there," and he hung up.

Josh started looking around the flat; feeling an added intrusive presence with the possibility that someone could be watching, or listening to him. He didn't feel he had any privacy anymore, and felt his mood change for the flat that he loved. Now he was suspicious of it.

He quickly undressed from his uniform, and put on some old jeans and a t-shirt. He grabbed his jacket and car keys and walked out of the flat. As he closed the door behind him, he noticed scratches around the keyhole that were obviously made by the intruder; picking the lock. For some reason seeing those scratches made the whole incident more real to him, that it was much more than what he initially thought.

Josh walked down the stairs and out of the main door. He looked across as he usually did at Sofia's house, hoping for a quick glimpse but she wasn't there. He walked to the end of the road and around the corner where he had left his car. About to open it and get inside he suddenly thought, "What if this is bugged as well?"

He was becoming paranoid and suspicious of everything; his attention was becoming split and dispersed. He needed Mac's help. He decided to use his car and that he was just being overcautious. But he also thought that none of what had happened to him in the last couple of days was anything of the ordinary. He still needed caution, and his wits about him.

Whilst driving, Josh repeatedly looked in his rear-view mirror to check if he was being followed. The roads were busy with rush hour traffic, making it more difficult to tell, so began practicing what he knew of anti-surveillance tactics to be sure. He had never been trained in these tactics, but picked up a few tricks working with other agencies during his career.

He pulled up to a set of traffic lights that were showing red. He looked in his rear-view mirror at a car that had tailed him for a couple of miles. It was two cars behind; he couldn't see the occupants. Josh indicated to turn left to see what the car would do. The car's left indicator also started flashing. As the traffic lights turned to green Josh pulled off, still indicating left but instead of turning drove straight ahead. This, he knew, would confuse the tail. It would force them to turn left as they were already indicating their intention to turn; otherwise, it would blow their cover. If the car didn't turn, he would know it was likely following him.

He watched closely in the mirror as the car he thought was following him turned left; finally, he could see the most unlikely spies inside—an old couple. Josh sighed as he felt a sudden release of tension that had slowly built up. "Bloody hell! Come on Josh, pull it together," he said to himself. Seeing the old couple eased his mind a little, but not altogether. There was still someone out there spying on him, and for whatever reason he didn't know.

Josh continued his journey, constantly checking and re-checking for potential tails. After driving around for a while, he felt satisfied that no one had followed him. And after doing a couple of last-minute U-turn manoeuvres, decided to go to the pub where he and Mac used to hang out.

Driving into the car park, Josh spotted Mac a mile off, sitting in a flashy top of the range sports car. He pulled his car up alongside Mac's and looked across at him. He was sporting a big smile with a deep tanned look—obviously from his last assignment in Saudi, and obviously doing well financially. Getting out of his car, Mac walked over, and Josh stepped out to greet him.

"Just like the good old days, hey Josh?" said Mac in a loud voice.

"Yeah, just like the good old days Mac. Except you're no longer in the army, and I've been promoted twice since you've left. And you're obviously earning a shitload more than me."

Mac laughed. "Still got that shitty attitude of yours I see though. That hasn't changed, has it?" said Mac, smiling.

One thing Josh liked about Mac, was that he was always chirpy, and would hardly ever be in a bad mood. He was a positive guy on a natural high; a very capable guy that could have gone a long way in the army. Together, they both made the rank of lance corporal, whilst on the same course, and were good friends from then on. He upset a few people in the regiment, after passing the course with distinction, but then turned down the promotion. At the same time, he handed in his termination notice.

"How are you doing Mac?" said Josh, smiling. They took each other by the hand and shook to their welcomed friendship.

"I'm great. Like my new car?" Mac was a real bragger, but never arrogant. He would never shove his success down your throat, or use it to make you look inferior. He was one of those guys you couldn't help but like and admire.

"Yeah, looks great," replied Josh. "How can you afford it?"

"With the compliments of His Royal Highness—Mr Saudi himself," he said smiling, but said no more. "So Josh, what's up mate? You been playing around with ya platoon commander's wife again?" Mac laughed at his own wit.

Josh smiled and explained, "I had a break-in this morning at my flat. I caught some guy and think he was tampering with my phone lines. There's a small device that looks odd, attached to the wiring, and I knew you did that course when you left the army on bugs and stuff."

"Technical Surveillance Counter Measures course Josh," said Mac didactically, with a big know-it-all smile. "Okay Josh, let's cut the banter; what's going on?" Mac was in his detective persona now.

"Look Mac, can you come and just take a look. If it's nothing then fine, if it's something I'll tell you." Mac agreed.

Before they left Mac explained that there were two ways of dealing with the listening device. The first option would be to remove the bug—which would either alert whoever was listening in that it had been found, or that they would believe it was damaged and come back to either fix it or plant another. The second option would be to feed it false information in the hopes of flushing out who was behind it. Josh knew they wouldn't be back as they had already been rumbled, but if there were any other devices that had been planted then he would use them to try and flush them out.

"Right Josh, once in the flat I don't want any talking. I'm not there, do you understand? Just let me do what I need to do without question. Okay?"

"No problem, I'll just behave as I usually do," Josh replied. "But what about my car?"

"Your car's fine," replied Mac, "I've had a portable radio frequency scanner on the whole time we've been talking. I've been scanning you and your car for radio transmissions. You're clean."

They got into their cars and drove back to Josh's place. Parking up on the road, Mac walked around to the back of his car, opened the boot, and pulled out two silver metal cases. He then joined Josh and both proceeded into the foyer of the block of flats. Mac instinctively walked over to the lift and pushed the call button, but Josh beckoned him to use the stairs.

"Geez Josh, like you said, I'm not in the army anymore. I'm not as fit as you, so let's use the lift, huh?" Mac waited for the door to open. "Which floor?"

"Fourth," replied Josh, and waited with him.

The lift door opened and they stepped inside. Mac put the two cases down and pushed the button for the fourth floor. They both stood in silence as the door closed and the lift started to ascend. Josh was remembering back to his childhood and how he got stuck in the routine of never using the lift. He thought it strange how something in his past was still routinely affecting him in the present; as though he was unknowingly being controlled by past events. What else, he thought, was controlling him that he was unaware of?

The lift came to a halt on the fourth floor. Mac grabbed his cases and they stepped out; Josh leading the way to his flat. He opened the door and they went inside. There was no talking, as instructed by Mac earlier.

Mac placed the two metal cases side-by-side on the living room table, unlocked them and lifted the lids. Josh looked inside. Inside one case was a built-in computer, unlike any other he had seen, with various dials, buttons, and a headset. The other case had an assortment of handheld devices.

Mac started to remove the equipment; placing it next to the cases. He then motioned to Josh, who showed him to the cupboard, and the suspect device he discovered on the wiring. Mac studied it for a brief moment, walked back into the living room and returned with a pair of wire cutters. He leaned forward and snipped one of the wires connecting the device to the cabling; disabling it but leaving it in place. He then motioned to Josh, to follow him out of the flat to a secure area to talk.

"Josh, what the fuck is going on?" Mac was more serious than Josh had ever seen; his usual big grin wiped from his face. In fact, he looked white with worry.

"What do you mean?" Josh was also starting to feel anxious.

"This device is top class equipment. You don't buy this on the open market."

"So, what—what are you trying to say?"

"I've only seen this once before, from a tech-head who had some involvement in making it for certain organisations a year or so ago. It was a training session, a lecture I went to, giving details of some really sophisticated shit—surveillance devices that were only used by intelligence agencies. It was actually a hush-hush training lecture, if you know what I mean: secret stuff. I knew someone, who knew someone, that got me in. And I'm not afraid to say it, but there were some pretty scary looking characters there. Anyway, this device is one of those high-tech creations. It's not just your usual room bug. It can pick up all transmissions, including visual display. It can "see" what you're looking at on your computer. You've got some serious people watching you Josh!"

Josh was trying to process everything that was going on. It made sense to him what the device was, and the possibility of some agency watching him. It was tying together, but he only had the edges of a puzzle that was vast in size. It all connected somehow; with the stranger he got involved with in his teens, the two government agents visiting him at the barracks, and the assassinated C.I.A. officer. But how was he involved and for what reason? There were still too many questions and too few answers.

"Anyway, I've disabled it, so someone may or may not come back for it. Likely they won't, but you never know. But I still need to sweep the rest of the flat. It might take some hours to really dig around, especially if the devices are like that one. Do you need to get going? You can leave me here on my own to work."

"Yeah sure. Thanks Mac. I need to get to the barracks pretty soon, so I'll just get changed and go. You've got my number, so give me a call if you find anything. I'll be able to get away easily enough; the boss is away."

They went back into the flat, Josh got changed and left Mac to it. Walking out of the flat, Josh had so much on his mind that he forgot to close the door. He walked down the stairs, as his routine dictated, through the lobby and out the main front door.

While walking to his car he heard a shout, "Josh!"

He turned. It was Sofia, standing by her front door.

"Hi," Josh replied, and he walked over to her.

"I see you're back. Well, I saw you come back with that other guy carrying the cases. Is everything okay?" she asked.

Josh's deceptive ability quickly came in to play, as he didn't want to reveal anything about what was really going on, especially to her. He felt he needed to protect her from the truth, for if she knew what was going on, she could become involved in some kind of danger. What that danger could be, was not entirely known to him. He didn't fully know the scope of what he was involved in, and so he couldn't take any chances, not with her.

"Yeah, everything's fine Sofia, thanks. I decided to take your advice and call the police. He's a forensics man. He's up there taking fingerprints and trying to find clues, that's all. I've left him to get on with it, as he may be some hours and I must get to work."

Josh hated deceiving someone he really cared about, but felt it was for the best.

"That's good. Hopefully they'll find something. Well Josh, don't let me hold you up, I don't want to make you later than you already are. See you around," and Sofia went into the house.

Josh smiled, not because he had managed to fool her, but because he was starting to really fall for her.

CHAPTER 8

JOSH ARRIVED AT THE barracks. His platoon was drilling on the parade square with corporal Compton as acting drill sergeant. Compton was shouting and double-marching them around the square; a good indication the platoon was messing up and needed waking up.

Josh parked his car, got out and walked briskly to the office block as he knew he was late. He hated lateness and setting a bad example. He knew how bad examples and poor performers spoilt a unit, causing unit sloppiness to spread and potentially unnecessary casualties in war. He walked into the platoon office.

"Ah! Sergeant Brannon, nice of you to join us," said Lieutenant Giles, the platoon commander, who was sitting at his desk.

"Morning sir!" said Josh sharply with a salute, "I thought you were on training today sir?"

"Obviously sergeant."

Josh could sense the unexpressed resentment, with a hint of "I've got you now" flow in his voice, and knew he had to play it cool. He couldn't let the past between him and his superior get dredged up again, as he was always the one to end up paying the price.

Josh's transgression with his platoon commander's wife was a drunken mistake he would never make again. His life had been made a living hell ever since, and the rift between him and his boss never mended. Every so often his boss would make the odd indirect dig just to remind Josh of the mistake. He used it as a means of control. He had Josh exactly where he wanted him; that was his way. Despite being cowardly, he was deviously clever.

"What time do you make it sergeant Brannon? I mean, you do realise you were supposed to be drilling the platoon this morning. But instead, you took it upon yourself, in my suspected absence, to have what—a lie in? You do look a little tired. I hope you feel well rested now."

Josh could feel himself seething inside, not because of the bollocking he was getting—if one could call it that, as he could handle those easily enough—but because of the slimy way it was being said. He could take a full-frontal tirade of abuse, but one thing he couldn't stand, was a snivelling coward—only brave enough to make hidden jabs or sarcastic comments.

How Lieutenant Giles became an officer was beyond anyone's understanding at the regiment, particularly the lower ranks; they could spot a weak link a mile away. There was talk that he was transferred from another regiment due to his abysmal command; command that led to two men getting seriously wounded while on active service. The story that circulated, was that he lost his bottle during a contact with some insurgents, and his platoon sergeant had to take over. It was always suspected that this was the reason for him being assigned to a strong platoon sergeant—Josh.

"I had a break-in at my flat this morning sir," replied Josh, setting his boss straight.

"I see. Did you call the police?"

Josh knew his boss didn't want to know out of concern, but simply to corner him somehow. So, with the subtle attack, he had to figure out what angle his boss was coming from. He certainly couldn't tell him that he hadn't reported it, as he wouldn't be believed about the break-in. Deception was needed.

Luckily, at that precise moment the office phone rang, to Josh's relief, giving him a stay of execution. Lieutenant Giles picked it up and answered. He suddenly adopted a meek manner to a one-sided conversation, speaking only a couple of words to acknowledge compliance of orders: "Yes sir! Yes sir!" After a brief but seemingly impinging conversation, Lieutenant Giles hung up the phone. He looked as though his nose had just been put out of joint.

"Well sergeant, it appears as though I, being your superior, am the last to know about a transfer of yours. It seems as though you have taken it upon yourself to circumvent my authority. You seem to be doing that a lot lately, but never mind. The C.O. has requested your immediate presence at battalion HQ. I do hope you enjoy your new posting sergeant."

Josh could see through his boss's façade—the forced smile and fake pleasantries—and knew he wasn't happy about losing his hold over him, or being kept out of the loop.

"So, where has the army felt fit to post you then, back to Afghanistan?" continued Lieutenant Giles.

He was fishing for information and Josh knew it. "It's classified sir," answered Josh abruptly, feeling a sense of satisfaction in not telling him.

Lieutenant Giles looked ready to explode; his lips puckering up like shrivelled raisins. He expected people to obey him at all times and expected an answer, even if it was a personal matter.

"Sergeant Brannon, you are still under my command! Now where have you been posted?"

"It's classified sir," repeated Josh, with a deadpan face.

He could see it was winding his boss up and enjoyed every moment of it. But in truth, he didn't even know what his new posting was going to be—just found it amusing to push his boss's buttons. Josh was standing, holding a fixed expressionless gaze, but inside was kicking himself with enjoyment at the torment he was causing. He could feel a resurgence of power which had been lost ever since the marital mistake he had made, and was enjoying the experience.

Josh loved the army and the adventurous lifestyle it gave him, but he couldn't shake off the idea that it was somehow making him into more of a "robot". What little individualism he had, before joining, has been slowly eroding, right from basic training. In part, he has been rebuilt into a non-thinking machine, programmed to accept and carry out any order without question. This way of operating Josh was used to—during his early years at home; but at least then he was able to escape it to an extent. Being in the army was different, only being allowed to think within certain limitations that didn't go beyond his rank. Josh felt restricted in his abilities and was hoping his new posting would give him some added freedom, while still doing the job he loved.

"I see," said Lieutenant Giles, his face looking stiff with resentment at Josh's disobedience. "Go and see the C.O., he's expecting you!"

Right to the end he was trying to keep Josh on a leash, giving him one last order, trying to kid himself he was still in control.

"Yes sir!" replied Josh and gave a salute.

"I'm sure we'll get a suitable replacement before you go. Well done, hope it all goes well."

"Thank you sir," replied Josh, however recognising the lack of sincerity in his boss's words. He turned and left the office.

Josh didn't care one way or another for his platoon commander's empty wishes of good fortune. He promised himself that if ever he left the army and saw his boss, he would tell him exactly what he thought of him; if that meant a couple of right hooks to get the message across then that's what he would do. There were a few guys in the platoon that felt the same way. In the meantime though, Josh was effectively still under Lieutenant Giles's command, and so had to keep biting his tongue and playing it cool.

Walking to regimental HQ, Josh was in deep thought about the break-in and what Mac had told him about the listening device. He was focused on trying to come up with answers as to why he was being targeted, and by whom. His only prime suspects were the two gentlemen he had just accepted a new posting from, and possible connection to the C.I.A. He started over-thinking the situation and his mind began throwing up all sorts of random possibilities. He simply didn't have enough facts, and was really just guessing to fill in the gaps surrounding what little information he had. And these were big gaps.

He walked into the adjutant's office where he was made to wait. He took this rare opportunity to have a look around at the photographs and trophies of the regiment. He looked at the most recent battalion photograph and noticed Lieutenant Giles, sitting three seats away from the commanding officer in the front row. Josh smirked with contempt.

While standing, perusing the pictures, the assistant adjutant walked in. She put a smile on every low ranker's face as she was attractive and "out of bounds"—due to her rank as second lieutenant. The barrier of rank seemed to make her more appealing to the troops.

"Good morning ma'am!" Josh snapped to attention and gave a salute.

"The C.O. will see you now sergeant Brannon," she said, returning the salute.

"Yes ma'am!"

Josh marched sharply into the C.O.'s office, snapped to a halt and carried out another salute. The C.O. was sitting behind his oakwood desk, his shirt pushed to the limit by his oversized belly. Tea and biscuits were placed within an arm's reach, so he didn't have to exert himself too much. Josh wondered how "Jabba"—which was what he was secretly called by his troops—could be in the position and rank that he was.

"Ah—sergeant Brannon; it appears as though your services are wanted elsewhere damned sharpish. This transfer of yours has been pretty quick through the pipeline of bureaucracy. And I'm surprised, as much as you will be, that you are to report first thing in the morning. Your transfer has been approved effective from today. You need to get yourself sorted and report at 08:00 hours tomorrow. All the details are in the transfer order." Jabba passed Josh the typed orders.

"Well good luck to you Brannon, you will surely be missed at the regiment. And you can offload that burden of yours onto someone else; that's if I can find someone to take the challenge. It's difficult working under a 'sewer rat'", he continued with a serious face.

Josh was completely surprised to hear Jabba talk bluntly like that, and knew he was referring to Lieutenant Giles. The C.O. wasn't as useless as Josh had pegged him to be, but had correctly estimated his platoon commander's personality with precision. Josh suddenly gained some respect for his C.O. and knew he was sincere about his good wishes—unlike the "sewer rat".

"Thank you sir," replied Josh.

"Okay, that will be all," said the C.O. and dunked a biscuit into his tea.

Josh sharply saluted, made a right turn and marched out, back into the adjutant's office.

"Good luck sergeant Brannon," said the assistant adjutant, smiling.

"Thank you ma'am," replied Josh and he continued walking out of the office.

While heading back to the platoon he read the details on the transfer order. There was no mention of what unit he was transferring to or his role, just an address of where to report to and the time. He wondered exactly what it was he was getting in to.

Back at the platoon office, Lieutenant Giles was still sitting in the same position as when Josh had left him. He was the biggest hypocrite ever, with his feet up, gazing out of the window, and obviously hadn't been working.

"Alright sir!" Josh half shouted in a bid to scare his boss.

"Oh, um, yes," replied Lieutenant Giles. He was startled. He quickly took his feet off the side and pretended to be checking the cleanliness of his boots. He continued the pretence by brushing one boot with his hand, as though wiping off dust, then picked up a piece of paper lying on his desk and faked his interest in it.

"I didn't see you come in sergeant. I was just going over the training plan for the week. I've booked us in for some Close Quarter Battle training on Thursday—the C.O. will be watching. You can polish up your command of the platoon in battle situations. You could do with a bit of time management too sergeant Brannon," he slyly added.

"Bull-shitter," thought Josh. "I'm afraid you're on your own for that little adventure sir," he said out loud.

Josh happily began to inform his platoon commander he was off. But was even happier to let him hang himself on Thursday; he knew his boss would fail miserably commanding the CQB drills.

"What do you mean?" questioned Lieutenant Giles.

"I've been transferred, effective immediately from today. I've been ordered to get going by the C.O.," and Josh started to collect his things from his desk, placing them in a box he kept underneath.

"But that's very sudden. Who's your replacement?" Lieutenant Giles was panicking at the thought of having to command the platoon.

Josh didn't know and didn't care; just as long as he was out of the way of the "sewer rat".

"I've no idea sir. The C.O. said he would need to get someone of a high calibre to look after the platoon, that's all he said. Oh, and he mentioned something about a 'sewer rat', but I didn't catch on to what he was talking about, being a lowly sergeant, SIR!"

Josh knew he was pushing the boundaries. He sensed his freedom and the release of his platoon commander's grip on him, and was starting to express the grievances he had bottled up over time. He was starting to dig back but still had to be careful about rubbing his boss's nose in the dirt; he hadn't left yet.

"What do you mean by that sergeant?" Lieutenant Giles demanded explanation.

"By what sir?" replied Josh, while still packing his things and pretending not to know.

"With what you just said about what the C.O. said?"

Lieutenant Giles was becoming insecure by the comments made by Josh—which of course was the purpose of relaying what the C.O. had told him. He wanted his boss to know what their commanding officer actually thought of him—without directly saying so.

"Just telling you what the C.O. said sir. I thought you wanted to know all that was going on?"

Josh was enjoying the cat-and-mouse game, except this time he felt like he was the cat. He could see his boss looking perturbed with his lips screwing up like shrivelled raisins again. His boss had lost control of him and he knew it. Josh finished collecting up his private effects and put the box under his arm.

"Right sir, I'm all packed and off. I hope you have a good time commanding the platoon on Thursday sir," and Josh gave a final salute. As he was about to leave the office, he turned with a parting shot, "Oh and say goodbye to your wife for me sir, thanks," and he sharply walked out of the office.

He couldn't resist a good wind-up with that last comment and half expected to be called back, but surprisingly no action was taken. He knew the "sewer rat" had swallowed a mouthful and had "drowned". To his satisfaction, Josh walked away smiling.

On his way to the car, corporal "Billy" Compton was walking towards him. He had given the platoon a bit of a breather from marching up and down the parade square.

"Alright Josh," said Billy with a nod.

"Alright Billy; how's the drilling going?"

"Bloody awful, we've got a long way to go. What happened to you this morning?"

Josh didn't want to go into it, so pulled rank a little, "Personal stuff corporal. And by the way, it looks like you might be acting sergeant for a little while longer." Billy frowned with confusion. "I'm off," revealed Josh, "I've finally got my transfer and I'm leaving right now; hopefully never to come back."

"Bloody hell Sarge, you're not leaving me with that waster are ya!" moaned Billy.

Josh smiled. He knew no one in the platoon liked Lieutenant Giles.

"He's all yours to babysit now corporal Compton," he said in his sergeant's voice, but then continued in a friendly manner, "You'll do fine mate. Watch your back with him and don't give him any more information than necessary. Just look after the rest of the lads. And if you get any problems with him...."

They looked and nodded at each other. Billy knew exactly what Josh was thinking, they had already discussed it in detail. The regiment was going on operational tour to Afghanistan in six months, and they had already worked out the details of how to get rid of their boss—if he became a liability again. Josh had decided none of his troops were getting their legs blown off, because of a cowardly incompetent officer, and he and Billy were prepared to do what was necessary to prevent it.

"You better get back to the platoon, looks like they're getting bored," said Josh.

"Thanks sarge. You look out for yourself, whatever you're doing."

Josh extended his hand and they shook a farewell. Corporal Compton turned and marched back to the platoon that was goofing about.

Josh got into his car and gave a final look around. He looked over at corporal Compton who was giving the platoon a good bollocking. Josh smiled to himself. Despite the odd bad apple in the regiment, there were still a lot of good guys, and he had had most of his best times in life with them. It was a bond of brotherhood that could never be replaced. But it was time now for him to move on, but to what, he was still unsure. He started his car and pulled off. He drove by the guardroom and out through the camp gate for the very last time.

Whilst driving home, he listened to the radio and the local news channel, to see if anything had been reported on the C.I.A officer who had been shot a couple of days ago; still nothing. He couldn't believe the media hadn't reported on a story like that; it was completely unusual. He thought that maybe he should listen to Sofia and contact the police. But he didn't want to blow his chances of finding out what was going on, and how the recent events are linked to his past. Somehow Josh knew that his new career would furnish him with new answers. He didn't know why he knew; he just did.

CHAPTER 9

DRIVING INTO THE END of the road, Josh could see several emergency vehicles parked outside his apartment block, accompanied by a small gathering of spectators. He instinctively knew it was to do with Mac and feared the worst. He pushed down on the accelerator and sped towards an awaiting ambulance and police vehicles. He drove towards a police officer, standing in the middle of the road in front of a stretched line of police tape—cordoning the road off to prevent public interference. Josh knew they only cordon off an area like this when a serious incident has taken place. He had done similar on operations, when needing to preserve the scene of an IED—Improvised Explosive Device—, or terrorist firing point.

As Josh approached, the officer put his hand out, palm facing forward, gesturing him to stop. He stopped his car in front of the officer, who then walked round to speak. Josh wound down the window.

"Where are you off to sir?" questioned the officer.

"I live here, in that block of flats," and Josh pointed.

"What's your name and flat number?"

"Josh Brannon, Flat 24. What happened here?"

"Wait there a moment sir."

The officer gave no response to Josh's question, but only spoke into his radio, giving Josh's details over the net. Josh could see the officer was receiving instructions by the slight nodding of his head, like he was actually talking to someone standing in front of him.

After the brief conversation, the officer returned his attention to Josh, and asked him to wait as someone was coming to meet him.

Less than a minute later, a tall man dressed in a dark grey suit walked out of the building towards the officer. He approached the officer, who pointed Josh out. The man walked up to Josh and identified himself.

"Mr Brannon, I'm Detective Inspector Giles."

Josh momentarily hesitated on the name "Giles", wondering if he was related to his, now former, platoon commander. "What are the odds?" he thought.

"What's happening Inspector?" enquired Josh.

"Please sir, can you come with me," requested the inspector.

Josh parked his car and joined him. They headed towards the flats.

"Can you tell me who is in your flat Josh? You don't mind me calling you Josh, do you?"

"No that's fine. Um, it's an old friend of mine from the army; Mac." Josh knew something was wrong. "What's happened?"

"Let's go inside shall we." Both Inspector Giles and Josh entered the building.

It was the second time that day Josh was forced to use the lift, as he and the inspector made their way up to Josh's flat. Outside the flat door, a uniformed officer stood guard. He acknowledged DI Giles with a nod as he and Josh entered. Inside, uniformed officials were busy working the scene. The forensic specialists were taking photographs and bagging items from the flat. Mac's two metal cases were still positioned on the table, not having moved much since Josh had left earlier that morning.

"Where's Mac?" asked Josh, looking at the inspector.

Just as he had asked the question, two paramedics came through pushing a stretcher with what appeared to be the form of a body sealed inside a body bag. The medics pushed past, wheeling the body out of the flat. Josh felt a sudden emotional drop inside his own body, as though he had just lost something precious.

"That's Mac, isn't it?" Josh solemnly asked the inspector.

"Yes, I'm afraid it is. Can you tell me what happened?"

Josh gave no response. He was hesitating for two reasons; the sudden shock of bad news about his friend Mac's death, and the trouble he was now facing. He had to start thinking of some serious credible lies for this one. He still had his bloodstained clothes in the laundry basket; blood from the murdered C.I.A. officer the previous day. He couldn't get involved in that. But he knew the forensic team would go through the place with a fine-tooth comb and discover them — if they hadn't already.

"Sorry Inspector, just a bit shocked." Although genuinely shocked, Josh was also using the situation to gain a little thinking time.

"I left him here this morning and went to work. We met up earlier, as like I said we were old friends from the army."

Josh knew he was leaving big holes in his story, and was desperately trying to think of how to close them. He knew the inspector would use probing questions to fill in the missing details himself.

"What happened to him Inspector?"

"He has gunshot wounds to the body. Two shots, small calibre. That's the preliminary assessment, but I will know more later with the pathology and forensic reports. So, he was alive when you left for work?"

"Yeah." Josh knew to keep the answers short and sweet; not to say more than was necessary. Just answer the question and no more, to avoid tripping himself up.

"Tell me, why was Mac here?"

"I had a break-in this morning; some guy had gotten into my flat. I disturbed him when I came back from going to work, and he clocked me one in the face and ran off. I told my friend Mac about it who said he would help me secure my flat for me. He's a private investigator, and knows all about this kind of thing."

"I see. Did you report the break-in?" asked the inspector.

"No. Nothing was taken so I didn't bother. I didn't get a good look at the guy; it was very quick, and as I said, he hit me in the face which dazed me."

"Yes, I can see the cut. That must have hurt," said the inspector sympathetically. "You should still report the incident Josh, even if you didn't get a good look at the suspect. We will need to go over it to get some details of this person; whatever you can remember. Incidentally, what time did this occur?"

"It was around 8ish I guess; maybe a bit before."

Josh felt it was going smoothly and started to relax a little, but Inspector Giles had other ideas. He was a professional that liked to get his prey nice and relaxed, to catch them off-guard.

"Do you know what this equipment is for Josh?" The inspector pointed to the two metal cases on the table.

"They're Mac's, he brought them with him. I guess its equipment to help secure my flat. Mac didn't say exactly what he was going to do, as I left him to get on with it."

"I see. Well, would it surprise you to know that the equipment in these cases is for the purpose of detecting listening devices, or bugs?" said the inspector, analysing Josh's face for tell-tale signs of his knowledge of them.

Inspector Giles was good at reading people. He had been in the force for years, and had conducted thousands of interviews, so knew when he was being fed lies; even the small ones.

Josh countered the Inspector's question, "Why would Mac bring that sort of equipment here?"

"Well, that's what I want to know Josh. Were you aware of what this equipment is for?" The inspector was still analysing Josh's reaction to the question.

"Um—no," replied Josh shaking his head slightly. "All I thought he was gonna do was fix the broken lock, and install some kind of alarm or something." Josh was feeling a little edgy, but knew he couldn't expect the inspector to just walk away, so had to keep a cool head.

"I see. Can you show me the broken lock?"

Josh led the inspector to the flat door and showed him the lock. It had already been processed by the forensic team and was covered in black fingerprint powder.

"Sorry, you said it was broken?" said the inspector, looking thoroughly at it.

"The lock was picked," corrected Josh. "These are the marks he made from picking it," and he directed the inspector's attention to the scratches around the keyhole.

The inspector looked closely; "Picked the lock hey? That's quite a professional burglar to be picking a lock for a break-in; and in broad daylight at a time which would be considered highly risky, especially with people going off to work. A professional burglar would know that. It's a very busy time to risk getting caught, don't you think Josh?"

"I guess so."

Josh was now beginning to understand the inspector's tactic. He sensed the inspector was just playing along with him, skirting around the edges, letting out a little rope to allow Josh to hang himself. He was beginning to realise he was the one under suspicion of Mac's death.

"Tell me Inspector, how did you find out about the shooting?" Josh wanted to get a few of his own questions answered, as he didn't trust anyone, especially not now since his friend had been killed.

"We're still working on that one. We received an anonymous call about an hour ago from a woman," revealed the inspector. "We haven't been able to trace the call yet, but suspect she used an unregistered mobile phone. Any idea who it could be?"

"No… no idea," replied Josh.

Despite not knowing the caller, Josh knew this was related to the unusual past events he was involved in. He had to work out a way of getting the inspector off his back, but that was like trying to separate a Pit Bull from a bone—it wasn't going to be easy. He also knew that if he came across as defensive the inspector would be more suspicious, and grill him even harder. He had to play it cool, but not too cool, as that would also get him noticed. He learnt from experience that when in trouble, always play the "grey man"—someone that draws no attention and is easily overlooked. Not being too forthright and not being too sedate, but being the person in-between that no one cares about. This was one of his many methods of getting by in life—a survival mechanism.

The inspector looked in thought. "Okay, so what time did you contact the deceased?"

"It was sometime just after nine this morning. I phoned him and he said to meet at our old drinking place."

"Why didn't you just meet here? Why did you meet there?" asked the inspector.

Josh needed to come up with a plausible answer. He didn't want to tell the inspector that Mac had instructed him to meet away from the flat because it was being bugged.

"I don't know; it was Mac's decision. Maybe he wasn't sure where I lived, and thought it would be easier to meet at a place we both knew," replied Josh. Even he knew his lie to be pretty lame. He was giving the dog more bones to chew on.

"I see," said the inspector. "But it seems a little odd that a private investigator wouldn't be able to find your address, after all, that's what they get paid to do. Wouldn't you say?"

"Yes, you're right," answered Josh, feeling a little stressed on the inside but still keeping a cool exterior. He needed to up his game. "Sorry Inspector, but I can only guess as to why he wanted to meet there. He's dead, so I can't ask him. Is it really that important?"

Josh was starting to get back on form; trying to invalidate the inspector's line of questioning as irrelevant, hoping he would drop it. It didn't work. Josh was up against a real hardball. Inspector Giles had been up against some of the best liars in the game, and always came out on top. Without distraction, he continued.

"So, tell me again Josh; why you both decided to meet away from here?"

"I guess he thought it would be easier to meet there. Plus, I think he wanted to flash off his new car to me. He was a bit of a poser, and had a new top of the range car he bought with the money from his last job in Saudi. It was some hush-hush job he couldn't tell me about."

Having to think on his feet, Josh thought he would try and deflect the inspector's attention elsewhere—to Saudi and Mac's work. He thought he would try and drop a false lead into the inspector's lap with the hope he would latch on. He knew he couldn't suggest it as a cause though, as that would be too suspicious, but needed to let the lead come out naturally, so the inspector would believe he had discovered it.

"Saudi Arabia, I see. We already have officers looking into his work files at his office. We'll find something there if it comes up," replied the inspector.

The "pit bull" was already one step ahead. He wasn't letting go just yet, and Josh suspected the inspector had something more up his sleeve he wasn't saying.

"Tell me Josh, you're a sergeant, so I assume you have access to most areas in your barracks?"

"Yeah, that's right," replied Josh. He knew where the inspector was going with his question.

"So, I can assume you have access to all types of military weapons?"

Josh was right. He guessed the inspector's enquiry was leading right to him. "Yes Inspector, I have access to all types of weapons, including small arms pistols with small calibre rounds."

Josh was getting fed up with the game the inspector was playing, and wanted him to just ask the question that was on his mind.

"What is it you want to ask me Inspector? Did I do it? Well, the answer is no!"

"I see," said the inspector, suspiciously.

It seemed as though he had already decided Josh was guilty, and had him walking to the gallows; so much for impartiality, and being innocent until proven guilty.

"Mr Brannon," the inspector changed his demeanour and sounded more official, "my forensic team found bloodied clothes in you washing basket; can you explain?"

Josh knew the noose was tightening, and if the inspector linked him to the shooting of the C.I.A. officer, he would surely link him somehow to Mac's death. It was all starting to add up against him, even though he hadn't carried out either crime. He was now feeling cornered and knew it was time to keep his mouth shut, and speak to a lawyer.

"I have nothing further to say Inspector," asserted Josh.

"Alright Mr Brannon, I have to caution you:

> I'm arresting you on suspicion of murder. You do not have to say anything, but it may harm your defence, if you do not mention when questioned, something which you later rely on in court. Anything you do say, may be given in evidence.

Do you understand that?" asked the inspector.

"Yeah," replied Josh, feeling like he had nowhere to turn.

The inspector beckoned an officer over, who proceeded to place handcuffs on Josh's wrists. The officer searched Josh thoroughly for weapons and sharp implements, then escorted him downstairs to a waiting police car. As Josh was placed in the back seat, he looked across at Sofia's house. She was looking out of the window straight at him. The officer closed the car door and Josh turned his head away. The car slowly drove off, passing through the cordon and nosey spectators, taking him straight to the local police station.

The journey to the station was short. Josh had been looking out of the window the whole time, but not really looking at anything; his attention was introverted. He felt like a condemned man. The car drove into the police station compound and stopped. The officer driving stepped out of the car, opened the locked door for Josh to get out, and escorted him into the building to be processed. The duty sergeant behind the counter looked up as they approached.

"What's the charge?" asked the sergeant—a fat man sipping on coffee.

"Suspicion of murder Sarge," replied the escorting officer.

"Full name?" asked the sergeant, while putting his coffee down to fill out the arrest report.

"Joshua Brannon, no middle name," replied the officer.

The duty sergeant looked at Josh, "Is that correct?"

"Yeah," answered Josh.

The whole process was neatly systematic, lasting only several minutes, as they completed the report and placed Josh in a locked cell. For the officers, it was just an everyday occurrence they were used to, but for Josh, not so.

Sitting for what seemed like hours, in a white boiler suit—after having been stripped of his uniform to be forensically processed—Josh had time to think. He was concerned this would ruin his chances of finding out more about the past events, and was trying to think of ways that would distance him from the inquiry. He knew forensics would likely come up blank on a blood-match for the C.I.A. officer's blood stains on his clothes, and they certainly wouldn't match it to Mac's blood; but he would still have to explain it somehow. He knew the local police wouldn't be privy to information on the death of a C.I.A. officer, if they knew about it at all. So, in spite of all the evidence, there was no evidence at all to hold or charge him. This thought gave him hope.

In the corridor outside, Josh could hear footsteps approach his cell, then the clinking of keys and the unlocking of the door. The door opened. It was Inspector Giles, with a duty officer.

"Mr Brannon, you are free to go," said the inspector, resentfully.

"I don't understand?" said Josh, who was even more confused.

"The charge has been dropped. Your clothes will be returned, and you can collect your things at the duty desk on your way out."

Josh stood up. He didn't need telling twice.

"Well, it seems like you have well connected friends Mr Brannon. I was instructed by my superior to release you without further charge. If I had my way, you would be banged up for good."

"It's a good thing it's not up to you then Inspector," answered Josh.

He could see the inspector's nose was put out of joint, but didn't care, just as long as he was out of there; but how? Josh was just as surprised as the inspector at being released. He thought he would be there for a long time yet, and he hadn't even explained to the inspector about his blood-stained clothing. This was becoming more confusing.

Josh was escorted to the duty desk, and handed a plastic bag containing his uniform and personal effects. He signed for his belongings and was taken to a room to change. Dressed again in uniform, he was pointed to another room by the duty sergeant.

"There's someone waiting for you Mr Brannon."

Josh opened the door. He looked in bewilderment at Sofia, who was sitting at a table, dressed in a smart professional looking suit, with briefcase by her side.

"I don't understand; what are you doing here?" he asked.

"I saw you were in trouble and came to help. I'm a lawyer."

Josh smiled. All of his worries just dropped away. He could feel a strong sense of admiration for her, for being his guardian angel.

She stood up, and took hold of her briefcase. "Shall we go?" she said calmly, leading the way out of the room.

Josh couldn't help but stare, as she walked past him. She didn't even look at him, but knew he would be watching her; she was used to men admiring her beauty. But for Josh it was different, he saw something else in her. He followed her down the corridor, towards the scornful Inspector Giles, who was standing by the exit, eyeing him all the way. Josh nodded to the inspector—a triumphant nod, and followed Sofia outside.

CHAPTER 10

OUTSIDE IN THE POLICE station car park, Josh followed Sofia to her car. She put her case in the boot, turned and looked at him with utter aplomb; a look that went straight through to him.

"Are you going home now?" she said.

"Yeah, I have things to sort out."

"You'll want a lift then. Get in."

"Thanks." Josh opened the door to a well-polished Audi. "Look, I don't know what you did to get me out of there... but I owe you."

"Yes, you do," she said smiling confidently, and got into the driver's seat.

Josh grinned, stepped into the passenger's side and seated himself. He fastened his seat belt and she pulled off, leaving the police compound. She drove fast, breaking the speed limits, which surprised Josh, being that she was supposed to be an advocate of law. She was much more than she appeared, at first glance.

The journey home was quiet; the silence between them permitted Josh to relax and forget everything. However, the calm of oblivion was momentary, as they pulled up outside her home, and back to reality. Josh looked across at his flat; he felt somewhat abashed at the upset caused to the rest of the tenants, due to Mac's death in his flat. He felt a sense of responsibility of being the cause of everything that had happened, but wasn't sure why. He hadn't killed the C.I.A. officer, he hadn't killed Mac, but something in his head was telling him it was all down to him.

"Are you okay Josh?" Sofia knew he was troubled.

"Yeah... just thinking about my friend Mac. I feel like I got him killed."

Sofia could see guilt was starting to eat away at him, putting him on a downward spiral of self-punishment, and she needed to stop it fast.

"You owe me dinner!" She quickly changed the subject, to get his attention off of Mac, and onto something more pleasurable.

"Pardon?" Josh's attention shifted easily; she gave him a new purpose to focus on—her.

"You owe me dinner. You said you owed me, so buy me dinner," she said outright.

"Er—right—sure. I can cook you a meal tonight at my place, unless you'd rather eat elsewhere. It's probably not the best of places to eat right now, considering what's just happened," he said.

Sofia wasn't squeamish. "No, that's fine. Seven o'clock?"

Josh smiled, "Yeah okay, seven it is," and he stepped out of the car. "See you then," and he slammed the car door shut.

As he walked over to the flats, he sensed people were watching him through their windows, despite not seeing anyone. He entered the building and began walking up the stairway. As he moved through the building he was "replaying" the whole incident back in his head—as though playing a recording.

He reached the door to his flat; this time there was no police officer standing guard, just police tape stretched across to keep people out. Josh pulled the tape off, screwing it up in a ball. Facing the door, he pulled his keys from his pocket. He paused momentarily, looking down at the black powder smudged around the handle where it had been dusted for prints. He inserted the key and opened the door.

The first thing to catch his attention was the smell of chemicals used by the forensics team. It would take a while to get everything back to how it was, but still, it wouldn't be right. The image of Mac being wheeled out by the medics was deeply ground in his mind. He couldn't wash that away as easily as the chemicals. He walked in and closed the door behind him, making sure it was locked.

Stepping further inside, Josh's attention was immediately drawn to the red spatter on the wall, that deeply contrasted the white paint. It looked like the start of a painting—a half-finished Pollock. He slowly dropped his gaze to a smear that marked the floor; a dried red stain. Josh couldn't fully accept the reality of it all; he had only been talking with Mac several hours ago. It was odd; he had seen death before, but couldn't think with the concept—something there one minute, then nothing. Not that he was religious, but to say that was it, you no longer exist, didn't make sense to him.

He looked around the flat. All of Mac's equipment had been removed as evidence, along with Josh's bloodied clothing. This troubled him greatly, the more he started to think about it. If they had made a serious investigation of it, and with the bloodied clothing, the police would have had clear evidence he was at the scene of another killing, only a day apart from Mac's murder. Surely they would have grounds to detain and question him on both deaths, even if he was innocent? And why was the inspector leaned on? And who was the mystery woman that anonymously tipped off the police about Mac's death? There were too many questions and no answers. Albeit in Josh's favour, it wasn't right, and something stank.

Josh set to, tidying his flat—putting the furniture back and cleaning all of the surfaces smelling of chemicals, or painted with fingerprint dust, and with some difficulty, Mac's dried blood. It was hard not to place the blame on him, as he was somewhat responsible. He didn't pull the trigger, but he did get Mac involved.

The cleaning of the flat gave rise to another question: why would the police let him back into his flat so early? He had worked with forensic agencies before, on operations. The army would provide a cordon, sometimes for days, so SOCO and forensics could pick their way through everything, looking for evidence. The investigation into Mac's death was too superficial and seemed to have been dropped, much to the disappointment of Inspector Giles.

Pausing for a moment, Josh remembered the exact reason for calling Mac in the first place—the bug! It had slipped his mind with everything that had happened. He went to the cupboard and looked in the junction box; oddly the device was still in place, just as Mac had left it. Thinking about what Mac had briefly taught him, on how to catch the spy, gave Josh an idea. It was a long shot, but he would leave the device in place, hoping whoever had planted it might come back to fix or remove it. This would hopefully flush them out. Josh replaced the junction box cover without screwing it on.

After getting his flat back into order, Josh started thinking about his date with Sofia. Or was it a date? He wasn't sure. But he had to cook a meal and wanted to impress her. She was clever. Her ploy in getting Josh's attention away from Mac's death was working.

In the kitchen, Josh prepared steak—covering them with herbs, sliced some potatoes, and for dessert, planned a chocolate mousse. He always took the time for dessert as he had a sweet tooth. He was a fairly good cook, or so he thought, and living on his own had helped him develop into a "master chef".

Whenever he went into the army cookhouse for a meal, it was like eating in a fast-food restaurant; everything cooked in bulk to get people in and out as fast as possible. The food was edible, but to Josh it was on par with his mother's impatiently made meals—lacking quality.

After making his culinary preparations, Josh took a seat, looking at the table he had set for them. He had placed a candle in the middle of the table but wondered if he was making a mistake, after all, he was still uncertain as to what this dinner meant. He didn't want the meal to come across as more than a sign of friendship, if that was all Sofia was expecting—friendship; but he also didn't want to show her he wasn't interested romantically, because in truth, he was. He decided to leave it and take a chance.

Seven o'clock approached and Josh was starting to feel a little apprehensive; a nervous ache began building in the pit of his stomach. He hadn't been on a date with someone he truly liked for years. Usually, he went out with girls he didn't care much about. It was easier that way; easier to break up with them. His difficulty to commit to another was an unresolved problem. His solution to the problem, one that protected him, had always been avoidance of people he cared about. It was a dumb solution and he knew it, but that was how he functioned.

DING-DONG! The door bell sounded. Josh went to answer it, knowing it was Sofia. He had dressed himself in smart trousers, a well-pressed shirt and tie, as though going on parade. He opened the door. Standing before him, dressed in a black satin dress, was the most stunning woman he had set his eyes upon. Josh knew he was staring but couldn't stop. All he could think was "WOW!"

"Are you going to invite me in?" Sofia asked. "It's a little chilly standing out here."

"Um—yeah—sorry. Come in." Josh was inadvertently behaving like a goof. He couldn't help but be stilled by her beauty.

She walked in, brushing past Josh as he closed the door; a slight scent of her perfume wafted in his face. He breathed in subtly, allowing her scent to have free passage to affect his senses.

"I brought some wine. My contribution to the meal," she said, holding the bottle up.

Josh smiled; "Great! I'll get the cork screw," and he disappeared into the kitchen.

When he returned to the living room, Sofia was standing, looking at his regimental photographs displayed on the wall. She was leaning slightly forward, her dress shaped tightly around her body. Josh couldn't help but stare with admiration.

"Do you like being in the army Josh?" she said, without turning around.

Josh was caught unawares. He didn't realise she knew he was standing there. He was surprised at how sensitive she was to her surroundings, but guessed that was a part of being a lawyer.

"Yes, I do like it. I feel it's where I belong, and most of the guys are great. It's like one big family."

"That's nice. Why did you join the army? I mean, you seem quite capable of doing anything; why the army?"

"I've always wanted to join, ever since I can remember. When I was a kid, I would pretend to be in the army. It's a kid's game still I guess."

She turned and looked at him. "So, you felt compelled in some way?"

"Yeah—I guess so," he replied, thoughtfully.

Josh considered her viewpoint, which impinged deeply. She opened his eyes a little. He never considered that his decision to join the army could be based on some compulsion. He began to wonder if it was actually his own determinism that caused him to join, as oddly, he couldn't remember making any conscious decision to do so. He always felt it to be the "thing" he wanted to do.

"Shall we have some wine?" said Sofia, interrupting his thoughts.

"Yeah, sure," said Josh, bringing his attention back from the past.

He took the wine bottle, twisted in the cork screw, pulled and popped the cork. He poured two glasses and offered one to Sofia. She took her glass.

"To a self-preserved future," she toasted, lifting her glass and waiting for Josh to respond.

Although somewhat confused as to what that really meant, Josh automatically repeated her words; "To a self-preserved future," and he likewise raised his glass.

Both sipped to the toast, but were interrupted by the sound of water boiling over in the kitchen.

"The food, I must go and check on it!" said Josh urgently. "You can put some music on if you like, I may be a little while," and he dashed into the kitchen.

After a minor culinary battle, he brought things back under control, and after another ten or so minutes the meal was ready. He wanted to impress Sofia, so carefully positioned the food on the plates as you would expect to see in a high-class restaurant. He carried the meals into the living room. Sofia was listening to some music she'd selected from his collection; something romantic. It was beginning to feel like a date.

"I hope you like it," said Josh, carrying the meal to the table.

"I'll let you know," she replied, with a cheeky smile.

Josh smiled. He enjoyed her honesty and unconventional first-date etiquette. She always seemed to say what she thought and meant what she said. She was so far apart from the usual dates he had been with.

They sat down at the candlelit table; the music still playing in the background. It was a nervous moment for Josh and the conversation dried up. The silence was echoing horribly in his head, making him feel uncomfortable. Usually, he would throw his food down his throat and not care about what people thought, but he was quite conscious of Sofia's presence, and wanted to make a good impression.

"Tell me Josh, are you nervous?"

Not wanting to lie, but not wanting to seem like a wimp, he shuffled in his chair, trying to put on a confident smile. His avoidance of the question was too obvious. He gave his answer in his actions and Sofia, without needing words, sensed his slight discomfort at the question. She pushed him no further. Josh was like a puppet with her and she knew it.

"So, how long have you been a lawyer?" he asked.

Josh wasn't very good at being polite, or conversing on an intellectually social level. He was used to having a laugh with his soldier mates, which would usually involve lots of swearing. There was never any social politeness; it was straight talking and to the point, whether you liked it or not.

"Oh Josh, we're not going to get into social chit-chat now, are we? That is so boring. And I know you're not that boring, or maybe you are?" she said, with another cheeky smile.

Josh was surprised. She definitely wasn't the usual type he picked up. She had hidden depths that made him want to know more. She made him feel at ease.

"Yeah, you're right, I'm no good at this social shit," Josh laughed at his own response, but felt more comfortable being himself.

She laughed with him. "That's better. I can see who you are now. People hide so much of their personality behind a coat of armour, and sometimes one can be surprised at who they truly are. People tend to cover their true self to be more socially accepted. Don't you agree Josh?"

"I guess so. My old platoon commander, he always put on a false front, but I knew underneath he was a sly coward. But that didn't stop him getting a commission and commanding a platoon. People like that shouldn't be in places of responsibility, just because they're intelligent, well connected, and can fool others into thinking they're decent, when in fact they're not. Many politicians are like that, they make hollow promises just to get into a position of power. I mean, politicians kissing babies on T.V. just for votes, that's devious. And the worst part of it all is, is that people believe it."

Josh was coming out of his shell the more he spoke, and his discontentment for superiors and authority began to show through. He was a non-conformist at heart, but with years of bad control at the hands of his parents, the authorities, and military leaders, he had been forced to conform—his spirit broken. Now, he's just another tool for the government to use, and the irony, he agreed for them to use him. Somewhere along the line he had decided to allow himself to be used, and without question. He had given up some of his freedom.

"You don't seem to like authority Josh, but there you are in an organisation that relies heavily on authority and pure blind obedience." She watched quietly as Josh thought about her words.

Her philosophical statement moved Josh to look in at himself and his life. She made him think deeply about his choices. But were they really his choices? He had never thought about his life so meaningfully before, or the fact that he blindly accepts the way things are, just because society says so. He always had the fixed idea that life was unchangeable and had to accept it that way; that he couldn't change it.

The evening continued with stimulating conversation, and the late of the night drew in fast. This was the first time Josh had never attempted to make a play for sex; as the evening finale. He felt too much respect for Sofia. Not to say he didn't find her sexually attractive; she certainly pushed the right buttons, but to him, she was more.

"I must leave now Josh, it's getting late. And you have your new job to start in the morning."

"How did you know I was starting a new job tomorrow?"

"You told me, remember? Josh, I think you've had too much wine tonight," she smiled.

She was right. Josh was slightly woozy, and agreed for her to leave. He also needed to get some shut-eye. They both stood up from the table. He walked Sofia to the door and opened it to let her out.

"Thank you for the meal, and interesting conversation. We're even now, you don't owe me a thing," she said, and stepped into the corridor.

"Maybe we can do this again?" said Josh boldly, before she walked away.

She turned round, walked up to him, and kissed him full on the lips.

"We will," she said knowingly, and walked off—leaving him wondering.

He watched Sofia walk to the lift door, push the button and step inside; she never looked back. He walked back inside the flat, reminiscing about their evening together; making him smile and causing a new-found feeling of joy. He hadn't felt real joy for many years; he had plenty of laughs with mates, but real heartfelt joy had been absent until now. Dare he admit it, but he was in love.

Josh walked to the window, pulled the curtain open slightly, and peered through the gap, to see Sofia safely home. He caught sight of her as she walked away from his block of flats, and watched her cross the road. She walked to her front door, opened it, and just before she entered her house, turned her head and looked directly up at Josh. She smiled, then stepped inside and closed the door.

Josh smiled, closed the curtain, and proceeded to clean up. He collected the plates and glasses and placed them in the kitchen sink. "I'll clean them tomorrow," he thought, as it was late, and he wanted to go to bed. He turned out the kitchen and living room lights and headed for the bedroom to turn in. He then noticed the light was on in the cupboard. He couldn't remember turning it on, let alone leaving it on. "Yeah, she's right," he said to himself, "too much wine."

He went inside the cupboard, about to turn out the light, when he noticed something different about the junction box. The lid was hanging wrongly; it wasn't how he'd left it. Inspecting it further, he pulled the lid away; the bug was missing!

Bewildered, Josh struggled to get his head around the listening device's sudden disappearance. No one had visited his flat since his return from the police station; which was when he last saw it in place. Slowly he was coming to realise. The unthinkable truth was in fact staring him in the face; a truth he was refusing to admit and accept. It was the only reasonable conclusion but he couldn't face it. The only person with access to his flat, the only person with opportunity, the only person who could have removed the device, was Sofia!

CHAPTER 11

JOSH WOKE FROM A restless night. He had to report for his new assignment and wanted to be fresh, but the idea that Sofia was somehow involved in Mac's death, not only kept him awake, but made him feel bitter and betrayed. It also didn't help that he'd fallen for her.

He was unsure what to do at this point, so decided to leave it alone and let things play out for a while. He had an upper hand at last. Whoever these people were, they didn't know that Josh knew about Sofia; this gave him an edge. He knew where she lived, and he had her confidence.

After climbing out of bed, Josh got going with his early morning fitness routine. He hardly used weights for exercising, just his own body weight. He knew being too physically bulky was clumsy and a hindrance in the forces. He needed to be fit for endurance and strong for potential battle situations. Josh wasn't built like a bodybuilder but was very muscular—compact and solid with great muscle definition. He was a powerhouse, with the ability to run for long stretches carrying heavy military kit. He wasn't one for showing off his strength by participating in macho sports, but kept low-key. His viewpoint was that the better trained he was—not just physically, but also militarily—the more competent he would be, and the better he would be in battle. Boiled down, it was all about survival.

After finishing his one-hundred crunches Josh went to cool off in the shower, then breakfast to build up his energy reserves again. He felt a bit more focused, and Sofia was off his attention, or at least in the back of his mind.

Having dressed in civilian clothes—as directed by his joining instructions—he was now ready to leave. He grabbed his keys and kit bag—packed for the training programme he was about to embark on. With a final look around the flat, he briefly thought about his friend Mac, then left.

It was early hours and Josh, standing outside, looked across at Sofia's house with scorn and suspicion. He walked to his car, opened it, put his kit bag on the back seat, got in and started the engine. He had a couple of hours drive to the location typed on his joining instructions; some place situated in the middle of the countryside. He clipped his seatbelt in, took another look at Sofia's house then drove off.

It was a long journey ahead, so Josh turned on the radio for some company. He was listening to the music when the news bulletin came on.

"Good morning, I'm Matt Dorsey with your early morning news. A man was gunned down yesterday evening in a drive-by shooting in Derby Road. The police stated the incident was drugs related and carried out by a rival gang. The identity of the victim is still unknown and police are still making inquiries. Other headline stories this morning; a local politician has admitted to fiddling his expenses and...."

CLICK! Josh turned the radio off. He knew the news report was fake, that it was really about the shooting he'd witnessed of the C.I.A. officer. It gave the correct road but the day was wrong—a day after the fact. It was a cover-up being blamed on a gang shooting. Josh tried to reason with the possibility that two shootings could have happened in the same location in as many days, but he wasn't stupid; finding it highly unlikely. He wondered what inspector Giles thought of it all. Without giving the news report further thought, he continued on his long journey.

Driving along the motorway Josh's exit was coming up next. Counting down the exit markers in his head he pulled off the motorway, just as the early morning traffic was starting to get heavy. He carried on along the quieter country roads. He passed through a small village, not unlike the village outside his training camp when he first joined the army. It was mostly green fields and hedgerows with small narrow roads; his final destination only a mile or two further on.

He wondered what exactly he was letting himself in for, and then thought about Sofia and the profound conversation they had had during dinner. He thought about how he was allowing himself to be controlled into doing something he had no knowledge of—a blind unquestioning obedience.

Following the map, included in his joining instructions, Josh navigated through the tiny lanes. The location he was heading for was in a remote area not drawn on any Ordnance Survey map, or listed in his satnav. Just to find the location was a test in itself. He took a right turn down a dead-end road which led to his final destination—a small training complex.

WHOOSH!

Josh immediately zoned out, losing control of his car, after being overcome with an intense feeling of déjà vu. Quickly pushing down on the brake pedal, his car came to a screeching halt in the middle of the road. Josh's mind was spinning with sudden flashes of remembering, followed instantaneously by the forgetting of some experience. It was the same intense reaction as in earlier times.

"I feel like I've been here before," he murmured to himself, but realising it was impossible. "What's going on?"

After spending a brief moment regaining his composure, he put the car in gear and continued to the camp entrance. He approached a gate, manned by armed security. Josh wound down his car window and a guard, who had approached, looked through at him.

"Yes sir, can I help you?" said the guard firmly.

"I'm sergeant Brannon, reporting for my first day."

The guard checked down a list of names on a clipboard he was carrying.

"Can you show me your identification card?"

Josh reached for his wallet, pulled out his army I.D. and handed it to the guard, who checked it over while looking at Josh—comparing him to the photo.

"What happened up the road?" asked the guard, referring to Josh's screeching stop.

"Some animal; nearly hit it," lied Josh.

"Thank you sergeant. You're assigned to Block Number 1, straight up the road and first on the left," and he handed back the I.D.

The guard signalled for the security barrier to be raised and Josh proceeded to drive in. While driving up the road as directed, he began checking the place out. There were a few people walking around, but no uniforms in sight. The only uniforms Josh had seen so far were the gate sentries. He parked up next to Block 1 and got out. He grabbed his kit bag from the back seat.

The camp looked like an old World War Two training facility, with overly large tin Anderson Shelters that had been revamped. Regardless, they looked old and uninviting and not very homely looking. But Josh had slept in worse places. Even this looked a step up from the rundown council flat where he used to live.

He opened the wooden door to the hut he had been assigned to and walked inside. There were four spring-wired beds with equal number of tall wooden lockers—one by each bed, a wooden table and four straight-back wooden chairs in the main room; a combined shower and bathroom and a small kitchen area. It was very basic. The floor was made of grey lino and the windows looked like they were from the 1940's.

Josh claimed a bed by putting his kit bag on top. Another kit bag was already occupying one of the other beds, which he assumed to be another trainee. He walked over to get a look at the name tag: "Pat Murphy". It was pretty obvious to Josh where this guy came from.

It was half an hour before he had to officially report, so started using the time to unpack. As he was pulling out clothes from his kit bag a woman walked into the hut. Josh looked up, giving a somewhat surprised look.

"Oh—hi," he greeted.

"Hello," she replied, with a strong Irish accent.

There was a short moment of silence.

"I'm Josh; Josh Brannon. I'm here on a training course."

"Yes, I know who you are; we're both on the same course. I'm Patricia Murphy, but you can call me 'Pat.'"

Josh assumed the 'Pat' on the name tag to be a male and not a pretty athletic looking woman.

"Are you supposed to be in here?" he asked.

"If this is Block 1 then yes," she replied. "It looks like we're sharing. Is that a problem for you?"

"Um no, just thought...."

"You thought because I'm a female I would be uncomfortable sharing with men," she interrupted. "Well don't flatter yourself, I've seen better," and she looked Josh up and down with a dirty look.

Josh laughed out loud at the plucky Irish dig. She had just gained his respect.

"So do you know what you've let yourself in for?" asked Josh. He began talking to her on an equal level, like she was now one of the "boys".

"Aye, but you know we're not supposed to talk about our individual assignments," and she started unpacking her bag.

"I didn't know that," he replied. "I don't know what my assignment is yet." He had the feeling of being left out of the loop.

"Well, that's courageous of you, going on blind faith. They must have something special for you then," she said, as she pulled out a handful of bras and panties, placing them on the bed.

Josh looked at her underwear and became a little embarrassed, but felt the idea of sharing with a female quite a novelty.

"So where are you from?" he asked.

Pat looked up, causing Josh to realise he was still staring at her undergarments, and so had to quickly shift his eye-line to avoid further embarrassment.

"I thought that would be pretty obvious; you being a soldier, and at your age having probably served at least one tour," she replied, without being specific.

"Well, your accent's obvious, but not necessarily meaning you're from there. For all I know it could be fake," countered Josh. "So, my guess, you're being trained to work undercover in Ireland."

She smiled at Josh's accurate assessment and continued to unpack.

"But the troubles in Northern Ireland have stopped. So why send in undercovers?"

"Not everything is all black or all white. There are still things you don't hear about. And there are certain things that need to be dealt with, if you know what I mean."

Josh sensed the coldness in her voice and her true character starting to show through. She came across as uncaring and unemotional, which was what was needed for the type of work she was to be trained for. Josh knew he could be a cold hard bastard at times and had been with his platoon when it was needed, but he wasn't emotionally deficient. With Murphy though, he just sensed death.

"Right, come on, let's AV you!" shouted a voice from the doorway. Josh and Pat looked over. A short stout fellow with a slight pot belly was standing looking at them both. "My name's Frankie. I'm your Directing Staff In-charge for the duration of your stay. You are Brannon and you are Murphy; correct?"

"Yeah," Josh and Pat answered, simultaneously.

"Good. I need you both over at the training-wing briefing room in five minutes. You don't need to bring anything, just yourselves. It's straight across the road in Block 5,"and without waiting for a response of compliance, Frankie left.

Josh and Pat stopped unpacking and left for the training-wing together. Outside the block were four others waiting, two of them smoking.

"Come in!" shouted Frankie, and all six entered the briefing room.

"You and you," Frankie pointed to two of the four that were already standing outside; "go back to your block, grab your kit, and fuck off. You're off the course."

The two men looked confused but Josh knew why they had been singled out; they were smokers. He knew if they were being trained as surveillance operatives they would be expected to live in harsh conditions; conditions that would necessitate a hard routine for days, or even weeks on end. That meant cold rations and no smoking. Josh hated smokers on operations. He knew the smell and sight of a burning cigarette at night could compromise a covert observation post; and a person who craved a smoke wouldn't have their mind fully focused on the task at hand. They were a liability; a liability to the group, and so he always gave a hard time to any of his platoon that smoked.

Looking disappointed, both men left the room without saying a word, followed by another D/S.

"Okay, does anyone else smoke?" quizzed Frankie. Josh, Pat and the remaining two stood silently. "Good. Take a seat." Each of the four remaining trainees sat down as instructed.

The room was cold and without heating. It was set up with individual tables and plastic chairs. A table was positioned near the front of the room; set upon it a detailed 3D model of the camp and surrounding training area. Taped to the hut walls were maps of the area and training posters covering military principles and procedures, such as field craft and weapon handling.

"Right, I'm D/S Frankie Bennett and I'm the senior instructor here. I won't be taking you through all of your training myself, but will instruct some of it along the way, with my staff. I'm also here if you have any problems. However, that being said, don't come to me with your problems. If you can't handle your own shit then you shouldn't be here. The first rule here is that whatever rank you have outside of this facility, no longer applies. If you're an NCO, an officer, or even a bloody General; you no longer have the privilege of rank. I kid you not gentlemen and lady; this will not be a picnic. Do you understand me?"

Josh nodded along with the other trainees. He felt like he was sixteen again and back in basic training, having been knocked down a peg or two.

"You each have an induction pack in front of you. Take it with you, read and digest. Okay you two," Frankie pointed to the other two trainees, "are on the Surveillance Specialist course and will go with D/S Pretty over there. Your stay here is for the duration of eight weeks intensive training. Okay, off you go."

Both men stood up like it was their first day at school and walked off with their trainer. Frankie turned his attention to Josh and Pat.

"You two. You're here for the full basic, intermediate, and advanced specialist training courses. You will both be here for a period of six months intensive training. You will not be permitted to leave the confines of this training facility unless instructed. Do you understand?"

"Sure," Pat responded, nodding compliantly.

Josh spoke out; "I wasn't given any prior briefing of my training program. I wasn't told what it involves and didn't know it was for six months or that I won't be able to leave the camp. I will need to handle a few things first."

"Okay, go back to your block, grab your gear, and fuck off. You're off the course," said Frankie bluntly. He gave Josh the standard response he gives to all trainees that fail to meet any standard of his course.

Frankie's response immediately created an intense ridge in Josh; an explosive emotional ridge. He began seething, wanting to rip Frankie's head off. Josh stood up but couldn't hold his temper back; "Fuck you, you wanker!"

Frankie looked slightly amused at someone having the balls to front up to him. "You wanna pop at me do ya?" he said. "You ain't got the balls."

All wound up, Josh lunged, targeting Frankie with a right hook to the face. But before his fist made any impact, Frankie reacted fast, pinning Josh down—his nose stuck in the 3D model on the table. Josh's arm was twisted inextricably behind his back, and despite being in a no-win situation, refused to concede or show pain. Face down, he realised that his strength wouldn't always overcome someone else's fighting skill—even if they looked an easy target with a pot belly. He was learning fast: the hard way.

At that moment, another door opened, whereby a man partially entered the room. Josh could see a set of well-polished black shoes and trousers up to the knees, but little else from his current position. Frankie released Josh's arm, leaving him lying face down as he walked over to the man.

Josh eased himself off the table, slowly twisting his pained arm back to its rightful position. He stood up, looking over at Frankie and the unknown man. This guy had cold looking eyes with a hardened stone-like face, who looked out of place wearing a suit. He looked like a criminal that would be more suited wearing a prison uniform. Josh watched closely, trying to listen in to the faint conversation they were having; but it was too indistinct. The man obviously had some importance though, because Josh noticed Frankie appearing to take orders from him; nodding at what was being said.

Finishing their conversation, the man walked back out through the door, and Frankie returned to Josh and Pat. Josh was expecting another round with Frankie, or at least a bollocking. But Frankie made no mention of the fracas between them, and instead carried on as though nothing had happened—as though it had just been erased from his memory.

"Right, both of you will need to go to the storeroom and draw some clothing and equipment. The storeroom is in Block 4 next door. You are expected. Once you've drawn your gear, take it back to your block and be back here in fifteen minutes, dressed in PT kit. And then we'll see what you're made of. Okay, go!" ordered Frankie.

Josh and Pat walked out together, not saying anything in the presence of Frankie, and began walking to Block 4.

"What the fuck was that all about?" asked Pat. "One minute you're getting kicked out and having your arse kicked by a fat dwarf, and next some strange guy comes in and starts throwing his weight around, and that's the end of it, you're back in, no questions? There's something fishy for sure."

Pat was a little over the top with her exaggerated observations and conclusions, but she was right. Josh was thinking the same thing—who was that man, and why did he intercede when he was being shown the door?

They went inside the storeroom to draw their gear. There was a wooden counter with shelving and storage racks behind it, laden with equipment. The place had a stale musty smell, as though they didn't get much in the way of people passing through to warrant cleaning it often. A man was waiting behind the counter—another short stocky fellow with a pot belly.

"Frankie's brother," murmured Pat sarcastically.

"Over here," said the storeman. "Here ya go, here's your equipment. Check it off and sign the sheet." He had already prepared their equipment and slid it across the counter at them, along with their checklists.

Josh grabbed his bundle and looked it over, while ticking it off against the list:

1. Khaki boiler suits, x3

2. Wet weather clothing, set of, x1

3. Webbing, set of, x1

4. Backpack, x1

5. Sleeping bag, x1

6. Bivvy bag, x1

7. Ration packs, 24 hour, x3

8. ....

The items on the list were limited to the basics, but Josh was already prepared; bringing much of his own stuff: assorted maps, navigational aids, survival kit, camouflage cream, and other basic and essential equipment. He had been on a number of training courses and knew it was always best to buy his own gear; not rely wholly on the army's.

"You will return your equipment at the end of the course. Make sure it's clean. Any weapons and specialist equipment will be issued on a day-to-day basis," said the storeman.

Josh signed for his gear, opened his back pack and stuffed what he could inside. He flung it on his back and carried the rest in his arms. He and Pat then left the storeroom together, with their arms full, and walked back to their block. Josh dumped his gear on his bed.

BANG! Suddenly the door flew open, banging hard against the wall. Frankie, along with two other instructors, stormed into the room shouting.

"RIGHT!" blasted Frankie, "get into your running kit NOW!"

Josh was suddenly reminded of his first days in army training, when the platoon NCOs would bawl at them to enforce control—shouting and swearing that would make any hard-man break. It was tough, and he knew this was the start of the next six gruelling months.

CHAPTER 12

JOSH WALKED UP THE road where he used to live. He looked up at his old flat which was now reoccupied. The curtains were different, and children's toys were placed on the window sill. He wondered if the new occupants knew the history of the flat; the murder of his old friend—Mac. Knowing what the neighbours were like, they were probably made aware right from the very beginning.

Josh had been gone for a year; six months intensive training and six months induction into his new role. It seemed like yesterday when he remembered living there, and his last day before going off for training. He wasn't permitted to return to sort the flat out, and he ended up losing all of his belongings. The landlord probably thought he did a bunk, and in some way he did; but not to avoid any rental payments. Still, the upheaval and loss of all his possessions was worth it. The loss of his belongings was a small price to pay. He was now in a position that, to him, was second to none.

The only thing he regretted, and the one thing he came back for, was Sofia. Although he knew she was not all she had led him to believe, Josh couldn't get her out of his mind. She was the only reason that pulled him back. There was something about her that compelled him to reach out again. He wanted to pick up from where they left off a year ago, not only to see Sofia, but to find answers. He was sure she was somehow connected to the bug in his flat, and, in all likelihood, the murder of Mac.

Walking to her home, but not wanting to appear obvious, Josh did a walk-by; looking briefly but intensely through the front window as he walked past. He couldn't see much through the window, but on the outside, the place and its surroundings looked different from a year ago. He stopped a little further up the road and turned around. He walked back to the house, up to the front door and rang the bell. Thirty seconds or so had passed and still no answer. He rang again and this time there was a response.

"H−e−l−l−o," a frail voice spoke from behind the door. It sounded like an old lady.

"Hi, I'm looking for Sofia!" said Josh loudly, through the door.

There was a noise of the door lock slowly turning on the other side. The door partly opened but was stopped by a security chain attached on the inside, preventing the door from opening any further. An old lady poked her head through the gap.

"I−don't−want−a−sofa," she slowly replied.

"No, 'Sofia'. A woman called 'Sofia'. She used to live here about a year ago." Josh looked through the gap, trying to see inside; again, it looked different.

"No−she−doesn't−live−here," the old lady replied, and without saying anymore, pulled her head in and slowly closed the door; locking it behind her.

Josh stood back, wondering where Sofia had gone. He walked round to the neighbour's house and rang the bell. This time a young woman promptly answered the door. "At least she'll have her marbles," he thought.

"Hello," she said.

"Hi, I just spoke with the old lady next door and she said you might be able to help me." Josh fibbed; trying to build a rapport. "I'm looking for the woman that used to live next door. She lived there about a year ago, called "Sofia". Do you know where she moved to?"

The woman squinted and frowned as she thought for a second or two. "Um, I remember her but didn't know her. We never really spoke. She just seemed to have vanished; one minute she was there and the next she had moved. Yeah, about a year ago, I think. The old lady has been there for about ten months now. I don't know any more than that," she said.

"Alright, thanks." Josh turned and started to walk off.

"Oh, and there were a couple of men looking for her as well; around the same time she left," she continued.

Josh immediately turned back around; "Do you remember who these men were and why they were looking for her?"

"No; just two men asking the same question as you—where she moved to. Is she in some kind of trouble? Are you the police or something?"

Josh ignored her questions. He was looking for answers, not giving them.

"What did these men look like?" he asked softly, so as not to put the woman off talking to him. He already had her confidence and let her talk freely.

"I can't remember much really. The only thing I do remember is one of them. I only remember him because he made me nervous. He was very cold; I mean his eyes looked cold like he was staring right through me. He had this look of stone or something, and I felt very uncomfortable with him. I didn't like him at all. He did most of the talking, not that he said much. The other man didn't say anything, just stood there."

"And where did they say they were from?" Josh enquired.

"They didn't. I think they might have been police though, as they were dressed in suits and looked official-like. As soon as I told them she had moved and didn't know where to, they walked away. They didn't even thank me; quite rude they were."

"Thanks, I appreciate it," smiled Josh and walked off.

He couldn't help but think about what she said about the man with the "cold eyes". For some reason, his attention went straight back to when he first encountered Frankie at the training facility; the run-in he had had with him at the start, and the man that intervened in the termination of his training. That man also had cold eyes and a stony hard look. Josh began identifying both "stone-faced" men as one, but in reality, the man who visited this lady could have been anyone. However, Josh's instincts told him otherwise, and his instincts were now very highly tuned.

Josh had been on leave for the past two weeks, after completing his training and induction phases. He needed to report for duty first thing in the morning. He had been through the most gruelling training of his life—pushed beyond his limits, both physically and psychologically.

He walked to the end of the road to his new company car—a sleek design worlds apart from his old model, and with a few interesting modifications. The government issued saloon had additional features purposely fitted to meet the requirements of the job. It was built with bullet resistant glass and a bomb proof shell. The shell was made of light but very strong armour plating, designed to flex and absorb low-to-moderate blasts. His car, designed as an SQRV—surveillance and quick reaction vehicle—housed an array of weaponry and military grade equipment unavailable on the open market.

Josh now carries a 9mm Sig P226 pistol under his jacket at all times—a requirement in his new-found profession, due to the high risk of compromise and potential capture by hostile foreign intelligence agencies, or terrorist groups looking for information. During his training, he underwent hostage capture, resistance, and interrogation drills, to experience the likely methods of extracting information by an enemy; a reality he didn't want to experience first-hand. He had contemplated—if he couldn't shoot his way out of a situation—of using his last bullet for himself, but that idea didn't sit well with him. He would prefer to go down fighting, even if he had to fight tooth and claw.

Because of this threat, Josh must always keep himself ultra-aware of his surroundings; a physical skill that comes with a downside—exhaustion. One trick he learnt well, over the past year, was the ability to switch off and on at will; to unwind without compromising his reaction time and ability. He learnt it out of pure necessity, as at the start of training he was constantly wound up, causing stress and exhaustion which, unbeknown to his instructors, nearly put him on the road to the spin-bin. Luckily for Josh though, the psychiatrist missed it in his periodic psych evaluations—utterly useless. Josh honed the ability well, turning himself on and off in an instant—able to easily relax in the absence of danger, but react fast in its presence. He could flick his biological switch like turning a light bulb on and off.

Before getting into his car, Josh surreptitiously looked around for hostile surveillance operatives—an ingrained tactic completely natural to him now. He knew the likely surveillance points an enemy would use, and if he didn't like the look of something, he could call it in with a "Threat Call". The response of which, would be a fast-arriving hard-hitting task force of plain clothed small-arms reaction units.

The area was safe, so Josh got into his car. He had decided to look for Sofia that day, which violated company protocols. Once being introduced and accepted into his new occupation, he was instructed to leave behind everything he once knew. His detachment from his old life helped from being compromised and potential danger; but Sofia was the only thing he wanted from his old life.

He drove by, looking at Sofia's old house. He thought about his old friend Mac and the incident with the bug, wondering if he would ever find out what really happened. To him, it was unfinished business.

The following day, Josh reported for duty at headquarters—an office block in the city that from the outside looked like any other; the inside however, was something else entirely. No one would suspect the suited comings and goings of staff, through the front door, were government spies, intelligence officers, and special operatives—some carrying weapons under their attire. The whole set-up was an elaborate façade, hidden by the shell of a fictitious company.

During Josh's six-month induction phase, working out of HQ, he was given mid-level tasks that would test his skills and abilities. Usually, trainees on induction would be assigned low-level tasks, but Josh had proven himself ten-fold that he was an exceptional asset, so was upgraded in operational status quite rapidly. Graduating with outstanding results, Josh was given a permanent position at government headquarters, rather than be assigned elsewhere. His new role would have him working mostly alone on intelligence gathering missions; collating and evaluating whatever information he finds. This suited Josh down to a T, as he preferred working alone, but there was only one downside to it all: his new boss.

"Brannon, your first official assignment," said Harris, the Case Officer In-charge, and Josh's new boss.

Harris was an arrogant man and promotion hungry with it—a bad combination in Josh's eyes that made for someone he couldn't really trust. Educated at Oxford University at the behest of his well-off parents, and with a bought and paid for honorary title, Harris had a sharp eye for detail. His lofty upbringing was far up from the world that Josh had lived in, and his new boss was quick to exploit it—slyly rubbing Josh's face in it from time to time.

Harris pushed a brown file across the table to him. He had a look of self-importance and Josh knew he wanted him to mess up. Unlike Josh, Harris never had to go through the same harsh training; he was recruited directly from Oxford and had no field experience whatsoever—he was an office dweller. Josh considered him as just a pen pusher, and despite being sharp, so was Josh. He had already spotted one of Harris's weak points; the need to prove himself better than the field agents, because they had skills and abilities he didn't. It was a problem for his ego. Josh knew Harris's ego would at some point bring him down; it was just a matter of when.

Josh took the file and opened it. Inside were but a few pages including a summary of the case he was required to work on, along with pertinent data on the main target.

"This is an important assignment Brannon, to start you off with. There's not much intelligence but that's what you're here for. Do you think you can handle this one?" said Harris pompously.

Josh was scanning through the paperwork; "It doesn't mention anything about why they're to be investigated. Who are they and what are they suspected of doing?"

"We don't know that. The case has been sent to us for evaluation. They could be a group of right-wing nationalists or a terrorist cell. It's your job to work it out. It's what you get paid for."

Josh knew this was a bullshit first assignment. If it was suspected to be of anything like a terrorist cell, they wouldn't be sending in just one operative: to sniff around like a dog to be caught cocking its leg up a tree. He considered this was a further test of his skills and so had to just grin and bear it.

Harris's phone rang as Josh was re-reading the report more thoroughly; familiarising himself with the case. Immediately though, while thumbing through the file, he put his attention on Harris as he took the call—without making it known he was listening in. Harris was called to go and see the Section Chief urgently, so left Josh alone in the room to carry on.

Discontent with his first assignment, Josh began looking around and noticed Harris's briefcase on the floor; the flap was open. Inside, Josh could see a batch of several brown files similar to the one he was given. "Case files," he thought. He stretched down and pulled the batch from the briefcase. He placed them on the table next to his own, remembering to keep them in the same order so Harris wouldn't know he had been spying. He noticed these particular files were given a red tag, whereas his own had yellow. This was clearly a colour code—signifying importance level, and that his "yellow" coded assignment was likely low level. He smirked, as he proved himself right about his own case.

Josh picked up the first red coded file from the top of the pile; there was significantly more information than that of his own. The file contained an additional heading: "FILE TO BE DESTROYED". In fact, all of the red coded files had the same heading and were earmarked for destruction. Opening the first file, he began to read the summary report:

TOP SECRET
IG/167 File Summary
Condition – Green

The Census Program is designed to implement a viable method of locating disaffected nationals through the use of the National Census. Its purpose is to enforce every citizen to provide their personal details for use by National Statistics, but more importantly, to be used by intelligence agencies. All completed census papers are not as important as the absent ones. It is concluded, that those persons who refuse or protest at completing the National Census paper, are disaffected nationals, or non-conformist. They are to be marked and placed on the intelligence watch list. These individuals will be monitored by IG Internal Communications, and if necessary, further action will be sanctioned.

This use of the National Census will aid in determining the degree of population control and tests the current methods of control used. Once determined, this can facilitate the implementation of socially unpopular legislation.

As Josh read down the page, he had a feeling of disbelief and rejection of its content. He knew that working in the intelligence community would have its secrets, and as part of being privy to those secrets, he had been bound by the Official Secrets Act to not disclose them. In the army, he had been privy to restricted material, but these related to terrorists—fanatics wanting to destroy the country. The material he had just read was in conflict with the survival of its own country. Fascinated, Josh opened the next file. He wanted to know more.

TOP SECRET
IG/192 File Summary
Condition – Green

The World Health Organisation and psychiatric associations, along with allied pharmaceutical corporations, have built an effective alliance facilitating the population control agenda. The pharmaceutical industry continues to develop its psychotropic drugs, being used widespread to successfully speed up the increase of docility and lowered mental ability in the user. Reported harmful reactions are significantly high, but allied damage control measures are being run effectively. If necessary, to prevent public attention and unrest, outspoken opponents of the alliance will be discredited through the usual media channels via IG Internal Communications.

The W.H.O. and psychiatric associations have strategically positioned allied personnel in its own ranks and that of governmental advisory boards worldwide. These key personnel are instrumental in successfully influencing government policy and forwarding the agenda.

"I don't understand," thought Josh. Again, he couldn't help but read with disbelief and confusion.

He never considered himself to be naïve about life and what people were capable of, as he had seen his fair share of crazy, but this was on another level. This was a hidden assault on populations. But what Josh was slowly coming to realise, and the most uncomfortable part of it all, was that he was now a party to that agenda. Although unwitting, he had allowed himself to be blindly led without question. Josh realised he had been naïve, and by allowing himself to enter into it, now made him just as guilty. His failure to find out what he didn't know was his mistake, but now the hard part; just by having that new knowledge, Josh had to decide what to do with it. All he wanted was a career he enjoyed and was good at. He never thought any further than that. He never thought about consequences of his life, the ripple effect of his actions or inaction. In truth, he didn't really care about his country and was just out for number one: himself. But now, his eyes were starting to open, and he began to see what was in his blind spot. With the problem of knowing, came the problem of responsibility. He didn't like it, but there it was.

Josh closed the file and placed it back in the pile. He picked up the batch, making sure they were in the same order, and slid them back inside Harris's briefcase. But for some reason, he became curious, and picked out the file at the bottom of the pile. He placed it on the table and opened it.

TOP SECRET
IG/242 File Summary
Condition – Red Top Priority

View Corp has continued to operate undetected. It is suspected they have strategically placed informants and active cells in governmental departments. All communications are being monitored by IG Internal Communications for relevant hot list keywords, which will be flagged by national and international monitoring stations. This terror organisation still needs to be infiltrated despite earlier failed attempts. Intelligence needs to be gathered and an upgrade in resources has been approved.

"View Corp," he whispered. Josh was further woken by the brief reference to "View Corp". He hadn't heard any mention of it for the past twenty years, but suddenly now, he was faced with his past. Was this a coincidence? Floods of unconscious memories and questions he used to have, which were all but buried, began to surface again. He remembered the stranger and his death; the bunker and the explosion. His mind was in full flow, with all thoughts converging and leading to one important question: "What is View Corp?"

CHAPTER 13

WORKING ON HIS NEW assignment, Josh was feeling misused. "This is bullshit," he thought, while sitting in a café across the road from an electrical shop—his new target's location.

His first real case appeared to be some kind of job initiation, simply to watch the comings and goings at the shop. He was dressed in the disguise of a workman, wearing old clothes and florescent jacket. There were road works going on in the area with genuine workmen all over the place and his disguise suited. The only difference was that these workmen wore hard hats and carried shovels, whereas Josh carried a 9mm pistol under his jacket.

He was on his second cup of tea whilst pretending to do a crossword puzzle in the daily newspaper, but was actually making notes of people visiting the target property. Jotting down descriptions and number plates was the highlight of his day so far, until suddenly a familiar face came into view. It was Sofia!

Josh suddenly perked up, his heart racing a little through the excitement of seeing her again, but when he saw her enter the electrical shop, he couldn't help but think suspiciously of her. Was it just a coincidence she happened to go into the place he had been assigned to watch? He knew from before he had some doubts about her, but seeing her go inside gave him the certainty not to trust her.

Watching closely, Josh waited another twenty minutes before Sofia reappeared; leaving the shop. She was carrying a small parcel and looked a little tense. Josh knew from her actions she was doing something she shouldn't and decided to follow her; going against his assignment instructions.

He quickly stood up and dumped his florescent jacket on his seat; he wanted to blend in. He had been trained to adapt quickly to any type of situation or environment. "I'm coming back," Josh told the girl behind the counter, "just going to check on my guys." He was living his cover.

He walked out of the café and started following Sofia from the opposite side of the road. He was quick to spot a close protection team around her. Any ordinary person wouldn't have spotted it but Josh was no longer any ordinary person.

Three men were strategically positioned around her: one in front, one behind, and one to her side. All three were looking extremely vigilant, continually scanning and watching their surroundings. Josh knew that if he got too close he could be spotted, so kept a good but effective distance between him and them. He watched as they walked along the busy road; analysing their form and body-guarding technique. From their movement and positioning of their hands he knew they were carrying weapons.

Josh had been taught in training to understand body language from a tactical viewpoint, to anticipate someone's actions. He had also been trained to do the opposite—so another person or hostile operative couldn't easily predict his. He observed the close protection team were tense; wound up like springs inside despite trying to seem composed on the outside. He knew he could use that to his advantage; knowing that when someone was wound up, they don't think clearly and make mistakes.

He followed the group to a multi-storey car park and watched from a safe distance as they entered the lift together. As the lift doors closed Josh moved in quickly to see what floor they were to arrive at. He watched the numbered light panel above the lift door.

One by one the light moved along: one, two, three, the numbers and lift stopped.

"Third floor," he thought. He knew they would have to leave by the only exit, so decided to wait outside and get their registration number as they drove out. He could then follow up by checking the registration plate through the Police National Computer, and obtain the details of the registered owner: as long as the vehicle plate was legitimate. Josh stood away from the car park exit, watching while hidden in a fire exit doorway.

BANG! BANG! The sound of two gunshots rang out in close succession.

Josh identified the shots fired were coming from within the car park location, and knew instinctively from which floor. He raced back into the car park and drew his 9mil while launching himself up the stairs. His training kicked in hard and fast.

BANG! BANG! Another two shots rang out, closely following the first. Three flights of stairs seemed to merge into one at the speed Josh moved to reach the third floor.

BANG! BANG! Two more shots fired. Josh already knew the six shots were for each of the close protection team, two a piece, but who was doing the shooting?

Reaching the third floor, Josh purposely slowed up so as to quickly evaluate the scene, and not become a statistic himself with the next two shots. Holding his 9mil up in the alert position, slightly out from the front of his body, he looked across the sea of stationary cars. Tactical split-second decisions were streaming through his head, influencing his every action. "No sign of movement," he thought.

He moved tactically around the parked cars, scanning the area for signs of the contact. He knew there was a high probability of being only one shooter, based on the pattern of gunfire. More than one shooter would have produced a series of randomly scattered gunfire sounds from different weapons. And if it was one shooter, he knew they were good; getting all three bodyguards without them getting a shot off takes skill.

Josh saw an arm lying on the ground, stretched out from around the side of a car's rear wheel. He stooped down low and looked underneath the car to get a better view. The three bodyguards were all lying motionless on the concrete floor. Josh got up and moved in closer; there was no sign of Sofia.

After a fast but thorough sweep-and-clear of the area, with no sign of the shooter, Josh went back to the bodies. Each one had two gunshot wounds centre mass of the body; still flowing blood. Only one bodyguard had been able to pull his weapon, although he wasn't quick enough to get a shot off.

Josh knew the police would be on their way so needed to quickly search the bodies for intelligence. One by one he hurriedly checked their pockets and pulled open their jackets, revealing small bore bullet holes puncturing their bodies. Not one of them carried any form of I.D. or documentation. They were I.D. clean. He stood up and looked for the shooter's empty gun cartridges, but again nothing. The shooter even took the time to collect his casings. This was an extremely professional hit!

Looking around, Josh found a discarded empty beer bottle. Using a dead bodyguard's clothing, he thoroughly wiped it clean of grime and proceeded, in turn, to press each of the bodyguard's fingers onto the glass. He would later have forensics at HQ lift the fingerprints from the bottle, and check for their identities using the company's intelligence databases. It was more civil than cutting their fingers off.

The sound of sirens wailed in the near distance; a warning for Josh to get going. He gave one quick look around and speedily walked away. Reaching the bottom of the stairs, he exited the car park, walking casually so as not to draw attention. Running would cause him to be noticed; making him look suspicious. Two police cars turned the corner and sped past him. He knew the sight that awaited them.

As Josh was walking back to the café, he couldn't help but think about Sofia and whether she was safe. He knew she was dirty somehow but that didn't stop him from feeling the way he did about her. He needed to know. His new assignment was not such a waste of time after all. Something was going on at the electrical shop and he needed to find out what. In some way—his instincts and gut feeling were telling him—the shop, Sofia, the murder of his friend Mac, the murder of the C.I.A. officer a year ago, were all linked. He knew it was also connected with View Corp, and the wild encounter with the stranger when he was fifteen.

Sitting back in the café across from the electrical shop, sipping on another cup of tea, Josh had resumed his workman undercover role when he received a call on his phone. It was Harris.

"Brannon, what's your location?" Harris demanded immediately.

Josh knew this was about the shooting moments earlier and replied, "I'm at the café."

"There's been a gangland shooting near your location. The police are in attendance. Have you heard anything?"

"Do you need me to attend? It's better than sitting here doing nothing." Josh expertly deflected the question and even Harris, with his first-class education, missed that Josh never gave a direct answer.

"No, stay there and continue with the assignment," and Harris hung up.

Josh didn't know Harris all that well, but he was a good judge of character and didn't trust him at all. Maybe he just didn't like him because of his arrogance and the way he looked down on his subordinates; but something Josh sensed about him didn't feel right.

He continued his surveillance on the shop, but with greater interest this time. He knew something was amiss there and wanted to find out what. But he also knew he wasn't going to find out anything by sitting on his butt drinking tea, pretending to fill-in crossword puzzles. He stood up and put his fluorescent jacket on. He decided to go into the shop and have a look around, in spite of his orders.

Before he left the café, Josh asked the girl behind the counter for a bag. She was more than willing to oblige. Unfortunately for Josh, she had been eyeing him up ever since he asked for his first cup of tea. She wasn't subtle about hiding her feelings even though they were not reciprocated. Being handsome did have its downfall when trying to be inconspicuous. Josh took the bag and ignored the girl's loving smile. He removed the fingerprinted beer bottle from his jacket and dropped it into the bag.

"Thanks," he said, and walked off.

Walking out of the café, he put his full attention on the electrical shop, and casually walked across the road towards it. He couldn't see any activity inside through the window so decided to enter. He opened the shop door. JINGLE! JINGLE! An old brass bell fixed above the door sounded, alerting the proprietor to customers. He stepped inside and closed the door.

It was a small old-looking shop with old ways. The floor was made of century-old dark stained pinewood. The old wooden shelves were jam packed with electrical items, placed without any discernible order or system. Josh hated disorder. He liked things done in set ways and liked things stored tidily. This was something that was drummed into him throughout his time in the military. The shop looked in a somewhat messy confused state.

Josh began poking around. "Nothing out of the ordinary," he thought; not even security cameras, which was unusual for a shop these days.

"Can I help you?" A voice spoke from behind. Josh turned to face an old man looking at him.

WHOOSH!

Josh suddenly became fixed—standing on the spot. He was immediately dumbstruck, unable to answer the man during a sudden and deeply impinging wave of déjà vu. A rapid succession of mental pictures flashed instantaneously through his mind, causing a reeling sensation.

"Can I help you?" the old man repeated.

"Um—who are you?" Josh was hesitant; trying to compose himself.

"I own this shop," said the old man. He was standing behind a tiny counter, half hidden amongst the mess and confusion of randomly placed items. He looked as though he was in his seventies, with probably a similar number of wrinkles on his weather-beaten face.

Still staring at Josh, he asked again, "Can I help you?"

Josh came right out and said what he was thinking; "Do—do I know you?"

"I don't think so," replied the old man. "I've been here since just after the war; me and my shop, but I don't think I've had the pleasure."

The old man came across pleasantly enough, but Josh couldn't work out why he felt he knew him, and why he triggered the déjà vu feeling in him. Back to his senses, he realised he shouldn't have gone inside. Although he hadn't blown his cover, he knew he was behaving oddly. And even if the old man hadn't picked up on it, Josh would have to be more careful.

"Damn, I'm here now so better make the most of it," he thought. Josh needed to make a clean exit without arousing anymore suspicion. "I'm after 50 metres of 7 core armoured cable." He used his cover and background training of electrics—knowing the old shop wouldn't store that type of cabling, or if it did, certainly not that amount.

"I'm sorry but I don't stock that here; just the simple things. You will need to go to the big hardware and electrical store just up the road. You can get it there," suggested the old man.

"Okay," said Josh. "Hey, did you hear about the shooting up the road a little earlier? Apparently three people got shot in the multi-storey."

Josh decided to dangle some bait to see what reaction he would get from the old man. He was good at reading people and the instant look on the old man's face easily gave him away. The sudden look of fear he was trying to hide, along with the slight blood flush to his cheeks, suggested to Josh the old man knew something.

"I haven't heard anything. We get all sorts of things happening around here. Well, thanks for your visit." The old man was trying to look unaffected and seemed to want to get rid of Josh.

Josh knew the old-timer was trying hard to cover up his knowledge of the three men and Sofia, but didn't want to press him for answers. That could expose him. "Thanks for your help," said Josh, and he casually walked out of the shop.

He walked up the road but a few steps when he heard the old man lock the shop door. Josh turned his head and watched as he put up a "CLOSED" sign. This was highly suggestive the old man was somehow involved. But involved in what exactly was still unknown.

Josh casually began walking up the road in the direction of the hardware and electrical store the old man recommended. He wanted to seem genuine and that he was taking the old man's advice in case he was watching. Further up the road Josh crossed over and doubled back to the café, to the delight of the young girl who was serving. She instantly came to his table, asking if he wanted another cup of tea. Josh willingly accepted.

He waited, anticipating the old man would leave at some point; but no sign of him. Another hour passed by and Josh was beginning to feel like part of the fixtures and fittings of the café. This was a problem, as he would start to attract attention from staying in the same place for too long. He knew he needed to move location. And besides, he was getting too much unwanted attention from the love-struck waitress.

Josh decided to call it in to Harris. He was a stickler for knowing who was where and doing what. He wanted absolute control and bitched like mad if not kept informed. His bitching wasn't wholly upfront though but more subtle, with undertones of contempt in his well-spoken voice. Josh speed-dialled Harris's number and waited for an answer.

"Harris!"

"This is Brannon. I'm moving to location two; this one's warm." He waited for the know-it-all response.

"Oh, too warm," said Harris sarcastically, "How can it be getting too warm when nothing is happening? Stay at your current location Brannon."

Josh knew how to put Harris in his place without seeming to overstep the mark. "You haven't done surveillance work before have you? You should know that there are two basic reasons a surveillance op goes tits-up. One: is the number of times you are seen and two: is unusual behaviour. I think sitting here all-day drinking tea and doing nothing else is slightly unusual wouldn't you say?"

Josh could pick-up on Harris's reaction down the phone without the need to see his face. It was something he could picture quite easily.

"Brannon, move to location two and message me when you get there. And you can call me 'Sir', as I am your senior." Harris immediately hung up.

"Yes sir!" said Josh smugly to himself; still holding his phone to his ear.

He put the fingerprinted beer bottle inside his jacket, and packed his props away inside a plastic carrier: newspaper, florescent jacket, hard hat, and measuring tape, then upped and left the café.

During the planning stage of the assignment at HQ, he had already chosen a secondary observation post in the local library. He would have an excellent frontal view of the electrical shop, just as he did in the café. There, he would change his cover from workman to bookworm—pretending to read whilst spying on the shop through the window.

Walking a couple of shops distance, before reaching the library, Josh looked across at the electrical shop, noticing movement inside. It was indistinct but appeared as though there were two figures. He knew there were no customers inside, as the "CLOSED" sign was still up, and he hadn't seen anyone enter since the old man locked-up. So he decided to do a walk-by, to see who else was there. He dumped his bag of props in a street bin and walked across the road. Walking past the shop-front, he gazed through the window. There was no sign of movement or anyone inside, so he went around the back.

The back area was pretty well closed off, with no real access to the shop. All deliveries and customers went through the front door. There was however a small yard, where access could be made by scaling a six-foot high moss-covered wall.

Standing on tiptoes Josh looked over the wall, noticing the back door wide open. His instincts kicked in as he knew something smelt off. For a split second he thought about his orders, which were specific in him having no contact or involvement of any kind with anyone in the shop. He was there solely to record comings and goings. But he had already made contact with the proprietor—the old man. He then thought about Harris and how pissed off he'd be for going against his orders. "Ah, what the hell," he thought, and decided to take a look. He quickly and easily scaled the wall, quietly jumping down to the other side.

Josh's senses were on full alert as he approached the open door. He pulled his 9mil from its holster—quietly cocked it—and slowly entered the back room. There was no noise or sign of any occupants, so moved further into the room. He pushed open an inner door leading to a study area; papers had been strewn across the floor. The drawers had been tossed as though someone had been searching for something in a great hurry. He moved stealthily through the room checking it as he went, but nothing; no sign of the old man and no sign of the second figure he had seen through the shop-front window.

WHACK! A fast sudden movement from the side with a hard thump struck Josh's hand, causing him to lose grip of his 9mil. With instant pain permeating his hand, through to his fingertips, his weapon fell to the floor. A figure of a man had swiftly exposed himself from a small cupboard room before Josh had time to clear it. Instantly, the unknown figure moved in on Josh with a rapid succession of extremely painful strikes to his side. He was propelled across the room from the force, further hitting his body against a hard wooden desk.

Josh's mental switch flicked to extreme, automatically shutting off the pain. Situational calculations were rapidly being computed in his mind, and pumping out mathematically sound tactical equations. His mind, his awareness, and his training, worked in conjunction to build a split-second picture of the situation, along with solutions to survive.

Pushing hard against the solid wooden table, Josh used momentum and force to propel his body towards his target. Not allowing the force of motion to stop, and using physics to his advantage, Josh retaliated—attempting an elbow thrust to the man's face. The man adeptly moved back a step, taking the steam out of the oncoming strike. This man also knew how to use motion and force.

Both he and Josh fought: deflecting, punching and counter-punching, for what seemed like hours; but only a minute or so had passed. Josh knew he had met his match; that he was up against someone of considerable strength and skill as himself. He needed to step up his game. He was no gentleman when it came to self-defence, this wasn't Queensberry rules boxing, there were no rules except one—survive. He played dirty and he played to win. With a couple of moves Josh pushed his attacker off balance, and with a rigid hand and stiff pointing fingers—as though holding a cup—gripped the man's jugular, squeezing deadly hard. The man's face instantly went pale, and after a few seconds he collapsed to the floor; a coarse gargling sound coming from his mouth. Josh had crushed the jugular vein as well as the man's throat.

Josh looked to the floor and picked up his 9mil. He quickly regained his composure; reduced his own heart-rate, re-analysed and re-calculated the situation from a newly acquired viewpoint. His tactical calculator didn't fail him.

He recognised the man now lying on the hardwood floor. It was the same man he briefly saw at the training facility, when he first started. It was the same hard-faced man who had intervened when receiving a good kicking by Frankie—his instructor. And the same stone-faced man he suspected of inquiring about Sofia's whereabouts; described by the neighbour he questioned.

Without delay, Josh continued searching and clearing the rest of the shop, in case of other surprises. The only other surprise though was the old man, prostrate on the floor. From the angle of his head and bruising on his neck, it looked as though his neck had been broken. Not really knowing why, Josh felt a little disappointment, as the old man was, in his eyes, okay. And to see him meet his fate like that was a little saddening, and so he felt justified in terminating "Stone Face".

Josh picked up a cloth from the floor and wrapped it around his hand—not to cover any wound but so he could search around without leaving fingerprints. He went back to "Stone Face" and began checking the body for identification. Bubbles of saliva were still coming out from his mouth. It looked as though he was still fighting for his last breath. This wasn't the first time Josh had to expire someone, but it was the first time in doing so up close, and with bare hands. The strange thing about it, he felt nothing for what he had just done. It was part of the job.

"Nothing, no ID," Josh thought to himself. He wasn't at all surprised. He had also been drilled into not carrying any physical identification when on a job. The training instructors said it was for security reasons but Josh knew that was bull; he wasn't stupid. No identification meant easy deniability if things went wrong. Instead, Josh was made to memorise his I.D. number in case he ever got stopped by law enforcement. The police officer could check it against the Police National Computer. All that would come up would be a photo and title "Government Employee" with a directive to release if stopped.

The only intelligence the corpse was giving up was the 9mm semi-automatic still strapped to its body. Why "Stone Face" hadn't used his weapon on Josh was a mystery; one that now could never be revealed, at least not by the man he'd just snuffed out. Josh removed the pistol from its holster and removed the magazine. Pushing down on the top round, Josh counted at least six rounds missing. He put the magazine back and replaced the weapon in its holster. He was pretty certain that this was the same weapon used to take out Sofia's security detail—the three bodyguards in the car park earlier.

"Good. Another set of finger prints," he thought as he removed the beer bottle from his jacket; which somehow had miraculously survived unbroken. He added "Stone Face's" prints to the collection and put it back inside his jacket.

Josh began searching around, through papers and files the old man had kept, some dating back many years. He couldn't find anything that was out of the ordinary. They were mostly business related: tax, customer orders, invoices, stock inventories, papers one would normally expect to see in a shop. There was nothing unusual or suspicious, apart from the two dead bodies. There had to be more, but what?

Standing back for a few minutes, to take a fresh look at the room, Josh noticed a dislodged panel in an old antique wall cupboard. It was possible it had been knocked and dislodged during the fight. He pulled at the loose panel, letting it fall to the floor, revealing an old locked box in a hidden space. Pulling the box out, he placed it on a table. Probing for weaknesses he tried to break it open; even though it was old it was still very strong. He had to take it with him. He couldn't waste any more time at the shop as it was becoming riskier to stay. He needed to leave before customers became suspicious, as the shop was closed when it should be open for business.

Quickly, he found a basin and washed his face and hands of blood. He tracked back over the shop, thoroughly wiping any surface he had been in contact with. He knew the forensic team would be all over it, so he couldn't leave any of his blood or fingerprints behind. Lastly, he walked over to "Stone Face", knowing his prints, although latent, were now embedded in his throat. Josh pulled out his knife and cut out two strips of skin, one from each side of the throat, that had clear impressions of his deathly squeeze. He wrapped the strips in a cloth, and pushed it inside his jacket pocket. His job was done.

Josh holstered his weapon and concealed the box he found inside his jacket, along with the beer bottle. He glanced at the human debris on the floor, turned away and walked out the way he came in. He jumped back over the wall, brushed himself off, and calmly walked away as though nothing had happened. Josh headed for the library across the road—his secondary OP—went inside and took a seat next to a couple of patrons. With their noses stuck in books, they never looked up. They were oblivious to the man with bruises now sitting next to them; a man that had just taken the life of another human being.

Sitting by the library window, looking across at the electrical shop, Josh knew it was pointless being there. What had happened had happened, but he couldn't let on to Harris. He would have to continue his pretence until Harris found out, through other official channels, that the electrical shop assignment was blown. Until then, he would wait for orders to abort the surveillance op.

In spite of everything, Josh was feeling content. He now had some good leads to follow up on—with the four sets of prints on the bottle. He also had the locked box—but not knowing if it held any importance in his own case. Hope was resting on these to explain the unearthly experiences he was having, and has had in his past. Hope was resting on these to reveal the elusive answer to the question stuck in his mind—what is View Corp? Or would there simply be more pieces of a grander puzzle that was too big to understand?

CHAPTER 14

JOSH CEASED SURVEILLANCE ON the electrical shop for the day and left the library. As per his assignment instructions he was only to stay on the plot until 16:00 hours. He found it strange that the surveillance task was scheduled for only one operator and only during daytime hours. But who was he to argue, he was just doing as he was instructed by Harris. And he wasn't employed to be a "thinker", just someone to carry out orders—mostly.

"Just do as you're told," Josh said to himself. But this always left him with a bad taste of resentment. He hated being a puppet for someone else's play. He wanted to pull his own strings but always felt he couldn't. He felt tangled and trapped with the idea that this was how things were; this was his lot in life. His work he enjoyed. It was miles apart from the usual routine of working in a factory or sitting behind a desk, but always felt something was missing. He always felt something wasn't right.

Josh arrived back at HQ and parked up. He left the locked box he recovered from the shop under the seat of his car. He wasn't going to hand this over as it would expose him to the fact that something had happened at the electrical shop, something which he failed to report. Finding the truth was more important than explaining to Harris why there were two dead bodies lying on the floor.

The two strips of skin he had removed from "Stone Face's" throat had become a welcomed meal for a starving stray he had spotted on the way back. The incriminating evidence, linking Josh to the kill at the shop, was now being slowly digested in a scabby flea-ridden dog.

The beer bottle covered with the fingerprints of the dead; Josh kept with him. He needed to find out who they belonged to, so he could follow-up on any leads they produced. He would have to show the tech-heads the bottle if he wanted to find out whose prints they were, but they were sure to log it and report it to Harris; except for Flash.

Flash works in T-Branch—Technical Branch—the company's department responsible for the research and development of new equipment. His specialty is computer technology, although his abilities extend way beyond the knowledge of computer science. With an extraordinary mind, most unlike the average smart geek, he functions like an organic super-computer. It was rumoured he gained his position in T-Branch after being suspected of successfully hacking classified government servers—although never proven. Instead of letting him loose, he was seduced into working for the government, with opportunities of using his skills for the good of the country. Just like Josh, Flash didn't care about patriotism; he just wanted to get his hands on new technologies not yet released to the public. That was his obsession.

Walking past building security, Josh headed for Tech, ensuring to avoid Harris along the way. T-Branch was situated in the lower levels of the building, one up from the dreaded basement level. Built underground, basement level was solely for prisoner containment and interrogation; no unauthorised personnel dared venture there. It was the one part of the facility nobody wanted to know about. Josh always became aware of it the closer he got to Tech.

Josh entered the large office space of T-Branch. "Where's Flash?" he asked Tomblin—a member of tech support.

"He's playing with algorithms over there," and Tomblin pointed to a corner of the room. "He's developing a better way to synthesise...."

"Yeah thanks," interrupted Josh and he walked off. He had no time trying to decipher geek-speak and headed for the corner.

"Flash, I need you to do something for me," requested Josh quietly.

"Oh, hello Flash, nice to see you," replied Flash sarcastically. He was busy with his nose in a book. "You've been in the wars I see," referring to the noticeable scratching and bruising on Josh's face and hands. It was company policy not to ask questions about other operative's assignments, unless they were themselves an active party to it, but Josh and Flash had an understanding. Josh got to know Flash during his induction phase and took to him for his hidden disrespect for authority—a shared reality.

"I need you to identify some prints for me," and Josh pulled the beer bottle from his jacket. "There are four sets on the body; mine will be on the neck. And I need it done yesterday."

"Hmm, this sounds sinister," commented Flash. "Okay, put it in this bag." He reached out with an open evidence bag and Josh dropped the bottle inside.

"This is between us Flash; no one needs to be informed on this one, understand?" Josh stated quietly with a firm stare, to impress upon him the need for secrecy.

Flash smirked. There was one thing he enjoyed most when it came to his employer, and that was breaking the rules. Although he was working for the government, he still considered it an opponent, and anything to go against the grain was always willingly accepted.

"Good, we understand each other," Josh acknowledged, after accepting the smirk as agreement.

"Hey, have you seen my latest development?" Flash changed the topic excitedly. He pulled out a small handheld computer device from a drawer and showed it to Josh.

WHOOSH!

Josh suddenly blanked out, losing his senses. He could see a vagueness of the device he was being shown but his mind was spinning off elsewhere. Many indiscernible images were fast popping in and out through his head. "Josh, Josh." Josh could hear the muffled sounds of his name being spoken but was too absorbed in his trance-like state.

"Josh, Josh," repeated Flash, "are you okay?"

Using Flash's voice as a guide, Josh mentally pulled himself back to the present. "Where did you get that?" snapped Josh, looking at the computer device.

Flash was a little startled by Josh's tone. "I've just developed it. I was asked to come up with an integrated...."

"I've seen it before!" interrupted Josh.

Flash looked confused. "You can't have. I've only just finished constructing it. Where do you think you've seen it before?"

Josh was certain but wasn't going to disclose where. This was the same computer he saw in the hands of the stranger—the man he got tangled up with as a kid. Was this just a coincidence?

"I must be mistaken," Josh lied, "there are so many computers out there. I'll be back for the fingerprint results later."

Josh turned and walked off—leaving Tech. He was still thinking about the device he was just shown. He had no doubt in his mind that that device was the same one used by the stranger, those many years ago. He remembered it clearly when in the room of the derelict building; just before the shootout and having to escape when the stranger was shot. It was stuck in his mind like a splinter, a moment he couldn't forget. But what he couldn't understand, and what didn't make sense, was Flash saying he had just built it. This gave rise to more questions.

"Brannon! My office in five!" It was Harris's sharp voice, suddenly from a doorway in the corridor.

"Right sir," said Josh, hoping Harris hadn't twigged he had just come from Tech.

Josh went to relieve himself before his meeting with Harris. All of the tea-drinking in the café had had its toll on his bladder, and he knew the meeting could be long and drawn-out, so didn't want to have to hold on. Going to see Harris was standard after going out on any operation, no matter how meaningless it appeared. It was usual procedure to get debriefed on the day's activities so all intelligence—no matter how trivial the information seemed—could be collated, evaluated and passed to the relevant departments for action.

Josh knocked on the door of Harris's office. He could hear voices inside; Harris and one other.

"Come in!" snapped Harris.

Josh opened the door and entered the room. His eyes were immediately drawn to the familiar looking man standing in the corner; his hands in his pockets. It was the man who had recruited him from out of the army; the same man who had handed Josh's file to the C.I.A. officer who was shot in the street shortly afterwards—and the file taken.

"Josh, take a seat," asked the man.

Josh felt put at ease by the man's politeness and by the use of his first name, but nevertheless remained suspicious of him. He took a seat as asked. He quickly figured out that Harris was a subordinate where this guy was concerned, due to his lack of conversation and uneasy look on his face. He seemed to be waiting for the man to make the moves.

"Tell me what happened on your assignment today Josh?" the man continued.

Josh now knew the focus of the meeting. The two bodies must have been discovered and reported.

"As per my assignment instructions I was on the plot from 08:00 to 16:00 hours. As instructed, I kept observation and noted down the comings and goings at the target address. I changed location from OP 1 to OP 2 at 13:10 to continue "obs" on the target as OP 1 was getting warm. I called in the change to Harris by phone," reported Josh, but leaving out the most important facts of the day: the two bodies left lying on the floor in the electrical shop and the three in the car park.

"How did you get that bruising and those scratches?" The man was looking at Josh's face and hands—the injuries caused during the fight with "Stone Face".

"Working out with Mohammed," Josh replied.

Mohammed was the company's martial arts and self-defence instructor Josh had gotten on well with during his induction phase. Both had come from similar backgrounds. And anticipating he would be questioned about his battered appearance, he had asked Mohammed to cover for him, saying they had a full contact sparring session that morning before work.

"I see," said the man. "For the duration of the op, did you encounter anything unusual or suspicious?"

"Nothing from where I was situated," replied Josh.

"Why did you say it like that?" stepped in Harris.

"What do you mean sir?" countered Josh.

He knew what Harris was getting at and needed to throw the question back to gain more thinking time. He needed more time to counter the repeat question he knew was coming up. Harris had picked up the sense, from Josh's answer, that he had not strictly followed his instructions, but had wandered from his OP without authorisation. Harris was right of course, but Josh couldn't tell him that as he would dig in with more questions—possibly leading to the truth about what really happened that day. It was a game of cat-and-mouse and Josh knew, as the mouse, he had to turn the table and become more cat.

"Why did you say, 'from where you were situated'?" Harris came back with the predicted question; his question implying Josh had been at other locations.

The man, listening intently and waiting for a reply, never took his eyes off Josh. It was as if he was trying to stare a hole into his mind to get some telepathic insight into what Josh was thinking, or at least spot some sign of lying.

"A surveillance op like this should have had at least two people, one to watch the front and one to watch the back. It's obvious this was a waste of time!"

Josh criticised the lack of resources and poor planning of the surveillance operation in front of the man, knowing full well the attention and blame would fall on Harris. Craftily thought out, he purposely watched and waited before saying anymore. The man's stare released from Josh and landed on Harris. Josh knew his tactic had worked and Harris was now in the spotlight. He quickly took this opportunity to ask his own question.

"Has something happened I should know about sir?"

Harris looked to the man for guidance but the man said nothing.

"No. Write up your log and pass it on for analysis. That's all Brannon," ordered Harris.

Josh took the opportunity to leave. It certainly wasn't the usual debriefing and he knew they were both lying. He stood up and walked to the door.

"Same assignment again tomorrow sir?" enquired Josh, knowing full well the assignment was blown but was trying to elicit any information he could.

Harris paused, seemingly fishing for an answer. "Just report here, first thing."

Josh nodded and exited the room. He knew from Harris's demeanour he was hiding something. He took too long in coming up with his response and hadn't even answered the question. Josh could spot bullshit a mile away; after all, he was an expert at it.

He decided to take another look at the electrical shop that evening, but needed to do so in secret without using his company car, as these were fitted with GPS tracking. If Harris checked the car's tracking logs, he would be discovered.

Josh visited the debriefing room and got down to writing his report as instructed. He knew he was going to have to alter the time-line of events and needed to make sure they followed seamlessly—with no time gaps. Removing the two incidents—the attack on Sofia's security detail and "Stone Face's" death—there wasn't much else to write up. Most of the day's surveillance he could simply put into blocks of time. He thought about writing just one entry in the report: "From 08:00 hours to 16:00 hours; sat in café drinking tea. Nothing further to report." He smirked, knowing it would irritate Harris.

Finishing his report, Josh had managed to stretch it out—covering over any knowledge or involvement with what had happened at the electrical shop, and the shooting in the car park. As far as the report stated, he was in the café and the library as per his instructions. He also added the point about the waitress's affection towards him, at the café, as a compromise to the OP. He made his false report as "factual" as possible; one that could stand up to Harris's scrutiny.

It was starting to get late and Josh was eager to return to the shop. He picked up his report, filed it in Harris's tray and headed out of the building. He got into his own car and drove out of the secure compound, heading straight for home after employing standard anti-surveillance manoeuvres—a mandated procedure used by all operatives in case of a tail from the "office".

He pulled into the underground parking of his apartment block and reversed into his parking bay. He routinely parked his car with the nose facing frontwards, giving him the best advantage and responsive time in an emergency. He got out of his car, locked it with the remote and manually checked it was secure. He lived in a decent area compared to where he grew up. He promised himself never to go back to that low standard of living again.

Josh went up to his flat to eat and clean himself up. He was waiting for the evening to draw in more, before setting off for the shop again. He liked working in the dark; it somehow felt safer and protected him.

Leaving his flat to begin the night's activities, Josh walked back to his car. As he approached, he scanned the area for anything unusual. Reaching it, he crouched down, pulled a penlight from his pocket and searched underneath. This was also standard procedure. It was company protocol to check for explosive devices and hidden vehicle trackers. Josh knew the likely hiding places and tell-tale signs as he had also been trained to use such methods on others.

"All clear," he thought, then opened the car and jumped in. He started the engine and pulled off, heading straight for the electrical shop.

He was quick to reach the shop, facilitated by the low level of night-time traffic. It was quiet. He slowly drove by, looking through the front shop window as best he could for that time of night; nothing, no lights or activity. He pulled up in a side road, a couple of roads down from the shop; he didn't want his car to be spotted.

He exited his car, locking it behind him, then ran his hand over the outside of his jacket to feel the presence of his 9mil pistol tucked inside. Feeling it gave him a sense of security, power and confidence. There were seldom occasions he would go anywhere without it. The only time he would have to relinquish his weapon was on undercover operations, where the likelihood of being searched was high. The highly aware targets were always cautious.

Josh walked back up the road he had just driven down. He could see the shop front from a distance so slowed his pace to have a prolonged look while walking towards it. Still no activity; not even police at a crime scene. He looked at the nearby buildings, checking for possible observation posts. To his trained eye, nothing stood out to suggest the electrical shop was under further surveillance from another team, so he decided to enter the building from the rear again. He casually walked around the back and stood by the wall. Lights were still on in the nearby homes so he had to be careful about being seen by a neighbour. The last thing he wanted was a call to the police.

He only stood by the wall long enough to make sure he wasn't being watched, then with a quick heave of his body, pulled himself up and over. If you're going to do something then do it, don't hesitate, was what Josh had been taught. In his line of work hesitation could get a person killed. His decision-making process had been finely tuned to quickly and accurately observe, evaluate and decide. It became an instinctive process, refined in training, that would serve to keep him fully operational.

He approached the back door: it was closed! He knew someone else had been there that afternoon as he had left the door open—how he had found it. Being prepared, Josh put on some gloves and pulled his 9mil from his jacket. He gripped the door handle, turned it slowly and pushed—it was unlocked. He gradually opened the door while peering through the gap for danger. He entered the backroom. From what he could visibly see in the darkness, it had been cleaned. He closed the door behind him, pulled out his penlight and turned it on. There were no papers strewn across the floor as before. He walked further inside, into the room where he had left "Stone Face". Clean! He walked to the room where the old man's body should be. Nothing! Someone had meticulously cleaned up, making the shop look normal, as though nothing sinister had taken place.

"Who could clean this up so quickly?" he thought.

He knew the local authorities had no inkling of what had occurred, as the forensics mob would still be all over it like ants. There would have been police standing guard with cordons up, and although it was late, a few sickos would probably still be hanging around to catch a glimpse of any bodies.

"Cover-up," he reasoned.

Looking no further, Josh retraced his steps out of the shop, leaving it exactly the way he found it. He concealed his weapon and climbed back up over the wall. He walked casually to his car and as usual performed his security checks before leaving the area. Driving home, Josh could only wonder what had happened to the bodies, and who could have sanitised the scene so quickly, and so professionally. He could only answer his questions with more questions; unable to satisfy his void of absent facts.

Josh was now pinning his hopes on Flash; in finding out something with the fingerprints he had given him. But it weighed on his mind that they wouldn't reveal any identities, and all would be just another dead-end. Still, there was also the locked box that he hadn't had time to break into yet, maybe that contained some answers. It was time to find out.

CHAPTER 15

As Josh was driving home from the electrical shop a call came through on his phone. It was Flash.

"Yeah, what is it Flash?"

"I've found something, can you come in?" Flash sounded concerned.

"On my way," replied Josh and he hung up.

He immediately changed direction and drove as fast as he legally could back to HQ; skipping through a few red lights on the way. He pulled into the secure underground parking, parked his car and headed straight for Tech. On route to rendezvous with Flash, Harris collared him in the corridor; "Ah Brannon!"

"Don't you go home," thought Josh; he didn't have time for this, whatever "this" was. "Yes sir?"

"I thought you went home? I need you in at seven sharpish tomorrow," said Harris.

"Yes sir, seven sharp," answered Josh but avoiding the first question.

"What are you doing here so late?"

"Getting some target practice in at the range sir."

Harris didn't even acknowledge him but walked off. His arrogance irritated Josh no end but that was nothing new. He continued on his way to meet up with Flash.

Flash was tucked away in his corner as usual and looked up as Josh approached. His face was beaming a double-look of concern and excitement. Josh knew Flash had found something with the fingerprints he gave him, but what? He was hoping for tangible leads he could follow which would take him to answers and not more questions. Answers he hoped that would explain what "View Corp" is and the connection to the stranger in his past; and more importantly to the recent events involving Sofia.

"Back so soon," said Tomblin inquisitively, once he set his eyes on Josh. He began hovering where he wasn't wanted. "We don't often get visitors here, let alone twice in a day." Although he wasn't saying it outright, he was trying to find out what Flash and Josh were up to.

"Go back to your cage Tomblin," snapped Flash, "and stop bothering us."

"You dickwad Flash," protested Tomblin and walked off mumbling to himself.

Now in peace, Flash pulled out a folded piece of paper from his pocket and handed it to Josh. "I kept this off official lines like you wanted but wasn't so easy. You could have given me photos; it would have been easier."

"Sure, I'll remember to take photos next time." Josh was being sarcastic; knowing that stiffs weren't very photogenic. But the real reason and what Flash didn't know—that Josh had been tipped off about by another operative when he first started—was that all images scanned through the Facial Recognition System were flagged to operational managers, and that meant Harris finding out.

Josh unfolded the paper Flash gave him and started reading the details quietly to himself. It was a one-page report on the fingerprint results.

"The first three sets couldn't be identified—no criminal records—but the last one was a positive ID!" Flash butted in before

Josh had a chance to read it fully. "Look at the one identified!" he continued excitedly.

Josh looked. "Hoffman S. No first name. It says here he died five years ago."

"Exactly!" said Flash, "But what's a dead man's fingerprints doing on a bottle I presume you took recently?"

The first three unidentified sets of prints belonged to the three dead bodyguards and the fourth to "Stone Face", now identified as Hoffman. Josh kept silent, not telling Flash he had met this Hoffman briefly on his training—after his supposed death, as well as making his death official just that afternoon.

"It says here he worked for the government, a government employee, but doesn't specify which department. Did you get anything else? Was there a photo?" Josh questioned.

"No, that was all. The rest of his file is classified and I can't get access without a higher authority."

Josh gave Flash a look, a tacit look asking him to do something he shouldn't.

"Look, I don't do that anymore. If I get caught hacking government files, I'm in trouble!" Flash quietly protested.

"Wow, that's not the 'Flash' I heard about when I first arrived. The 'Flash' I heard about was a fearless hacking genius; no firewall he couldn't penetrate, no password he couldn't guess. I must have heard wrong." Josh was playing with Flash's ego.

"I know what you're doing Brannon and it won't work," Flash rebuffed the challenge, "I'm not stupid."

"No problem, I was just playing with ya; I don't want you to get into trouble. So, who do you know could do it? What about Tomblin? He's pretty good, isn't he?"

Josh continued his manipulation on a more serious level, now pretending to overlook Flash as the best contender. He knew Flash wouldn't approve of Tomblin, or anyone else for that matter. He wouldn't approve not because of getting someone into hot water, but because of the need to feel the best. Undoubtedly, he was one of the best, but his weakness, one that he couldn't bear, was having someone beat him at his own game—especially Tomblin. So Josh pushed his button, knowing he would win. His manipulation of people was a mastered art; easily able to spot and exploit someone's Achilles heel.

"Hmm—maybe I could do this one simple one," Flash reconsidered, not realising the second trick Josh played on him and having landed right into his hands.

"How long will it take?" Josh was eager to find out more.

"It won't take long using this," and Flash reached into his drawer, producing the handheld computer device from earlier.

Josh was curious to see it again. Oddly, this time round, it had no immediate effect on him. It seemed to have lost its influence over him and was now just another interesting puzzle piece, put in its rightful place.

Flash connected the device to the company's intranet via his computer. He activated a special type of computer surveillance key-logging program—one that could trace back encryptions and user information that had already been input into a computer. In effect, it didn't have to be installed on a computer prior to monitoring a user in real-time to obtain information; it could be used any time after the fact. It was like a computer hound-dog that could sniff out trails of information.

Having tapped in some data, he then pushed a button. The device began searching and almost immediately started to produce a string of numbers, symbols and letters. After a couple of minutes, it stopped, and displayed the full encryption on the screen. Flash tapped the code into the main computer and a display came up: "ACCESS GRANTED". He typed the name in a search field on the computer: "Hoffman"—related to the fingerprint scan he had already input. A digital file popped up on the screen, this time displaying a wider profile of information that Josh could work with.

The first thing Josh confirmed to himself was the photograph. The photo was that of "Stone Face"; the man with the psychotic stare he had snuffed out at the electrical shop, and whose body was now missing. Josh felt he was finally getting somewhere and began to read his file with increasing interest.

The file gave the man's full name: "Stephen Hoffman", as well as other personal and operational details. The department he was assigned to was a special operations unit within the same government organisation as Josh. It listed his background training, specialist skills, assignments and operations. He had been on clandestine operations all over the world, in both hostile and friendly classed countries.

"This guy's been around," said Flash, whilst reading the detailed profile. "He's a one-man army. His last entry has him listed as 'Killed-In-Action' but that was five years ago. So where did you get his fingerprints?" Flash looked at Josh for an answer.

Josh wasn't listening but busy looking for his own answers, scanning down the entries on the screen, when suddenly his eyes and attention zeroed-in on a word he recognised: "View Corp". He clicked on the entry, opening the page and began to read. As he read, Josh was beginning to feel cold; he was in part, reading about himself.

The file spoke of the incident he had had with the stranger when he was fifteen; the underground bunker where the nuclear device had been destroyed, and the stranger's death. There was no mention of the two men in white coats Josh witnessed the stranger kill; but a reference only of two blood types of unidentified sources. It was all there, except for who the stranger was—no name; nothing. He was just referred to as "Officer FAC12". This part was a disappointment, but he was relieved to see that there was no mention of him personally in the file. He had managed to keep under the radar and his anonymity safe.

Reading on, the file revealed how Hoffman was tasked in bringing down View Corp and was assigned solely to that task. The file mentioned View Corp as being an underground network of terrorists, intent on destroying and undermining governments to create instability and chaos. It continued to say that these were not ordinary terrorists using conventional terrorist methods, but relied on sympathiser support with infiltration into the very fabric of governments and high-powered organisations. The organisation was classified as "Extreme", with all efforts being made to de-cloak and terminate its members.

Josh began to hypothesise with what he was reading in the report, and with what he already knew. He began to think about Hoffman whom he had killed.

"Was that why he didn't use his weapon on me at the shop? He wasn't there to kill me. But why did he attack me? And why didn't he stop and identify himself?" he thought. Josh began to get a sinking feeling the more he thought about it; the closer he came to realising he had killed a "friendly"; one of his own.

He continued pondering: "The old man at the electrical shop must have been part of View Corp. And the three bodyguards Hoffman killed...which also means Sofia...." The idea of Sofia being a terrorist gave Josh an even deeper sinking feeling. "The bug in my flat that got Mac killed, must have been View Corp, and Sofia. But why bug me?" he thought. "They must have known about my new government job. They were trying to infiltrate the company?"

Everything was now dropping into place. The confusion he had lived with for so long was blowing away, with past and current events becoming clearer. The truth slowly revealed itself piece-by-piece. However, an incidental factor of knowing the truth was the anger that accompanied it. Josh was now beginning to feel hate towards Sofia and her terrorist organisation, especially with his friend, Mac, being murdered.

"But what about the C.I.A. officer who was killed; what was his involvement?" he thought. Josh wasn't sure, that was still a piece of the puzzle he didn't have. All he knew was that this man had been passed the file containing his profile. He also knew that he had been killed for that file. And he couldn't help but think that the C.I.A officer had been killed by View Corp—it made sense at this point that that was the case.

"And why did Sofia help me out at the police station? How did she manage to get me out?" he thought. "People on the inside...they've got influential people on the inside. That's what they want me for; they need me to be a mole. They want to recruit me. And Sofia was the bait."

Although answers were now dropping into his lap, so were more questions. There seemed to be contradictions of some facts as well as missing information. He had to keep at it; to push through the confusion if he wanted the complete truth. He knew the electrical shop, the fingerprints, and Hoffman were now dead ends. These sources of the investigation were now exhausted, so he needed to focus on other lines of inquiry.

One aspect he still didn't understand, was the link with the dead C.I.A. officer and the man who had recruited him. This was now to be his new line of investigation, and it needed to start with Harris. But Harris was no fool. If he sensed Josh was up to something he would have him placed on the employee watch list. So Josh needed to keep one step ahead.

"Flash, I'm going to keep hold of this for a little while," said Josh, as he disconnected the handheld device from the computer.

"No no, you can't have it, it's the prototype! I've got to perfect it and send it for operational approval before it gets issued!" Flash was eager to have it back; behaving like a child having his favourite toy taken away.

"It works fine, you did a great job Flash," praised Josh and stood up. "Tell whoever needs to approve it, you had some problems...and need to work on it a little longer. I'll get it back to you as soon as I'm done."

"But...." Flash tried to argue, but Josh had already tucked the device inside his jacket and was walking off.

Leaving Tech, walking along the corridor, he knew he needed to cover his back with Harris; the lie he told about staying on for target practice. There was a possibility Harris would check up on him, so he stopped off at the indoor range to see Smithy—the armourer and range controller.

"Hey Smithy," called Josh.

"Josh; haven't seen you in a while mate." Smithy was inserting 9mm rounds into a magazine. "You come to shoot some targets? I wanna win my money back."

"No not tonight, another time. I'll be glad to take another fifty from you though," said Josh.

Smithy smiled as he finished snapping in the last round and inserted the magazine into a Glock pistol.

Josh was the best shot in the company and he knew it. It was one of the reasons for his recruitment, or so he was told. But he wasn't just a good shot under controlled conditions on the firing range, he could also produce marksmanship scores in field conditions under intense pressure. To him, shooting was natural, like taking a leak.

"Smithy, if Harris asks, tell him I practiced tonight will ya?"

"Is he getting on your back again Josh? Man, you just have to know when to toe the line mate," replied Smithy, slowly shaking his head in judgment. "Yeah, I'll tell him. You were here for an hour and I won my fifty back."

Josh smiled; "Thanks mate."

"No problem. But I still need a chance to get my money back!" demanded Smithy, as he sharply cocked his weapon. Josh nodded and walked off.

Now was the time to find out what was in the locked box he found at the electrical shop. Still hidden under the seat of his car, he hadn't had any real opportunity to break it open to look inside, until now. He walked out of the building to his car, opened the door and climbed inside. He gave a quick glance downwards to where he had hidden the box and started the engine. He pulled off, driving past security and out of the facility, heading for home.

It was getting late as Josh reversed into his parking bay at home. Coming to a halt, he turned off the car's headlights and engine, then reached for the locked box under the seat. The travelling had caused it to move further back out of reach. He opened the car door, got out and walked round to the other side. He opened the passenger door and leaned in. He reached down under the seat and grasped the box with one hand, pulling it towards him, then began to rise to his feet.

THUMP! Josh felt a sudden sharp blow to the back of his head, quickly followed by excruciating pain. Although partially aware at this point, he could feel a dizziness kicking in fast; his eyesight starting to go black. He began to lose all senses and slumped back inside the car onto the seat. His last semi-conscious feeling was that of pressure; his body landing hard. He was out for the count: knocked unconscious!

CHAPTER 16

"Hey, hey. Are you alright?" said a voice, the words barely sinking through. Josh's mind was a blur and he felt fuzzy as he slowly became aroused by the words of an unknown origin. A walking stick was being prodded in his back.

"Young man, are you okay?" came the voice again with another poke.

Josh started to come round. His recollection of what had previously occurred that evening began to reboot in his memory. He was still leaning over inside his car where his last conscious memory had left him, shortly after the crack on the head. Instantly he started to fumble around under the car seat, looking for the locked box. It was gone! He pushed his body up off the seat, feeling dizzy as he stood up.

"If you're going to drink you shouldn't be driving! Shame on you!"

Josh looked to see an old lady standing behind him with a walking stick—a resident from down the hall where he lived. Seeing him lying in his car like that she put two and two together and came up with a completely wrong answer. She assumed he had been drinking. She was "blind" to the reality of it, not able to face the idea of someone being hit over the head and knocked out in her "safe" neighbourhood. For her, it was better to not face the stark reality but create a false one—one she could easily face.

"It won't happen again," said Josh.

He didn't want her to be aware just as much as she didn't want to be aware of what really happened. The blood-matted hair on the back of his head should have been an obvious sign of violence, but Josh was content to have her believe her own illusion. After all, he didn't want anyone involved, the police or Harris; especially Harris! If Harris caught wind of what had happened, he would be sure to ask deeper questions, and the knowledge of the locked box would lead him to the electrical shop and the two dead bodies—Hoffman and the old man.

"We don't like that sort of thing here you know." The old lady finished her moral lecture and walked away muttering.

Josh didn't give her a second thought. He had more important things to consider than that of a batty old lady. He checked his phone for the time; "Damn, seven-fifteen and three missed calls!"

He had been there all night, lying unconscious in his car. He was supposed to meet with Harris at seven for his assignment. It was time for a good cover story to get Harris off his back, but was in no fit frame of mind to concoct an elaborate tale to feed him.

BEEP-BEEP, BEEP-BEEP! BEEP-BEEP, BEEP-BEEP! Josh's mobile went off for the fourth time. It was Harris.

"Brannon," answered Josh; trying not to sound sluggish like he had just woken up, and desperately trying to think of an excuse as to why he was late.

"Brannon; well, I assume you have an adequate explanation for your lateness this morning, but explanations always follow failures, and failure Brannon is not something I tolerate." It was the second person in as many minutes trying to lecture Josh on principles. "Your explanations are not going to save your career. So, I suggest you be a good fellow and pop into the office; at your own convenience of course," he continued sarcastically. And the phone went silent. Harris hung up.

"Ha," expressed Josh with contentment. He hadn't managed to think of any excuse whatsoever for his lateness, and as it happened, he didn't need one. "Another half hour won't hurt," he thought and made his way up to his flat to get cleaned up.

He walked into the bathroom, stripped to the waist, and stood in front of the mirror while feeling the back of his head. He could feel a lump from the blow and dry matted hair—matted with crusty blood. The blow hadn't caused much external damage, and he knew the cut was likely small as it had healed fast with minimum blood loss. Luckily, he had a thick skull.

Grabbing a quick shower, putting on fresh clothes and throwing a protein breakfast of scrambled eggs down his throat, Josh was ready to get going again. He picked up his 9mil from the side-cupboard and pushed it home into its holster, under his left arm. He grabbed his car keys and left the flat. He made his way back to the basement parking, scanned for potential threats and jumped into his car. He started the engine and sped out of the parking bay, making a dash for the office.

His attention was on the pain in the back of his head and the slight damage done to his pride, at being jumped from behind. Even the best operatives couldn't foresee all potentialities in the field—an idea that consoled him. He knew that whoever hit him over the head was only after the box. If he was somehow a problem, they could have easily killed him. Disappointedly, this led him to the conclusion that he must be far off track in his investigations and not a threat.

He knew now that the only advancement in his personal investigation was through Harris and this unknown character that had recruited him. He had to start pulling on those threads to see what mysteries were attached. This pair, Josh suspected, knew more than they were saying. But he had to be careful.

Driving at speed into HQ's secure compound, Josh saw Harris talking with Tomblin. Both looked over as he parked up and got out. His immediate thought was that his late evening rendezvous with Flash—hacking Hoffman's file—had been discovered; but he had to let things play out to be sure. He walked over to Harris with the expectation of a good earful.

"Brannon; Tomblin has just informed me of a distant connection between the proprietor of the electrical shop and this address." Harris passed over a piece of paper with an address written on it. Oddly, the address was in Josh's old neighbourhood where he grew up. "It's simple enough; go and check it out and report back what you find. That's if you can manage it."

"What's the connection?" quizzed Josh.

"A communication intercept of an email that was routed to a computer IP at that location," replied Harris.

"What was the email content?"

"Need-to-know Brannon. Now check it out and get back to me on what you find," and Harris walked off bearing his usual contemptuous look, with Tomblin trailing behind like a puppy on a lead.

"Right, yes sir," said Josh to Harris's back. "Need to know... well I need to know," he thought. The government's interest in the case benefited Josh, as it paralleled his own personal interest. But it was more than just a strange coincidence now, as both interests crossed over; inexplicably connected.

He looked at the address again and memorised it; it wasn't hard, even with a sore head, as he already knew the area. He walked to security to sign for his Surveillance and Quick Reaction Vehicle. Everything in the company was signed for just as in the army, especially the hardware.

"All right Josh," the duty security officer greeted him. "Here ya keys. Everything's been ok'd by maintenance. You've got a full tank and full kit on board. Just need ya signature," and the officer handed Josh the vehicle log to sign.

"Thanks mate." Josh took the pen and signed for his gear. "Can you put this in the red one for me?" Josh gave the security officer the paper from Harris with his new target address—it was standard procedure not to leave the "office" with intelligence. The security officer—also bound by the Official Secrets Act—took the paper and pushed it into a sealed red bin; through a one-way opening. The red bins were used for restricted material pending destruction and couldn't be opened, unless you used a heavy hammer. The sealed units would be removed and incinerated along with their content.

Josh picked up the keys and walked to the fleet of company vehicles. The fleet was mixed: mixed makes, mixed models, and mixed colours—but mostly neutral. On the outside the cars were made to look ordinary and non-conspicuous, but underneath the ordinary appearance they were designed for speed, protection, and equipped with full tactical gear.

Unlocking the SQRV, Josh began his own vehicle and inventory check. As much as he wanted to have faith in his comrades, he remained untrusting. His philosophy—one he learnt the hard way in the army—was to always check his own gear and never take someone else's word. He opened the boot and lifted a cover concealing an arsenal of weaponry, spare ammo and technical equipment developed by T-Branch. This was the standard hardware in all of the company vehicles.

Josh looked over the kit, checking it off in his head: "MP7, spare Sig, ammo, wire-cutters, torch, rope, plasticuffs, first aid kit, T-Branch's bag of tricks..." and continued, mentally noting it all down. "All good," he thought, as he finished up. He replaced the cover and slammed the boot shut.

All set, he jumped into the car, started it up and drove out of the compound. He had mixed feelings about this assignment.

For one, he had promised himself never to go back to his old neighbourhood; it was in the past and that's where he wanted it to stay. And two, he had a strange feeling he couldn't put his finger on. But orders were orders, and if he could follow another lead to all that had happened to him then he was damn sure going to take it.

He drove around; back and forth a few times to make sure he wasn't being tailed, then picked up his mobile and speed-dialled.

"Flash speaking."

"Flash, Brannon."

"Do you know how much trouble you're causing me? I've got my boss breathing down my neck. I need that device back!" complained Flash instantly.

"I need a favour," said Josh, ignoring the complaints, "I need you to access Harris's computer for me."

"Look, I can't just go around breaking into people's computers. I work for the government now," protested Flash quietly. "And besides, you already have the means to do it."

"Your device?" answered Josh. "I need access to a secure computer."

"Now that I can do. I have a very special place, a place I had built to—um, well, progress my computer skills."

Before ending the call, Flash disclosed the location of a safe-room he had built during his hacking days, for evading the police's cyber-crime unit. Stupidly though, he never anticipated the government's National Cyber Security Centre would be interested in him; so much for using anonymous proxy servers and VPNs.

A room built with secure computer access would give Josh the perfect opportunity for using the device to snoop inside Harris's computer files. Here was a chance to find out what Harris knew about View Corp and what he wasn't letting on. It may also give him answers as to the man that had recruited him.

Given the details of the safe-room by Flash, Josh was surprised to hear that it was located in the town not far from his old neighbourhood. Was this just another coincidence? Now he had two reasons for paying a visit to the area where he grew up. But if he didn't want to arouse suspicion, he needed to kill two birds with one stone in the same time allotted by Harris. So, with no time to waste, Josh pushed down hard on the accelerator.

He drove fast, dodging the other early morning traffic. And as he drew closer to his old neighbourhood, things were becoming familiar to him again. He started to remember the times he had gotten into trouble, with his old school friend—Steve. And as much as he didn't want to remember the old days, remembering was making him smile. He then began remembering the times he would find his father, lying drunk in his own vomit; a common occurrence back then. His smile was wiped away and the unpleasant memories snapped him back to reality. Driving on, he finally reached the address given by flash.

WHOOSH!

He slammed hard on his brake; the car screech-stopped in the road. Luckily no other car was behind him, otherwise they would have ended up in Josh's back seat. He suddenly felt blind-sided; sitting statue-like with a semi-blank stare by what he saw. This was not just a flash of déjà vu but an actuality from his past. His past seemed to be coming full circle. He couldn't understand it or what was happening to him, but whatever it was, this was real.

Josh already knew the location; in fact, he knew it very well. He should, it was the same location he was taken to as a boy by the unknown stranger; the man he was forced together with. It was the same place where they had encountered the hit-team, where the stranger was shot. This was now becoming far too strange. It wasn't just a question of trying to solve the puzzle of View Corp, but also why he was now at a location he already knew.

He pulled into the industrialised area which, to him, looked the very same from when he first set eyes on it some twenty-odd years ago. He parked his car and—without using the instructions given by Flash—easily found the secure door to the safe-room, situated inside the old empty warehouse. He punched in the code on the keypad that Flash had given him and the door opened. He slowly stepped foot inside. It was all too unreal, yet real at the same time. The whole time, Josh was having flashbacks in his mind of what happened to him, during the time he was there before. He looked around the room. It was the same. The whole layout was identical to that of what he recalled from his visit those many years ago.

Josh was experiencing the whole scene in his mind twice over. He had parallel thoughts going through his head. Thoughts from the past and thoughts of the present were colliding with each other, overlapping, causing considerable confusion. It was as though he was living two lives at the same time. He remembered the lever he was ordered to pull by the stranger which released a door, giving way for an exit. He walked over to the wall. It was there, just as he remembered. He touched it to reassure himself it was real, that he wasn't just dreaming. It was real.

With a strange converged dual vision of past and present he continued to look around; getting reacquainted with the familiar space. The two computer terminals were there, exactly where they had been before. He walked over, turned one on and logged in with the username and password Flash had just given him.

BEEP-BEEP, BEEP-BEEP! BEEP-BEEP, BEEP-BEEP! Josh's phone began ringing. It was Harris.

"Yes sir?" he answered.

"What are you doing Brannon? Are you at the location I gave you?"

"Just stopped for a piss sir; on my way now!"

"Good," replied Harris and hung up.

Josh knew right away Harris was monitoring his movements through the SQRV's vehicle tracker, so he walked quickly out of the safe-room and headed back to it. He knew how to turn the tracker off but that would arouse too much unwanted attention, so he would need to come back later in his own car.

Standing by his SQRV, he glanced back at the warehouse; his old memories fading away to be buried again. He opened the car door and jumped in. He slowly drove away, getting back on with the task he was instructed with—the vague lead from Harris and the job of checking out the house.

After a short journey, he was back in familiar surroundings again; the familiar surroundings of his younger-years. Again, old memories surfaced. The old places where he used to hang out hadn't changed much over the years. It was as if they were stuck in some time trap—same buildings, same roads, and in places, even the same old graffiti.

Josh drove to his new target location—the house. He knew the area very well and parked his SQRV in a nearby side road. Leaving the car, he walked to the house, slowly passing it by to get a look through the front window.

"Nothing of interest so far," he thought.

From the outside it looked like a normal house. But he was trained to see things that others couldn't, when it came to safe-houses or properties that were made to appear "normal", but used for illegal purposes. But this house looked normal; nothing untoward at all.

WHOOSH!

Josh felt a powerful mental jolt, accompanied by a sudden whirling in his head. Déjà vu had struck once more, this time with significant intensity. Mixed with the bang on the head the night before, Josh felt particularly strange. He tried to control the effect on him, but it was difficult. He had been taught in training to control emotions and reactions when needed, however, this was uncontrollable. It took longer than usual, but slowly he was able to bring his senses back—becoming cognisant of his surroundings again. He wondered if the effect was caused by a late concussion from the blow. But he already knew. It was the same feeling and strangeness he experienced all those many other times—but greater still. Something must have triggered it; but what?

He looked around, and although he was very familiar with the immediate surroundings, knew that wasn't the cause. It had to be something more, more powerful. He walked away from the house, up a road that led towards a shopping centre, the very same shopping centre he used to visit as a boy. Reaching it, he stood still, staring at it and thinking about his past. Interrupting his own thoughts, he walked inside and began looking around.

WHOOSH!

Again, Josh felt the power of that feeling. He knew something was triggering it and searched intensely, scanning the many shoppers walking around. Then all of a sudden it was there. All of a sudden, he spotted it. He spotted him.

CHAPTER 17

JOSH WAS LOOKING AT a teenager inside a music store. He was wearing an old jacket that looked familiar. The hairstyle; everything about him was intensely familiar. The boy immediately stopped—frozen by the exit when about to leave, as though he had suddenly been turned to stone. He looked completely dazed.

Josh quickly walked away to a safe distance so he could observe him without being seen. He watched the boy, after appearing to snap out of a trance, walk back into the store. Looking through the window, Josh watched him remove a couple of CDs from his jacket and place them on a shelf. The boy then walked back to the front of the store and left in a hurry, looking extremely shaken.

Making sure the boy wasn't aware of his presence, Josh followed. Walking around the centre aimlessly for a short time, the boy eventually made his way to a café. Josh was finding it difficult, as he was still feeling somewhat dazed by the whole experience. And as much as it was crazy to think it, he already knew who this boy was. But how? It was impossible.

Josh watched him order a drink and take a seat in the café, sitting on his own. To blend in as a customer, Josh ordered himself a coffee and placed it on a table across from the boy. Looking at him was strange. He needed to find out if what he was thinking was true. So, taking the opportunity, he left his coffee on the table and approached the boy.

"Hey," said Josh, looking down at him. Josh felt a weird sensation throughout his body; chills and goose bumps all over.

The boy turned and looked up. He froze. He appeared stone-like again, same as he did when leaving the music store. He remained still, saying and doing nothing.

"Hey," Josh repeated, trying to grab the kid's attention.

The boy appeared to come round, although looking like a startled rabbit. "What do you want?" he replied defensively.

Josh immediately came up with a pretext; "The sugar," he replied.

"Oh, okay, yeah take it," said the boy nervously and passed it over.

Josh took the jar; himself in disbelief at what he was now experiencing. How? —was the biggest question stuck on his mind.

"Thanks," he said and walked back to his table.

He looked down trying to think it through, trying to resolve it in his head, thinking of the incredible, the impossibility unfolding before him. He had no answer to it, just as he had no answer those many years ago when he was sitting in the exact same spot where the boy is sitting. The exact same place —but different time—when he experienced the stranger approach him in exactly the same way he had just approached the boy. "What's happening? How can this be?" he questioned silently.

Josh knew what the boy was going through; he knew what he was thinking. He knew because he was looking at himself from ages passed—like a mirror of time. How? —was the question running over and over in his head. It was too fantastic, yet at the same time was the only plausible explanation to his life-long experiences of déjà vu, and the sighting of his "dead" friend who appeared in the stairwell that day—trying to tell him something. It was fantastic. And although a wild notion and seemingly crazy; it was the only
explanation that really made any sense.

The whole experience consumed Josh's attention; creating more questions than ever. He had never felt so shaken about life before. He had been indoctrinated with the idea that you were born, you live a number of years, and then you die. That was life. Period! He knew some believed in a sacred place and an "after-life", but that was for optimists. Physicists and scientists had everyone believing the limitations of the universe, and anything that couldn't be observed didn't exist. Theorists and out-of-the-box thinkers were criticised—looked down upon and made to look crazy—if proposing anything other than conventional science. Until now, he himself had never given much thought to science; except for bullet velocity and how to hit a moving target from a distance.

Josh had so many thoughts running through his head that he forgot about the boy. And when he looked up, he saw that he had already left. "Shit!" he said, springing up from his seat to go and look for him. But then he stopped. "I already know where he's going. I know where he's heading. It's crazy but I already know!" and with those thoughts, he left the café.

He headed for the shopping centre exit and waited. It wasn't long before the boy turned up just as he had predicted. He was right. Watching too closely, the boy spotted Josh; he looked straight at him but continued walking out of the shopping centre. Josh followed, leaving through another door so as not to spook the boy further. He already knew what he was going through.

As he left the centre, Josh was quick to zero-in on someone else taking a particular interest in the boy—a man, and from the way he was carrying himself, was armed. Josh watched the unknown male secrete himself inside an enclosed quiet space, out of view to passers-by and their untrained eyes. Josh on the other hand—who was highly trained—watched the man uncover a mini assault rifle with telescopic sight from inside his coat.

Josh knew who his target was and acted immediately. He force-marched towards the sniper, taking fast wide deliberate steps. He knew if he ran, the sudden movement would attract the sniper's attention. He wanted to stay low-key, with surprise on his side. As he homed in fast, he watched the man elevating the rifle into his shoulder, bringing it to a firing position. Moving in closer still, the sniper was already in the aiming position, with barrel pointing in the boy's direction. It was now or never.

Fast upon him and without thought, Josh slid the side of his boot down the back of the sniper's knee, causing him to buckle and lose his standing. The rifle barrel immediately pointed into the air from the sudden jolt. Josh grabbed the man's shoulder from behind as he pulled out his knife from his jacket, and without hesitation, thrust it deep into the back of the sniper's neck. With a forceful cross-motion jerk, he felt a snap as he severed the man's spinal cord. The man could only give a slight muffled gasp as he dropped heavily to the floor. Josh followed him down, removed the knife and looked around for spectators.

No one was aware of what had just happened. Nearby shoppers and passers-by were still going about their daily business — in their oblivious state. Josh cleaned the knife on his quarry's jacket and slid it back into its sheath, inside his jacket. He pulled open the dead man's jacket and quickly went through his pockets, searching for intelligence. Nothing. But his instinct was that the man belonged to View Corp, and they were after the boy.

Josh picked up an old soggy cardboard box lying nearby and threw it over the body, partially concealing it to make it appear as a homeless man sleeping. He then slipped into the street with the other pedestrians, just as though nothing had happened. Looking along the street for the boy, he could see he had already made some ground between them. Josh couldn't see any immediate threat from that distance but needed to catch up with him in case others were on his tail.

He raced round a back road and up a side-alley that led back onto the main street of the shopping centre. He waited in the alley, keeping out of sight. It wasn't long before he came into view; the person he was waiting for. Josh leapt out on the boy, grabbed him and dragged him into the side-alley. The boy started yelling.

"What do you want; I haven't done anything!"

"Shut up, you're drawing attention!" snapped back Josh, as he dragged him further down the alley.

Pushing the boy against a wall he started to shout out, so Josh gave him a light punch to the solar plexus to shut him up. He knew a punch to the soft spot of nerves and diaphragm would easily bring the boy under control. The boy immediately buckled over in pain, gasping for breath—having the wind knocked out of him. His loud shouting changed to quiet whining as he slouched to the ground, grabbing his body in pain.

With the boy successfully incapacitated, Josh quickly scanned around for other potential threats—looking back the way they came.

"It's safe," he thought to himself. No one had witnessed anything; or if they had, were too apathetic to care.

"Come on, follow me," Josh instructed and started walking. The boy automatically followed.

"Where are we going, what the hell is going on?" snapped the boy. Josh carried on walking at a fast pace. "Look if you don't stop and tell me what is going on I'm leaving!" the boy continued.

Josh had no time for a question-and-answer session so immediately turned, grabbed the boy by his jacket and pulled him along. The boy immediately shut up—doing as he was told.

Both walked out of the alley at speed; Josh still in control of the boy. He headed for his car; where he had left it parked a short distance away. He pulled out his key-remote and unlocked the doors. He opened the passenger door, pushed the boy inside and slammed it shut. He moved round to the driver's side, jumped in, started up, and sped off.

He drove around until he was satisfied he wasn't being tailed, but was concerned that Harris may still be using the tracker to keep an eye on his whereabouts. Should he leave it on or turn it off? The problem of the tracker quickly drifted to the back of his mind, as he instead started to think about the boy and what the hell was going on. He looked at the boy's clothes; they were exactly the same as his, those umpteen odd years ago.

"How could this be?" he thought—looking at himself from the past. He continued racking his brains over the idea whilst driving fast, until the boy started to shuffle around in his seat. This caused Josh to snap out of his incessant thinking of all the possibilities.

"Look, I don't know what's going on but people will be worried about me. What's going on?" said the boy nervously.

Josh replied to the boy's question, "Don't worry Josh your mother won't be concerned."

Without thinking or realising, he was imitating the stranger's words from the past. Josh was quietly astounded. Everything was almost the same; everything but a few minor details. The clothes, the circumstances, even the conversations—as best he could remember—were pretty much the same. There were slight variations but it was mostly like playing a recording; except this time, he was playing the other role.

The boy sparked up with surprise. "Who are you and how do you know my name?" he questioned.

"I know more than that," replied Josh. "I know where you live, who your friends are, your parents, about your father—who used to beat you, that you are to join the army soon and more besides. I know all about you."

"But how do you know? Who are you?" replied the boy frantically.

"We'll discuss it later. But in the meantime, I need your help," said Josh. "I need you to come with me; I have something to show you."

Sitting quietly, the boy agreed.

Josh knew the boy would follow along, just as he did in the past. The pre-recorded events appeared to naturally follow the same historic path Josh had been on. Although to him now—in the present—everything that was happening appeared self-created and self-determined by him; however, the truth of it began to reveal a different story.

CHAPTER 18

WITH ALL THE RECENT revelations needing explanation, Josh drove at speed back to Flash's safe-room, in order to gain remote access to Harris's computer. He pulled the SQRV up to the building inside the industrial complex and immediately jumped out. He paced quickly round to the passenger side and opened the door for the boy.

"Get out." Still looking anxious, the boy jumped out of the car. Josh closed the door, locked the car, and led him into the building—to the safe-room. He tapped in the security code for the door, opened it and went inside.

"In here and shut the door." The boy instantly complied. He was looking utterly startled and Josh knew why. The boy was experiencing the same feelings he had experienced many years ago with the "stranger" he had met.

"I feel like I know this place!" The boy was looking around the room like he had a big question on his mind. "I feel like I've been here before." Josh said nothing. "What's going on? What is this stuff?" the boy questioned further.

"Sit down," said Josh, pointing to a chair. Again, the boy did as he was told.

Josh stood looking at the boy in disbelief. He now had some time to take stock of the situation but it was too surreal for him to really understand. How could this be true? How could it happen? Many questions were circling inside his head. It then dawned on him what had happened those many years ago when he was the boy.

He began to see his future. He knew what was going to happen to him, as he recalled the incident with the hit-squad and the "stranger" getting shot. He was determined that that part of the future wouldn't come true for him and had to act fast. But in spite of knowing, he felt he had no real control over the forthcoming events. He felt the future was already set; resigning to the idea that it was going to happen anyway. He felt the future was already mapped out and he was a puppet having to play his part; play the part without a choice.

"Get a grip Brannon!" he thought, giving himself an order, then directed his attention back to the boy.

"I need your help," Josh said to the boy.

"But why do you want my help?"

"You've had some unusual experiences lately, haven't you? Things you can't explain?"

The boy looked shocked. "Yes, but how do you know that?"

Josh continued, "I can give you some but not all of the facts. But first you must tell me exactly what's been happening to you. I mean exactly."

The boy explained in detail whilst Josh listened and made notes. After the boy had finished Josh walked over to one of the tables in the room. He started reading his notes; comparing his experiences with the boy's own, to see how much they differed. The experiences were generally very similar, but there were the odd significant changes; changes that could be very important in the future outcome. This gave Josh some relief and a feeling of hope for his own destiny. No one would want to know when, where, and how they were going to die.

Josh logged-on to one of the computer terminals next to him. The computer file of Hoffman was automatically displayed on the monitor. Flash had sent the encrypted file to his own computer for Josh to find potential leads.

He walked away from the table and for a couple of minutes wandered around in thought. He remembered when he was the boy that the "stranger" had walked out of the room. He remembered stealing a look at the profile on the computer. Josh wanted to test the boy and the circumstances; he wanted to see the similarities and differences between the actions of the past and those of the present.

"Stay there," said Josh to the boy, and he walked out of the room—closing the door.

He gave the boy a few moments then quickly re-entered. The boy was sitting in the chair but in a shifted position, and Josh noticed the guilty look on his face.

"So, what did you read?" asked Josh.

The boy squirmed. "Read? What do you mean?"

Josh knew the boy was lying, just as he had lied when quizzed about the very same thing those many years ago. Everything seemed too identical; the whole situation didn't appear to have much in the way of flexibility. And he wasn't sure if he could cheat his foreseeable death.

Removing Flash's computer device from his jacket, Josh connected it to the computer he had recently logged in to. Using it, he was able to circumvent the firewall around the government servers used at HQ; but to access Harris's computer terminal and files he had to get his user and passcode. Josh was reluctant in using the device as that was a duplication of his past, but he had no choice.

"Let's see what else this thing can do," he thought. He typed "Harris" in the search field and tapped on a button. In a matter of seconds, the device displayed the results of profiles under the name of "Harris"; fortunately, only four. Clicking on each profile in turn, the device automatically sniffed out the user and passcodes to give Josh complete access—except for one. For some reason, the only terminal he needed access to was further blocked.

"Shit!" he thought, "I'll have to find another way," and promptly disconnected the device, put it inside his jacket pocket, and logged off the computer.

"I said; what did you read?" Josh repeated his earlier question.

The boy looked as though he was put on the spot, and Josh knew that was exactly how he felt from his own experience. The whole dialogue from what he could remember was all but verbatim. But it was exact enough to predict the future; a future that was fast coming and deadly for him. The boy mentioned seeing the name "View Corp"; as did Josh to his—now fully realising it—older self.

Josh revealed more to the boy about View Corp as did the "stranger" to him, when he was sitting in the exact same spot as the boy is now sitting. It was a real mind-bender, and Josh was still trying to steady the whole confusion.

FLASH! FLASH! — FLASH! FLASH!

Josh spotted lights flashing on the security panel and knew the company he was expecting were already there. The pre-determined event seemed to have come around faster than he thought it had before, so had to act fast.

Pulling his 9mil from his jacket, Josh sharply cocked it—pulling back the slide readying it for action—while at the same time moving to the computer terminals. He flicked a switch that Flash had explained to him in case of trouble—activating a hard-drive wipe. Time was now against them.

"Get up and do what I say!" directed Josh to the boy. "Stand over by that wall!" he pointed. The boy was putty in his hands, obeying every command; which was what Josh needed right now. Facing and pointing his 9mil at the main door, Josh was preparing for a room breach.

"That lever on the wall; pull it!"

Josh told the boy to pull the lever on the wall that he knew would open a secret door. Flash never told him about it but he remembered pulling it when he was the boy in the same situation. It was like playing cards and knowing what cards your opponents had, although it wasn't strictly going his way. His deal was a losing hand and he knew it.

The boy pulled the lever and the escape door opened. Josh moved fast with the boy into the adjacent room, closing the escape door behind them. This was the point of no return. He was trapped and knew what to expect. Josh had been wounded once before whilst on active duty, nothing serious but it hurt like hell. Something he would never forget in a hurry.

The whole event was playing out almost exactly as before, and although Josh knew it, he couldn't change it. He felt his actions were not his own anymore but was being pushed along a course not of his choosing. As much as he wanted to change it, it seemed he was doing the "right" thing.

"Follow me and don't make a noise. When I say 'move' you MOVE!" demanded Josh.

Both went to the back of the room to another door. Josh knew this was the moment and was prepared. He pushed opened the door and ducked back. A hail of bullets came cracking through, narrowly missing him, knocking out pieces of wall. The boy became frantic, shouting hysterically. "MOVE!" Josh grabbed the boy's jacket and pulled him through the doorway, against the anticipated second hail of bullets.

Zzp! Josh felt a sudden piercing force against his body, quickly followed by excruciating pain. As did his older self get hit, so did Josh. He knew it was predicted for him to catch a bullet at that specific moment, but still, he was not fully prepared for the pain. It felt as though someone had bitten a small chunk from his right arm. Sprinting and taking cover from gunfire, behind some old machinery, he quickly inspected his wound. It was only superficial but a deep enough gash to cause blood flow. Regardless, there was no time to treat it as they were still in immediate danger and needed to get out fast.

He cranked up his internal survival switch—blocking out the pain and heightening his tactical awareness. With his killer instinct up to full capacity, Josh ranged and zoned in on an armed target—a man—seventy-five metres away. Josh raised his weapon and fired two shots in short succession. It was instantaneous with both bullets landing where expected—in the target's chest. The target was pushed back hard, falling to the floor.

"MOVE!" shouted Josh.

He pulled the boy up, who was crouched with his head down, and both dashed for a nearby exit. More gunfire and bullet strikes bounced around them. Another target—a man firing a weapon—came into view, causing Josh to shoot on the move. BANG! BANG! He double-tapped two bullets centre mass of the target's body; like the first it dropped heavily. Running through the exit Josh had identified a third target in pursuit of them. He let go of the boy and immediately turned, taking up a kneeling position—BANG! BANG! He fired off two aimed shots, notching up a third kill.

Working on pure adrenalin, instinct and training, Josh got up, grabbed the boy again and dragged him to keep on running. They ran hard until Josh felt they were safe, then stopped in a suburban area. At this point the boy—out of breath and panting hard—went into hysterics. Josh immediately punched him in the side to shut him up.

"Why did you do that?" screamed the boy, wincing from the jab.

"You're losing it and you need to stay focused," said Josh calmly. In spite of it all, he had already regained his composure; there was no need to stay hyped up when it wasn't needed. "I think we're safe now but we have to keep moving, they know where we are."

"Who are they? You haven't told me a bloody thing!" the boy complained.

"They are View Corp. Now let's get going."

Josh concealed his 9mil under his jacket and pulled out the handheld computer. He covered his wound with his left hand, applying direct pressure to stem the blood flow and started walking; the boy following a few steps behind.

"Things are different," thought Josh, as he recollected and compared both events of the past and present. "The man I was with got hit in the left arm, but I got hit in the right. They're opposites." It was a significant difference. He continued to analyse the events in his head as he walked along a quiet road, cradling his injured arm.

They approached a line of cars and Josh knew he needed immediate medical attention, and that meant getting transport. He needed to get his wound sealed or he would faint from loss of blood. He looked around to make sure there were no onlookers, walked up to an old car and smashed the front passenger window with his elbow. Although he had been trained by the government in hot-wiring certain vehicles, he had also gained experience in his teenage years—stealing cars for joyriding.

Purposely choosing an old car, he knew it would be easier—newer models were not so easy to hot-wire. He opened the door, leaned in across the glass covered seat and looked at the steering column. He ripped off the cover to bear the wiring and pulled at the ones he needed. Stripping and reconnecting the wires for the starting motor, the engine kicked into life. Josh sat up and grabbed hold of the steering wheel, and with a forceful jolt of a turn, felt the steering lock break.

Josh pushed opened the driver's door for the boy, "I need you to drive."

"But I can't drive."

Josh knew he was lying; of course he knew, he was him. "You got into trouble with your friend Steve remember? Driving with no licence, so don't tell me you can't drive. Now get in and drive!"

The boy looked shocked at what Josh told him about his life. He didn't question though, just did as he was told; brushed off a few pieces of glass from the seat onto the floor and got into the driver's seat. He closed the door and pulled off before anyone saw them. "Where are we going?" he asked.

Josh had to get his arm patched up and he needed time to assess their situation. Although he had experienced this all before and knew what was going to happen, it was all running away too fast, too fast to change things. He needed a safe place. Working for the government, Josh had access to a number of company safe-houses; there he could buy some thinking time. He reached for his newly acquired device, courtesy of Flash, and tapped in some data. Flash's device had several useful functions including revealing the locations of safe-houses and access codes. Although Josh already knew the location of a local safe-house he needed the latest access code; they were changed remotely every twenty-four hours, regardless if they were in use or not.

"This will show you where to go," replied Josh, and placed the device—now functioning as a sat-nav—on the car dashboard for the boy to follow.

Now that things were calmer, Josh felt he could switch off a little more, or he would burn himself out. He knew his limitations. The problem now however was the pain. Coming down from the extreme tactical state he was in was like coming down from a drug-induced high. The drop in adrenalin—like the wearing off of a drug—allowed his attention to be focused on the pain; the pain in his arm. And he could feel it for sure. Now able to inspect his wound more thoroughly, he knew the bullet hadn't lodged inside, but it was still oozing blood. He ripped a piece of lining from his jacket and pushed it down onto the wound; grimacing slightly from the pain as he did so.

"How did you know about Steve and me; the police never caught us?" asked the boy.

"No; but your dad found out and gave you a real hiding; nearly put you in the hospital."

"But how do you know that?"

"I said before Josh, I know all about you. Now shut up and drive," replied Josh, finding it a little weird calling the boy by his own name.

He was remembering the whole incident when his dad beat him for stealing a car. He would never forget it. It was the day he decided to get away when he was able to do so. It was odd, while recalling the incident, as he then fully realised that his father was also the boy's father. It was sort of strange, like having a younger brother. Thoughts began drifting in and out of his mind, as he relaxed as best he could. He could feel the slow increasing effect of blood loss.

Josh suddenly opened his eyes. He had drifted off for a while, until he felt the car come to a stop. They had reached a housing estate. More alert now, he grabbed the computer device from the dash and ordered the boy to get out of the car. He purposely left the car some distance from where they were heading. He knew that eventually it would be reported to the police as stolen, and didn't want them tracking him.

So now on foot, they walked to a residential area and the location of the safe-house they could use. They walked up to the front door and Josh opened a panel, revealing an electronic keypad. He pressed in the access code hacked by Flash's device, unlocking the door. Pushing it open he stepped inside, with the boy following, and closed it behind them.

"Who lives here?" asked the boy. He was wide-eyed, looking around taking everything in.

"Me," Josh lied. He just wanted to get himself fixed up, not start another conversation. "Sit over there and keep quiet," he continued, as he pointed to a chair. The boy looked and sat down.

Josh left the boy alone and went into another room. He needed to sterilise and dress his wound. All of the safe-house layouts were similar with regards location of equipment and supplies; this made it easy for operatives to quickly locate what they needed. Josh located a medic pack in a cupboard, opened it, and set up a space to work from—laying out the medical supplies.

Removing his upper garments and making himself as comfortable as possible, Josh cleaned and sterilised his wound. The stinging was almost as bad as getting shot. He knew he could use a painkiller or local anaesthetic, but he couldn't risk being weakened by the effects of the drugs in any way; even mildly. But luckily, the bullet only grazed his arm, removing a little flesh. It wasn't such a big deal. Although difficult, he managed to stitch up the gash with his left hand—closing the wound and stopping the bleeding.

He finished cleaning it up and re-joined the boy in the other room, who began gawping at the stitched wound. He had been sitting quietly the whole time. Josh pulled open a field-dressing he removed from a cupboard, and began gently wrapping it around his arm to protect his wound: loose enough for it to breathe and heal.

"What is this place?" the boy piped up; still staring and hungry for answers.

Josh felt it odd that he couldn't come clean with him, that he had to keep things secret. But really, what had he to hide from him? Nothing. It was like he was lying to himself, being his own enemy and he knew it. He wanted to tell the boy, but the compulsion to not reveal everything was somehow firmly fixed. He had no control over it.

"What does it look like?"

"It looks like a home, but it's not. There are no pictures, family photos, nothing."

"Well, there you have it then, you already know."

The boy snapped; "What's that supposed to mean, 'I already know', know what? You haven't told me a thing, just leaving me to make guesses. You're really pissing me off!"

Josh gave him a killer look, as he was still trying to handle the pain in his arm, and didn't need the additional crap being thrown his way. The boy, seeing the deadly hint, simmered down and looked away. Josh finished wrapping the dressing around his arm, and put on his clothes from the other room. He was just beginning to feel hungry. He had expended a lot of energy which needed to be replenished if he were to continue. He opened another cupboard and grabbed an army ration pouch. He opened it, picked up a spoon and started eating the content—Beef Goulash.

He looked at the boy while chewing his first mouthful. He knew he was still pissed at him by the resentful look on his face—stewing silently and staring at the floor. "You hungry?" Josh asked. He was sure he would be.

"Yeah," the boy huffed.

Josh pulled out another pouch of food and threw it to him; a token of peace that would hopefully ease things between them. The boy pulled it open and looked inside.

"What's this?" he asked, screwing his face up at the mushy content.

"Army rations. Get used to it."

"You're in the army then?" The boy started up again. Josh ignored his question and continued eating. "So, what is View Corp?" continued the boy, who was determined to get his own answers.

That was the pointed question that caught Josh's full attention, and in some way, felt responsible to tell what little he knew. Josh explained to the boy, as did the "stranger" to him, what he knew about View Corp. It was like passing down a secret from generation to generation, except this was passing something down from himself to himself. It was like reminding himself of something that he already knew but had somehow forgotten.

"But what has all of this got to do with me?" asked the boy, as he spooned food into his mouth.

It was a question Josh couldn't answer, not because he didn't want to, but because it would be too unreal for the boy to understand, just as it was still unreal for him to fully accept.

"How did you find out about View Corp, and what do they want?"

The boy was inquisitive and wanted answers just as he did. The problem Josh faced, apart from being bound by secrecy laws preventing him from revealing much, was that he didn't have all of the answers.

"I found out about View Corp in a file I wasn't supposed to see, whilst working on another assignment. I discovered some kind of experimentation was taking place, something very serious but no mention of what exactly. There was also mention of..." and Josh stopped talking.

"What?" The boy's interest perked up, wanting to know more.

Josh was telling him titbits and had him hooked like a fish on a line. He knew the "lead" was a lead from his past. Ironically, his former self had already disclosed the lead he now intended to follow. He was looking to his past to resolve the present.

"I need you to help me. I may have a location where View Corp could be situated and I need you to come with me."

He knew the boy would be easily persuaded to go, just as he was back then. But somehow Josh felt he was being played, and although he knew the possible outcome of what was to come, he felt this uncontrollable compulsion to continue.

"Okay, so where are we going?" the boy eagerly replied.

Josh knew the boy was fully in, but for himself, he felt uncertainty. He knew the next step—the next lead in the investigation—proved fatal for the "stranger" those many years ago, and now, the same situation and possibly the same fate was presenting itself to Josh. It was a daunting thought he had to overcome.

Josh replied positively to the boy, "Follow me."

CHAPTER 19

KNOWING WHERE THEY MUST now go, where fate seemed to be leading them, Josh prepared as best he could. Luckily, Flash's new handheld device proved worthy with unhindered albeit unauthorised access to classified imagery. Josh was able to pull up satellite photographs of the area he now needed to investigate. It was a known location connected to View Corp and his only best lead.

Although Josh knew the area in question, as he had been there with his former self, preparation was absolute key. It was difficult to face as he knew the deadly outcome, so needed to cover all of his bases and potential scenarios. How much preparation his former self gave to this crucial moment he didn't know; all he did know was that clearly it wasn't enough. Josh was not about to get caught in that same trap. But did he really have a choice? He wasn't sure. Was this supposed to be the end of his days? Again, he didn't know. All he knew was what had happened in the past and that he was determined to change his future.

Viewing the image, Josh was able to quickly determine the best approach that would be tactically advantageous for them. He then realised it was the exact same approach he had taken with the "stranger" in the past.

"There has to be another way," he thought.

He began frantically in his head looking for an alternative route, an alternative choice. He couldn't find one. He knew from his training and experience this was the best tactical route; he knew it as did his former self before him.

"But what if I changed it?"

Josh needed to know he could change his future and that his life wasn't just some set path he was destined to walk. He was desperate to step out of the rut. As much as he looked for an alternative route, he knew he would be setting himself and the boy up for dire consequences. The conflict in his head between doing what he knew to be right and the feeling of needing to change his fate frustrated him.

"What if what I know isn't right but some already pre-programmed pre-destined response to this already laid out situation?" he considered.

Josh was analysing the situation from a new viewpoint. He knew that what his former self went through didn't work.

"So why would it work this time?" he reasoned. "It doesn't make sense to continue to do the same thing with the expectation of a different outcome. That's illogical," he continued, "That's the whole point! This whole situation is illogical!"

Josh came to realise he was trying to make sense of something that wasn't based on any contemporary logic. What he was involved in couldn't be perceived of in any normal sense. He didn't know why he hadn't thought of it before, but what he was experiencing wasn't based on traditional thinking. He was dealing with some kind of alternative universe; a phenomenon with powers and influence not recognised by traditional science. He knew now he had to think differently and this gave him confidence.

"Come on let's go!" he said to the boy who was sitting and waiting for orders.

They both grabbed their things and left the safe-house; leaving it the way they found it—minus some rations and medical supplies. Josh knew he needed to recover his SQRV for this next phase; he needed his weaponry. But the car was still near the industrial estate where he had left it and he needed transport to get there. His solution was simple.

Eyeing the cars along the road as they walked, he singled one out: a dented old banger. "That'll do," he thought. He scanned the area; all clear, no one around. He walked up to the window with the intention of breaking into it but stopped.

"My lucky day," he said, looking through the dirty window. The owner had left the car unlocked with the keys in the ignition; probably hoping someone would steal it so they could claim on the insurance, not that they would get much for it.

The boy stood by watching nervously as Josh simply opened the door, jumped in and turned the engine over. He looked over at the boy; "Get in Josh," he said. The boy, doing as he was told, jumped in and without delay they pulled away.

As they were nearing the industrial estate Josh's senses began to sharpen. He knew there was a possibility View Corp had found his car and set an ambush, or worse, an explosive device. He had to take the risk but it was one he had prepared for. And besides, he knew from his past that the "stranger" had been successful in retrieving it, so probability was on his side. He just didn't know what the "stranger" had to go through to recover it.

He pulled into a quiet side road and turned to the boy; "Wait here. I'll be back shortly." The boy said nothing; Josh could see he was scared.

He needed to go alone as the boy would be a liability if things went belly-up. He knew it as did his former self. He was now finding himself following the past actions of his predecessor a little too closely for his own comfort. He had to remind himself that all was not how it seemed and that he could change his future. But the subtle doubt of how much he could change crept in.

On full alert, Josh walked carefully into the industrial site, scanning his arcs to the left and right, looking into the old buildings for snipers. He placed his hand inside his jacket and kept it there, gripping the handle of his 9mil. Made ready with a round in the chamber, he was prepared to take action if he suddenly came under enemy fire. Walking further, his car came into view, looking exactly how he had left it. The surrounding area was quiet and showed no signs of movement.

Josh moved into a safe position by a wall and waited. He watched carefully for the slightest of movement, or anything out of place that would give an ambush away. He had to consider the worst-case scenario. Several minutes passed as he waited patiently. He knew if he was facing an amateur force, they would likely become impatient and attack—breaking their ambush cover. But if they were professional enough, they would be prepared to wait it out for as long as it took. It seemed possibly the latter, or there was in fact no one there at all.

He decided to move in. He pre-selected positions between him and the car, that if needed, he could use for cover from enemy fire. Keeping close to the walls and moving from cover to cover, while scanning around, Josh moved in closer. Still quiet with no indication of enemy presence, Josh felt a little relieved. Fairly sure the area was clear, he had to now consider the car had been booby-trapped, or at least fitted with a tracking device. Now close enough to see, Josh got down on his belly to look underneath.

"Clear," he thought and got up.

He walked the last stage to the car and, as a final security check, thoroughly looked it over for any signs of tampering. No devices and no sign of break-in. It was all clear. Josh deduced that the three-man hit-squad he had despatched earlier were the only ones. And it was likely their bodies still lay where he had left them, on the other side of the building. He got what he came for, now it was time to get going. The early evening was drawing in and he needed to get back to the boy—to himself. He jumped in the car, started it up and sped off back to where he had left the young Josh.

He sharply drove into the side road and pulled up alongside the old banger. "Get in!" he shouted, looking at the boy through the window. The young Josh promptly did as he was told and swapped cars. He was looking worried.

"You alright?" asked Josh.

"Yeah; just wondering where you were."

"I'm here now," replied Josh, putting his foot down on the accelerator; speeding away in the direction of the underground bunker, and the uncertainty of death.

They had been driving for about an hour, and daylight was just beginning to fade. None to very little conversation took place between them during the whole journey, but the internal conversations both were having with themselves wouldn't cease. They were trying to come to some understanding from their own viewpoints. The young Josh mostly had his attention on the so-called "stranger", of whom he was yet to realise was an older version of him. And the older Josh had his attention on the boy, still disbelieving his very existence as a younger version of himself. But regardless of what they were thinking, believing or disbelieving, they were somehow inextricably bound.

With the guidance of Flash's device, they reached the given location, off the main road and onto a dirt track in a wooded area. The surround was a mix of fields interspersed with a number of thick copses. Josh was finding it somewhat strange to be back. It was weird to know that the place he was about to visit had been destroyed in an explosion years before. It was also haunting to remember the death of the "stranger"—the "stranger" he had now become—and the death that was potentially waiting for him.

"These tracks are fresh," said Josh, noticing the imprinted tyre treads in the mud; a clear indication of presence. His alertness switched up a level and he began scanning the area for signs of life and View Corp.

"It could be a tractor, or a farmer or something," said the boy nervously.

Josh knew the boy was scared, and was trying to make a genuinely bad situation seem less dangerous than it was. But Josh knew the truth; he knew what danger lay in store. He pulled-in off the track, parking among some trees and bushes for concealment. He positioned the car ready for immediate escape, in case he did manage to get away. But he was under no illusion of what might happen.

"We walk from here," said Josh, as he turned off the engine and stepped out of the car.

The boy followed his lead. He watched nervously as Josh walked round to the rear of the car, opened the boot, and lifted the cover concealing the arsenal of small arms and ammunition. Josh removed his jacket, put on a tactical vest, grabbed his MP7 submachine gun and four spare magazines. He slung the weapon—strapping it to his body, and put on his jacket, concealing the submachine gun underneath, along with the spare mags of ammo he slotted into pouches on his tactical vest. He closed the boot and looked directly at the boy; seeing but ignoring his fear. Fear had no place in battle; it had to be controlled and had to be shut out. Josh knew it and the boy had yet to learn it.

"This way!" ordered Josh, and moved off with the boy in the direction of what he knew was to be the underground bunker—if his estimation of recent and past experiences were correct.

Josh followed the edge of a field, along the hedgerow, rather than risk walking through the open field. It would take a little longer but he knew it was safer: tactically. He knew the hedgerow would give them cover from view, from being spotted easily, and also cover from weapon fire, as they could use the banked hedgerow as a defence.

The boy trailed behind, quieter than ever. As they drew in to the target location, Josh got down into a ditch for cover, and pulled his MP7 out from under his jacket. He raised the weapon into his shoulder in order to look through the optical sight, but in doing so caused pain from his wound. Wincing, he could feel the pain taking over, and as difficult as it was, he managed to push it from his mind. He looked through the sight in the direction of the bunker. He could only see trees and undergrowth; no movement of people.

He stood up, and keeping his weapon in the shoulder—ready to fire—carried on. As much as it pained him to do so, Josh stopped every hundred metres or so to scan the area with his rifle's scope. It was a necessary tactical approach, regardless of any discomfort he was feeling, and kept it up until they reached the general location. He took up a final kneeling position and Josh scoped an opening in the undergrowth; indicating it to the boy.

"What is it?" asked the boy.

"An opening, through there," and Josh pointed with the barrel of his weapon.

The boy stared hard; "I can't see anything."

Josh knew why the boy couldn't see it. He was looking at the undergrowth, rather than through it. Military training had taught Josh to look through and beyond objects and spaces when searching for an enemy; not to just look at the near edge of a building or tree line but to look through it and into it—to look through windows and doorways and gaps between trees. An untrained eye would naturally stop at the first obstacle—the vision being prevented from extending further; which is why the boy couldn't see the opening.

"Look through the undergrowth, not at it," said Josh.

But he could see the boy was still struggling to see what he saw, so pulled at some bushes to reveal a hidden opening. Clearing the way, Josh pushed through without waiting for the boy; waiting was a luxury he didn't have right now.

WHOOSH!

Déjà vu justifiably impinged on Josh. A string of flashbacks swept through his mind, flashbacks of such intensity that put him into a light hypnotic trance. The dirty grey out-building of the bunker was still standing: untouched by past events. It should have been destroyed. He couldn't believe this was the same building that was supposed to have been obliterated—obliterated by the detonation of the device set off by his former self. It was as though that event never even took place. Fleeting thoughts ran through his mind trying to reason why it wasn't destroyed.

"Remember, there's no logic to this; no logic, no logic," Josh repeated to himself. "Keep going. Don't stop."

Reaching the out-building, Josh vaguely knew what to expect as he began partially recalling his own past experience of the same event. He was still feeling dazed, and as much as he could remember the general event, he lacked the detail. The details seemed occluded now and forgotten. He knew this was dangerous. In his game, details were the most important of all. He had a vague sense of immediate danger but was distracted by the thought of what was coming—what could in fact be his own finale. Josh moved in close to the heavy looking door into the building.

"Wait!"

Josh turned and saw the boy, who had just pushed his way through the undergrowth from the other side. Consumed by his past misty memories, Josh had almost forgotten about him and wasn't aware he had been left behind.

"What's wrong?" questioned Josh. The boy looked startled and dazed, himself battling to stay focused. They were both going through the same déjà vu phenomena.

"I don't know. I don't think we should go that way. We should go round the back."

Josh knew himself that something wasn't right, but couldn't pinpoint the danger. He needed to snap himself together. He realised he was going to have to take the boy's advice. He knew he couldn't just rely on his own wits, as they were being severely compromised, but needed the boy's help. Being helped was something he disliked. He never liked relying on others, preferring to do things himself, even if he had to struggle. This time though, he had to put away his pride, or whatever stopped him from accepting help. Help was what he needed to survive.

Listening to the boy, they moved up an embankment and round to the rear of the building, locating a small opening low down. It was easily missed as it was covered in brambles. Pulling the thorny plants out of the way, Josh was able to look through a small window. He remembered! There was an explosive anti-personnel device attached to the door on the inside. Had he breached the door he'd be peppered with shrapnel.

Josh started to realise the true danger he was in; the belief that he could change his looming death sentence appeared to be a lie. Was this to be his final mission? He couldn't help but wonder if there was another way, another lead he could follow. Maybe he could drop it altogether. He was trying to avoid what would be his toughest task yet. But he knew this was the biggest and only real lead he had, if he wanted to know the truth. He knew he had to continue.

The thick window was blast-proof, designed to withstand immense force and couldn't be smashed. Figuring out how to dislodge it, he began to work on the edges. He could see the weather-beaten bricks were the weak point. Pulling his knife out, he started scraping at the surrounding brickwork, weakening the window's edges. It was easier than it looked, and after removing enough concrete Josh lay on his back, kicking each side in turn to dislodge the window. It gave up. Josh squeezed through feet first. Once on the other side he helped the boy through. Both looked at the explosive device attached to the door.

"I knew something was wrong and I was right," said the boy excitedly. "But how?"

Without answering Josh smirked; he was just glad to be alive for a short while longer. "We can use this," he said.

He recognised the Russian-made mine, knew how to make it safe and got straight to it—inserting a piece of wire he found on the floor into the hole where the arming pin should go. Once disarmed and made secure he put it inside his jacket.

Again, he suddenly realised he was performing to the script of the past. Everything he was doing, the "stranger"—his former self—had also played his part. The way he had broken through the window, and how he had just dealt with the explosive device, was essentially following the same script. Although he felt with what he was doing was unique and in the moment, it was an illusion. Josh was operating on what seemed to be some kind of unknown auto-pilot.

Carefully walking down the concrete stairway inside the out-building, Josh remained extremely alert in case his memory failed to remind him of further traps. At the bottom they were met with the door made of heavy metal. Josh pushed on it in an attempt to open it, but it held firmly in place.

"What do we do now, it's locked?" said the boy. "There has to be another way in?"

Josh was remembering how the "stranger" had opened it in the past—by exploiting the wall around the hinges. The patchy broken concrete and exposed bricks were old, just like the wall around the window. Analysing it, Josh could see the weak spots, and just as his former self had, started scraping the wall away with his knife. Digging for half an hour, Josh exposed the locking bolts that kept the door secure. By sliding the bolts out of the wall, he was able to gain access. He pulled the door open as far as he could, then nodded for the boy to follow, before pushing his body through the gap to the other side.

The boy appeared through the gap and stood beside Josh. He was looking around—wide-eyed. "What is this place?" he asked.

Josh knew what it was, he had seen it all before. But he couldn't believe he was seeing it again, especially like this. "This shouldn't be," he thought. The bunker had not only been untouched by time, but had also gone untouched by the explosion the "stranger" had set off. That was one thing Josh remembered well, it was the time he was running for his life. Perhaps the bunker had been rebuilt? But he couldn't fool himself that it had been.

Memories were flooding in like they happened just yesterday. He recalled when he saw the "stranger" kill the two white-coated men, in the very same corridor he was now standing. He had the vivid picture in his head—the blood and bodies on the floor—and in a fleeting moment Josh started looking for them again, but that was in the past. He knew the immediate future of what was starting to become clear now. But something was gnawing at him. Josh couldn't help but think about changing his future: changing his destiny.

"Why did I kill those two men?" he thought; identifying himself with the "stranger". "I haven't got any reason except a suspicion they work for View Corp. And what the fuck is View Corp really?"

Internally, Josh was becoming unusually unglued, questioning everything, coupled with anger and frustration at not really knowing the truth. His judgement was becoming clouded and the pressure of having no time left was upon him. He knew the set future events that were laid out before him, but did he have to take the same path? It seemed that almost every action, every step he took, was an exact copy of the events from the past that his predecessor took. His life seemed a perpetual cycle of no choices. His life seemed as though it belonged to someone else, and he was only being allowed the appearance of being in control. This angered him more.

"Come on, get it together Josh, stop fucking around," he thought.

Remembering the string of events from the past, he recalled his former self searching through a particular file cabinet. He recalled seeing the "stranger" putting the file in his jacket and lying about having found anything: but why? Looking in the general direction where the "stranger" had stood, Josh identified the exact cabinet the file had come from.

"Check over on that desk and see what you can find," Josh told the boy. He wanted him out of the way.

"What am I looking for?"

"Anything to do with View Corp. Check for files, documents, anything."

The boy walked over to the desk and Josh, taking the opportunity, walked straight to the metal cabinet, and pulled open the drawer. He felt he was now looking through the eyes of his former self. He began feeling time was slightly apart but overlapping. He could see his past, his present, and his future, all-in-one. Time, and the end of the road, seemed to have converged.

The file cabinet was empty apart from one file; a file purposely placed flat on the bottom of the drawer. Taking the file in hand, Josh nervously opened it. The sole content was two pages clipped together—a brief bio and a one-line note attached: "CHANGE YOUR FUTURE JOSH".

CHAPTER 20

"CHANGE YOUR FUTURE JOSH"

The words echoed loudly in his head, filling him with astonishment and disbelief. The fact that someone already knew he would go to the bunker and look in that particular file cabinet contradicted his reality. For the first time, Josh was feeling irreversibly unstable; his being, his whole life had been flipped into confusion.

"What does this mean? I don't understand. How does someone know I'd be here?" he thought, his eyes glued to the note.

Lost for direction, something changed in Josh's universe. The revelation of this one note jolted him to such an extent he felt a radical change, but wasn't sure what. It was as though someone had pushed a reset button in his life—to start over again. It was at this point he snapped back to reality and started to recall the events of his past, his present situation, and the immediate threat of future-set events yet to unfold. Josh knew what was coming. He knew his former self had met with a fatal ending, and that that moment was fast approaching for him now. Without thinking, Josh pulled the note from the file—dropping it into the drawer—and stuffed the file inside his jacket.

"Come on let's go; there's nothing here," said Josh to the boy, who was still rummaging around over by the desk.

"Have you found anything?" asked the boy.

"No. Let's go!" insisted Josh.

He knew the boy was suspicious of him, as was he of his former self. He knew the boy had seen him conceal the file, just as he had seen his former self conceal it in the past. It was as though he was trying to hide something from himself that he already knew about. It was crazy, but that was how it was, and how it seemed it should be. There seemed to be no control over it. The set-recording of his life was in motion, and he was unable to change or stop it from playing the way it was supposed to be played.

Josh froze suddenly, becoming aware of a presence and the next part of the life-recording. He knew about the two View Corp scientists he was supposed to kill with his knife; just as his former self did.

"What is it?" whispered the boy. He was looking concerned.

Josh gestured for him to be silent, then pushed his own body into a wall space so he couldn't be seen. He automatically reached inside his jacket and pulled out his knife. He remained poised, gripping his knife, waiting for his prey. The boy, seeing Josh preparing for something, also backed up against the wall to hide. The look of fear on his face said it all.

"This is how it's supposed to be," Josh thought to himself. "I need to terminate them. I must take them out. I'm supposed to do this. I have to destroy View Corp."

Decisions were running through his mind; decisions that appeared to be of his own choosing. But something was different, something underlying felt off. He couldn't put his finger on the problem but began to doubt his self-direction.

"Change your future Josh," he whispered to himself. "Change your future. Change your future."

He iterated over and over to himself what was written on the note. He didn't fully understand and time was running out fast. He was used to acting without thinking: doing as he was supposed to do, and as he was trained to do. Conflict began growing in his head.

He could feel a solid mental ridge building inside of him. The ridge was being caused by the conflicting ideas of what he was supposed to do and what he felt he should do. Both ideas were pushing hard up against each other in his mind—in opposition. The ridge was causing uncertainty, confusion, and delay—delay he couldn't afford to have.

He suddenly snapped; intense anger consumed him, and without thought, pounced upon the two scientists that had already approached his lair. With knife in hand, Josh instinctively grabbed one of the scientists with one hand, while at the same time his other hand was swiftly cutting through the air toward his target. His pointed knife was destined to sever the back of his target's neck and spinal cord for quick termination. It was all reaction, unthinking reaction; Josh had no choice.

"NO! NO!"

Josh screamed out and suddenly stopped mid-action. For whatever reason he baulked; his body froze—knife barely touching the back of the neck of the first scientist. All life appeared to suddenly stop. Josh acted against all he knew to be true and against the set-recordings of his future. Something was now occurring that had been put in motion and couldn't be stopped. Time was appearing to change; time was appearing to unfold in a way that made a real future possible.

Wave flows of energy passed through the air. Images of the present appeared to wobble and pass through each other creating a confused distortion. Josh's mind was reeling, caused by images of the past, present and future, being mangled together. Mental images were flashing by so fast that Josh had no time to inspect them properly. Time was shifting around in monumental proportions as though straightening itself out. It was as though parts of the past, present, and future, had been overlapped in certain areas and now shifted back in line. The phenomenon seemed to go on for what felt like an eternity to Josh, but in actuality took only seconds to pass.

Overwhelmed and shocked, with his knife still in his hand, Josh was standing in the open—completely compromised as a government operative. He had given his enemy an advantage. This was an operational cock-up and he knew it. But something was different. He felt different. He felt he had changed his future. By not continuing to do what he was meant or trained to do, somehow allowed him to separate from a hidden control he was unaware of. There was a resurgence of self-determinism and freedom of choice he hadn't experienced before now. Josh felt he could now freely map out his own future.

"Hello Josh," the scientist spoke—the one who was about to feel the cold of Josh's blade.

"What... Who are you?" asked Josh, still reeling but ready with his knife in case he needed to use it.

"Apart from the man you were about to kill, my name is Stephen, Stephen Montague."

"What just happened to me? What are you doing here?"

Josh began throwing a series of questions at the two men, but who had no chance of answering. He then suddenly remembered the boy—his younger self—and turned to look for him. He was missing.

"Where's the boy, the boy I was with?"

"He isn't here Josh," replied Montague.

"Where is he? And how do you know me? What's going on?"

Josh was beginning to get agitated. He felt he was at square one with no more answers than when he first set out as a boy—with his older former self. The agitation grew, and he could feel the onset of a whirling sensation in his head. And although he could stand, suddenly his vision disappeared—going black. Josh's mind began shutting down; losing control of his body and feeling weak. He gradually lost all of his senses and blacked-out.

Waking up, Josh found himself lying on a bed in what appeared to be a hospital room. He had no clue as to how long he had been unconscious. He was still dressed, but his jacket had been removed along with his equipment—weapons, tactical vest, and spare magazines of ammo. His phone and Flash's device had also been confiscated.

He knew he had been sedated; his senses were dull and he felt a little groggy. The shitty feeling could have been from the fainting earlier, but he knew otherwise. One thing he hated was drugs. Still, he wasn't in any position to complain right now. And looking around, it didn't seem like he was in any immediate danger.

He sat up on the edge of the bed, looking around the room for exit points—only one closed door and no windows. The ceiling was solid with no crawl spaces to escape through. He was beginning to feel like a rat in a trap. He deduced he was still inside the bunker from the posters on the walls—similar to those in the bunker corridor. Plotting his escape and seeing what items he could turn into weapons; he was suddenly distracted by the opening of the door. In walked Sofia.

Josh calmed down when he saw her standing by the doorway. She was a familiar face who was purposely sent in to make him feel at ease. They knew what he was capable of; they had witnessed his deathly skills before—many times.

"Ah, the secret weapon," commented Josh. He knew their tactic, he wasn't stupid; though she still had the desired effect on him.

"Hello Josh," greeted Sofia, and she stepped closer towards him.

"Did you kill my friend Mac?" he snapped.

"No, I didn't." Sofia was cool-headed but knew she had to be careful; Josh was still in a volatile state.

"But you did call the police?"

"Yes. I found him dead when I went to your flat."

"Do you know who killed him?"

At that moment Stephen Montague walked into the room, accompanied by the other scientist Josh was about to terminate in the corridor earlier. This was Sofia's cue. She stepped back a little; her task successfully accomplished.

"Hello Josh. My name is Stephen. We met earlier, very briefly, before you passed out. How are you feeling now?"

"I want to know everything that's going on!" demanded Josh.

He was going to use this opportunity to get the many holes he had, filled-in—to complete his life-long mystery. But he knew the art of deception and so remained vigilant to what they would reveal; listening for the lies and half-truths they would tell. He was unsure who to trust at this point, and needed to listen carefully to the tiniest details of their tale. The minute details, he knew, were the glue that held a story together. Spies, intelligence officers and agents got compromised, not through lack of a good story, but through lack of the tiniest details that produced the cracks.

"Okay Josh," answered Stephen. "Let me try and explain things to you in a way that doesn't sound—how shall I say—odd. I am a professor of physics and this is Miles, Miles Balantyne, also a professor of physics. You are already acquainted with Sofia. We are a part of what you know as 'View Corp'. You have been indoctrinated into believing that View Corp is some kind of terror organisation. I can assure you it isn't."

Josh sat still, taking it all in. The general story was being sown but needed some rather large gaps to be filled.

Stephen continued enlightening Josh; "You have been experiencing—throughout your life—times you felt you had already experienced, or displacements of reality; seeing your old friend who is dead for example, meeting your adult-self when you were a boy, and more recently, meeting yourself as a boy again. These experiences are what we call 'Time-folds'. Time-folds are manifestations of altered time. These phenomena are created, in essence, from controlling and altering existence.

You have been an instrumental pawn in a game you had no choice in playing, with an outcome that had already been decided. You were made to feel you were in control, that your actions were chosen by you, and your thoughts were created by you. That was an illusion. You think you were stuck in a mouse-wheel Josh? You were!"

Although what Stephen was saying was wildly incredible, to Josh, it sounded that for the first time something made sense. He always felt his life wasn't truly under his control but wasn't more aware of that until now. But not being a fool, he kept his cards close to his chest; giving away no sign as to whether or not he believed their story. In truth though, he did.

"You said the Time-fold is created; who created it? And how?" questioned Josh. He was becoming more sentient as the drug effects wore off.

"Well, that's the million-dollar question Josh. We don't know exactly 'who', although we do know some key figures that have been trying to stop us. One of those key figures has been you. Every time Josh, you were the final impediment that would halt our progress. We tried everything to change your futures. We could adjust the sequence of events with some slight variations, but the outcome always ended up the same: until now. In some way, I am yet to fully understand, you broke the wheel. You changed your future."

Josh had been listening intensely to Stephen's story and needed time to think. He needed to adjust his reality from what he always "knew" to be true, to something he still couldn't fathom. Living in a world where people are told what to believe and what is true, all other realities become extinct, unbelievable, or laughed at as being ridiculous. Josh had done his fair share of ridiculing others about their abstract ideas—although not impossible ideas—that they dared to mention. Now the shoe was on the other foot. Who would believe him at HQ?

"So, what does this mean for me now?" Josh asked Stephen.

"Well, that's another big question. What do you want?" Stephen pushed the question back to Josh, in order to see where he now stood concerning View Corp.

Josh turned his attention back to Sofia, who had been standing quietly, listening to all that was being said. He never got his question answered about whether she knew who had killed Mac, and he wasn't about to let that go so easily—he wanted payback.

"So, do you know who killed Mac?"

He began analysing her response to the question. He knew body language could often tell a different story to what was actually being said. Josh was only interested in destructive lies and couldn't care less about the little white ones. Lying was an art he had mastered—mastered not only in being the deceiver but also in detecting deception. He was nervous she would fail his test; only because he still had feelings for her, in spite of everything that had happened. Josh watched her closely.

"The bug in your flat was put there by us Josh, simply to monitor you. But we didn't kill Mac. We believe it was whoever has been trying to stop us, but that's as far as we know. I removed the bug that night we..." and Sofia stopped mid-sentence.

Josh remembered that night very well, to him it was special, although now he couldn't help but believe it was just a set-up he had been conned into. He felt like a dupe—a fool, and he wasn't going to make the same mistake twice with her. He had since been trained to watch out for "honey trap" agents, as they were the most dangerous of all for government spies. He knew these types of agents—male and female—trained to use sex and emotion to entrap or get close to key figures; not only in government, but also within the intelligence communities of which Josh was a part.

As much as he wanted not to believe her answer, Josh knew she was telling the truth, and this made things more difficult. It would have been much easier to hate her than to love her. Still, Josh was not entirely sure as to her motives and that of Stephen Montague's; even more so, View Corp as a whole. There was still much that needed answering, and Josh was determined to find out—no matter how.

CHAPTER 21

JOSH HAD BEEN LEFT alone in the room to fully recover. "What now?" he thought, "Where do I go from here?"

Feeling motionless at a crossroads, unclear with no sign to follow, Josh felt stuck—even more so than before. At least before he had a direction, some purpose—albeit not his own, nonetheless a purpose. And although he had felt a huge release of restraining force, once he decided not to follow his pre-determined path, he was feeling lost. He didn't know what direction to follow or who to really trust. So, the result of his newfound freedom bore newfound difficulties.

Sitting on the edge of the bed he contemplated on what was next. He still had unanswered questions but did he care enough to discover the whole truth. He thought he could simply stick his head in the dirt and continue his new life; choose the easy option. But that wasn't the easy option—not for Josh.

The more he thought about the whole of his existence, the fact he had been pulled along like a puppet, began to boil his blood. Anger started to build in his bones, in his whole body, in his head. He stood up and began forcefully pacing back and forth, continually thinking about how he had been used and manipulated. He paced and paced, working himself up into an explosive menace. Everything he looked at suddenly became the enemy, and he wanted to destroy the enemy. Josh grabbed a cupboard, picked it up and smashed it into the wall. He grabbed every article, every object he could get his hands on and decimated it. And when he had no more objects, he began to punch the walls and door. Josh had felt anger many times before but this was pure rage. This was murderous rage he struggled to control.

With all the noise—crashing and banging, suddenly the door flew open with two brawny men racing in at speed, with the purpose of subduing him. One grabbed Josh by the arm—a big mistake. He countered the man's grip; twisting his arm so hard and with so much force it popped out of its shoulder socket. The man screamed out loudly as he sunk down and curled up in a ball on the floor; writhing in agony. Josh turned to the second target; nothing was stopping him now; he was a killing machine gone wrong. The second man, not feeling so tough on his own, was hesitant. Josh wasn't waiting, he was severely pissed. He lunged for the guy; he still had to purge his rage, and there was only one person left he could release it on.

"STOP! JOSH STOP IT!"

Sofia had quickly appeared in the room, springing in between Josh and the second man, holding her hands up to prevent him from causing more harm. She was an immediate salve to his rage, appearing to suddenly calm him down.

With his violent emotion subsiding fast, Josh looked around at the damage he had caused. The destruction was tantamount to a tornado in a jam jar. As he looked at the mess, he began to recognise something in himself that he had never felt before—when taking out a target—he felt guilt. He was able to discern right and wrong more accurately than before. He knew he was in the wrong; wrong for smashing up the room, and certainly wrong for pulling the man's arm out of its socket.

Josh's former actions were automatic—like a robot—taking away any and all responsibility for what he did. That was no longer the case. The automaticity of his actions had been lifted—lifted during his monumental episode in the corridor with the boy. The moment he decided to go against the hidden influence, he regained something of himself. The disconnected feeling he always felt when taking action—acting without a sense of responsibility—had gone.

"I'm sorry," he said. And for the first time that he could remember, he truly meant it. He was a government operative with a conscience, something no government intelligence agency would tolerate.

Josh looked at the man on the floor and knew from medical training how to fix what he had done. He walked over to him and placed a reassuring hand on the man's shoulder. "This will hurt," he said. And without saying anymore, or giving the man chance to think about what was going to happen, Josh felt the dislodgement, positioned himself, and with immediate force popped the arm back into its joint.

"You fucker!" yelled the man, his face screwed up from the intense pain.

"I know," replied Josh, with a sense of gratification he had righted his wrong.

Sofia walked up to Josh. "What happened?" She had a worried look on her face.

"Just finding my direction again," said Josh calmly. He felt better and immensely relieved.

Both men helped each other out of the room, leaving Sofia and Josh alone. It was their first real moment alone together since meeting up again. And it was awkward.

"Let me look at your hand." Sofia broke the ice; taking hold of Josh's bloodied hand he had used as a wrecking ball on the room. "You certainly made a mess here."

She walked him over to the sink, turned on the tap and held his hand under the running water. He could feel a slight sting through the numbness that permeated it, but was too distracted by Sofia to care. She washed the blood away and dried his hand with a hanging towel. She reached into a cupboard that was now half hanging off the wall – thanks to Josh – and pulled out a bandage. As she began wrapping it around his hand, she gazed at him and smiled.

"What is it?" he asked.

"I always seem to be patching you up. That time back at my old place when..." and she stopped herself again, mid-sentence. It was as though a truth of how she felt had started to emerge but was immediately shut out upon seeing it.

Josh remembered the incident with the intruder in his flat, getting knocked down and Sofia patching up his head. It was a moment he couldn't forget, not because of the injury, but because of her.

"Do you want to get out of here?" she asked.

"Yeah, I do."

She finished wrapping his hand and led him out of the room. "I need my things back." Josh was referring to his equipment that had been confiscated. "There'll be too many questions to answer back at HQ if I lose my things, if you know what I mean."

"I do," she replied, and led him into an adjacent room.

Laid out on a table was his jacket, weapons, and equipment. He walked over to the table and picked up his submachine gun, checked it over and made it safe – removing the round from the chamber – then placed it back on the table. He did likewise with his 9mil pistol then slotted it into the holster on his tactical vest. He put on the vest along with his jacket, picked up his submachine gun and quickly concealed it underneath. He felt he had to conceal what he was, what he was capable of, in front of Sofia. In her presence, he felt out of place carrying the tools of his trade. And he could see in her face the disappointment of what he represented.

Josh reached for the last piece of his equipment—Flash's device, and put it in his pocket.

"I want to know more. I want to know more about this place, what you're doing and View Corp."

"Okay," Sofia agreed without hesitation, "come with me."

Josh felt more comfortable now that he had his gear back, but knew he wouldn't need it. He followed Sofia out of the room, along another corridor he didn't recognise. He purposely memorised the location and direction to orient himself—what he had been trained to do; always get your bearings he was taught. He had been drilled hard by Frankie back in his training days, and taught that even in hostile unfamiliar ground—in order to survive—he should know the enemy's territory better than his enemy does. And as far as he was concerned, this was still enemy territory, until he decided otherwise.

Sofia led Josh back to familiar ground, the place nearby where he had discovered the file, and where he last saw the boy—his younger self. She took him to the room that he had seen as a boy himself, with the "stranger"—his older self: the room with the nuclear device that his older self had "destroyed". Josh was starting to get confused again, trying to resolve and reconcile the fact that he was all of those people; the boy and the stranger in the past, as well as the boy and himself—that stranger, now in the present. He was seeing everything, not only from a physical viewpoint of the present, but also from a multi-time-dimensional viewpoint.

Montague and Balantyne were standing by the device. Josh noticed them both appearing frustrated. As soon as Montague sensed Josh and Sofia approaching, he immediately removed the look of frustration and put on a more socially acceptable appearance.

"Josh, come in," welcomed Montague.

Josh wasn't fooled by his sudden facial change and pleasant attitude. He knew something was wrong and wanted to feel them out. Balantyne was less clever at hiding his feelings and pushed past Josh and Sofia, leaving the room with a face that looked troubled.

"So, what is this?" questioned Josh, looking at the device. "I know it has radioactive properties but it's not a nuclear weapon, is it?"

"Yes, you're right. I told you about the 'Time-folds'. This device is a Radio Frequency Adjuster, designed to disrupt the time overlap. We—Miles and I—have been working on a way to... er, straighten out time, is a simple way of putting it."

"Hang on, let's step back a bit." Josh had so many questions he didn't know which one to ask first, and Stephen could see he wanted to know everything.

"Well Josh, I don't want be rude but I have a lot of work to do. And as you are aware now, time is not our friend. So, I must ask Sofia to assist you with anything you want to know, so I can continue."

Montague nodded to Sofia for immediate compliance, then turned his back on them to focus on the device. But Sofia knew Josh; she knew he wouldn't accept the brush-off, and she was right.

"I see. Or perhaps I could just finish off my predecessor's work?" threatened Josh.

He was not going to be pushed away without an adequate explanation, making the threat thoroughly clear by revealing the arsenal tucked inside his jacket. Believing them or not, he was still a government operative. And besides, he wanted to be sure he was doing the right thing, by allowing them and their work to continue.

Stephen turned back around; his vision drawn to the weapon display Josh was showing off. "Ah—I think I understand." Sofia said nothing, but Stephen took the hint and continued to explain.

"Well, in truth Josh, we have never gotten as far as this. You were always the one to stop us. In order for us to continue, we had to somehow straighten out the wrinkle, the time overlap you were caught up in. We had to somehow stop you from stopping us. We tried on so many occasions but we failed.

The problem we face, is that the device produces an extremely high but detectable frequency, one we haven't been able to cloak. Every time we use it, we compromise our location. This is how we believe we get discovered. And then you arrive to... well, you know, you know what you do."

"But how do you survive? I — my predecessor killed you," said Josh, confusedly.

"Well not exactly," revealed Stephen, "you kill — facsimiles, copies, or time wrap-overs, as we call them. It all seems so real to you, but is more like being in a very realistic virtual game. The game can be played over and over. In effect, you — or rather your predecessors — have been killing energy created forms that are not real."

"So, right this moment, this is real?" questioned Josh, looking around the room.

"Well, what is real Josh? What is reality? Is it only something we can see or touch? Is it only something we can hear or smell? Is there something more than this? How do we know? You decide that for yourself," Stephen continued.

"Your experiences: those as a boy growing up, at school, your military training, you here with me now; those are real. The moments you experienced with your older and younger self were so-called: 'Time-folds'. They were merged realities; an interchange or co-existence of past and present. I know it flies in the face of what we're taught, but nonetheless, there it is."

Wrapping his head around the professor's explanations, Josh was finally starting to see the whole picture. Incredible as it was, it made perfect sense. "So, is there another me, existing right this moment, but in a different time?"

"In theory yes, though not only one, but thousands of you, split-seconds apart but existing in different dimensions; trapped in a kind of time prison, always following on, doing the same thing, one to another."

"You say 'prison'. Why?" asked Josh.

"Ah, I see the penny is beginning to drop. Well, we are not as free as we like to think we are. Some more than others perhaps, but we are in a prison; a prison that was created for us—one we have forgotten, or are unwilling to see.

Think of your life as a recording, a recording that can be paused, started, stopped, and even rewound to particular events or times in the past. Never fast-forwarded though, as fast-forwarding gives one their future: that is the key to undoing the trap. Give someone their future and you give them hope. Hope brings about self-determinism and realisation of the trap, or the 'prison' they're in. Once someone becomes fully self-determined, they become aware of the trap and are able to break free; just as we did, and just as you did Josh."

Stephen could see Josh was still somewhat confused. "Let me draw a diagram that I think will help you to better understand." He took a piece of paper from the side and drew a circle upon it. "This circle I have drawn is your life's path; well not just yours but everyone's. It's a life that goes around in circles—trapped, in a 'prison' of sorts. Now, this join where the two lines meet, well, they're not accurately joined, are they? That join is the wrinkle in the life—a 'Time-fold'. The Time-fold is when two time-dimensions overlap with each other, causing 'Cross-overs' or 'Facsimiles', such as your doubles—both young and old. What is caused by these folds, is a false reality. Once an individual's life path is straightened out, the altered reality vanishes along with everything in it. Such as the boy you were with; your younger self."

Josh suddenly remembered his wound—getting shot in the warehouse. He hadn't noticed it before now, but realised he couldn't feel it any longer. He pulled his jacket down from over his right shoulder to see what should be a bandaged wound: it was gone. His arm was just as it was before the shoot-out.

"These joins in time," Stephen continued, "these 'Time-folds', can be detected in various ways: seeing a duplicate of oneself or another, a strong sense or feeling like déjà vu, even a blurred wavy line or wrinkle in the air. There could be others but these are the most common.

Our purpose is to break the circle Josh, and straighten out the line. That's the function of this device—the Radio Frequency Adjuster. Now that we have appeared to have handled the continuous thorn in our side—you, we can advance our work."

Josh was beginning to fully understand. He remembered all through his youth, and even through his military career, the feeling of being controlled in a way he couldn't understand. He felt his life wasn't under his control, in fact, it felt that his life wasn't his. It was that moment, shortly before he was about to terminate Montague and Balantyne in the corridor—which was spurred on by the note left for him in the file cabinet—that he glimpsed he could change his future, and subsequently release his own trap.

That short conversation with Stephen held more truth than the whole of Josh's schooling: pushing aside the narrow-minded lessons that were passed off as truth.

Josh had two final questions to ask Stephen. "So, who is trying to stop you, and why?"

"'Who', is the ultimate question Josh. We're all under the control of a secret organisation; an organisation deeply inter-woven into every aspect of government, and key organisations, not only here, but worldwide. Our organisation—View Corp—has many members, but our influence and power is nothing compared to who we're up against. They have the power to keep populations down and ignorant, and we have been stopped many times. Through the manipulation of time and events, they control the game. And we have lost many friends.

So, who are 'they', you ask? Ask yourself Josh; you work for the government. It's unfortunate, but we only know the identities of a few of their disciples. One of whom you already know—your superior: Michael Harris."

CHAPTER 22

Josh and Sofia left Stephen to continue his work. Josh's life-long puzzle was finally beginning to look whole, but it still had some important pieces to be placed.

"What now Josh?" asked Sofia softly as they walked along the corridor.

He was still looking for gaps in their story and testing for weaknesses. He wanted all the details; he wanted to know the minute details that were gluing the storyline together. This he knew was where he would find the mistakes, the discrepancies, the lies.

"I was assigned to watch an electrical shop. My superior—Harris—led me to believe it was linked in some way to a terrorist organisation, but I knew he was lying and thought he was just testing me. The electrical shop was on Vine Street. There was an old man—the proprietor, who was killed. What's his connection?"

Josh was analysing Sofia for reactions, for attempts to delay in answering for lack of a truthful answer. She was stalling. She was silent for a moment, but not for trying to hide the truth or to come up with a plausible sounding story. Josh could see a reaction in her that was unexpected. Sofia's eyes started to tear up; a tear rolled down her cheek.

"That man was my father," she sadly revealed.

"I'm sorry," said Josh.

His authoritative tone dropped away and he genuinely became sympathetic. His guard was melting again. She had this way with him that disarmed him easily and it was beginning to become a problem. Josh was trained, moulded, programmed not to feel, or be weakened by emotion. Before, he wouldn't have cared; he would have only feigned sympathy if needing to get information from someone. He was trained to use emotion to get what he needed, that was all; his was a fake emotion. Now though, he truly felt for Sofia.

"I believe you owe me a coffee." Josh purposely changed the subject onto something much lighter. He wanted to pull her up, not see her sinking down.

"Through here," she replied sorrowfully, and they walked into another small room resembling an office canteen.

Josh reached for two mugs on a cupboard top and poured some ready-brewed coffee from a percolator. He still remembered how she liked her coffee from the first time he made her dinner back at his old flat. Those memories were precious to him, although he wouldn't admit it. He made her coffee and placed it next to her on the table she was sitting at. He took a seat opposite her. She seemed to relax a little and Josh couldn't help but simply look at her. Not saying anything, they sipped their coffee in silence.

As much as Josh was truly enjoying those few moments, he knew reality was to be faced. He needed to break the silence and get more answers, even if that meant upsetting Sofia.

"Sofia, how was your father involved?" he asked, but softly this time.

She half looked up, still holding her cup. "He supplied us with materials for the Radio Frequency Adjuster. I was reluctant to use him at first but he had the perfect cover. He could get hard-to-find and in some cases semi-restricted materials. Nobody would pay too much attention if an electrical store was ordering specialised components, and if they did, he had the perfect excuse."

Josh waited to see if she would reveal the moment when he saw her with the team of bodyguards.

"That was the last time I saw him," she said.

"What happened that day?" continued Josh.

"I went to see him for a component he was storing for us. As I returned to the car park we were attacked. I ran as fast as I could as my security detail was attacked. They were all killed. I never saw who it was."

Josh remembered the whole scene at the multi-storey car park, from hearing the first shot fired to making his own prompt getaway to avoid the local police.

"How did you get away?" Josh was looking for the specifics. He knew the shooter was Hoffman; the same man that had killed her father.

"I ran down the back stairs to the phone box on Carpenter Avenue. I was picked up by the two men you just attacked in the medical room and came back here."

So far, Josh was content with her story; it appeared to fit with what he already knew. He was also happy that Sofia appeared to be, in his eyes, on the right side; although what side exactly he was on wasn't clear to him yet. All he knew, was that the straightening out of his "Time-fold" anomaly, gave him a newly found sense of justice and ability to reason. He was no longer a gun-for-hire for the government. But he was also no mug; one to be manipulated by an underground organisation he was still suspicious of. He could now make up his own mind: make his own choices as to what side of the game he wanted to play.

"Did you hurt my father?" Sofia snapped.

She looked straight at Josh for the first time, since the upset of revealing the old man to be her father. Like Josh, she was also looking for an honest answer. And luckily for him, he was able to give her one; he didn't have to lie.

"No. The man who killed your father, was the same man who attacked your security detail that same day. And if it's of any consolation—he's dead."

"It still won't bring my father back," she said sadly. "How did this man die?"

Looking directly into her eyes, he gave her a frank reply: "I killed him."

Somehow that answer made them both happy. Somehow that answer brought them closer together. Josh wasn't looking for brownie points with Sofia, but he knew that that answer stacked up in his favour. Although she wasn't smiling with her mouth and lips, she was smiling with her eyes. A wave of emotional energy bounced back and forth between them as they looked at each other. Sofia blushed and looked down. She was always so self-assured but that moment weakened her.

Josh interrupted their moment. "What I don't understand is why your father, I don't know of another way of putting it, but didn't come back to life? Surely from what Montague said about the 'Time-folds', and creating these so-called 'Facsimiles', your father should have been, how shall I say, restored?"

"Stephen and Miles don't have all the answers. Stephen calls these unknown variables a 'glitch'—his answer for not knowing something. My father lost his life in his belief we could change the future; to free Man. It comforts me a little to think, that with you, we did just that, and his death wasn't a waste." Sofia smiled.

"We should go," she said, and about to stand up from the table, she paused. "Why did that man kill my father?"

Josh answered, but with one final test of her truthfulness. "He was looking for something. The shop was turned upside down. Any idea what it could have been?"

"Um—no; no, I don't," she hesitated.

"Okay," said Josh.

She failed the test. Not letting on, Josh was disappointed. He picked up on the lie as if it were painted across her face. During his subtle interrogation, Josh had been analysing Sofia's physical mannerisms when she told the truth. And he knew she was telling the truth prior to that final test, because he had asked questions he already knew most of the answers to. So, knowing what her behaviour and physical mannerisms were, while telling the truth, gave him a base-line to compare her other answers to. Asking her, if she had any idea what Hoffman was looking for, produced different reactions from when she told the truth. Josh knew she was purposely lying but didn't know why. He couldn't be certain, but suspected it was whatever was inside the locked box he found hidden in the electrical shop: the locked box that was taken from him in the parking lot, after being hit over the head from behind.

Sofia and Josh stood up together and walked out of the canteen. The two men Josh had trouble with earlier were standing out in the corridor, functioning as Sofia's chaperones. They were both your typical meathead bodyguard types—bulky and solid looking. Josh silently noted their stern unpleasant looks, particularly from the one who had had his arm dislocated. He knew they had an axe to grind with him, and any chance to get their own back would be pleasantly welcomed by them. Josh didn't need more enemies.

"How's your arm?" Josh asked, looking at the one who had had his arm popped out of joint. He knew genuine concern and sincerity would help to reduce their discord with him.

"No problem," replied the bodyguard.

Josh knew he was lying and trying to look tough. He could see through the thin hard-man veneer, but didn't want to cause him to lose face again; even though he needed additional training. Instead, Josh praised him, telling him he had a tough arm. And although the bodyguard didn't say anything, he appeared to simmer down; regaining his self-confidence.

It was surprising how one could improve a relationship, just by recognising and mentioning the qualities in someone. Josh didn't need any military training to realise that; he learnt it from a rough upbringing where "praise" and "encouragement" were considered "words of the weak". He knew that was bullshit, as he had observed first-hand that praise and encouragement of one's good qualities made a person want to do better, especially when encouraging soldiers. Praise and encouragement in the right direction made his platoon one of the best; it made them a strong cohesive machine.

Josh was satisfied that the bodyguards, although he wasn't their best buddy, wouldn't be an immediate threat to him anymore. An unspoken truce had been established. One thing Josh had learnt in his training, was to build more allies than enemies. There are genuine enemies out there, but there was no need to make enemies out of good people who could be a friend, especially when needed. There was a possibility he would need these two in the future.

"What's your plan now Josh?" Sofia asked as they walked on; bodyguards following a few steps behind.

"There's still too many unanswered questions; questions about View Corp, what you're trying to achieve and why."

"That's easy to answer," replied Sofia. "We're trying to stop a hidden organisation that has absolute domination over people, people that don't know it. We are trying to wake people up, to see how they are being manipulated every day without them knowing. We are trying to make this world a better place, where people are truly free and work together. That's what we're trying to do Josh."

Sofia's certainty and strength of character had bounced back.

"You don't have to believe me, or doctors Montague and Balantyne. All you have to do is look for yourself, and believe what you see. No alterations, no bias, no prejudice, just see what you see. You experienced what happened to you—the 'Time-folds', your life overlapping, meeting the different facsimiles of yourself, the sudden release you experienced in the corridor. Your choice now Josh, is to believe, or not believe."

He did have a choice. Josh was moved by Sofia's words but still he was suspicious, suspicion caused by the earlier lie. He could see altered truths or truths that were being held back. He wasn't blinded by his feelings for Sofia and knew she wasn't being frank with him, so he had to keep his cards pressed hard to his chest. He had to continue playing the game with her; from the standpoint of being enemies.

"I understand you—View Corp, are trying to undo this 'prison' caused by enemies unknown; and let's say for a moment I believe all this. What's it all for? Do you think people will be better off? Do you think people will change?" He began raising his voice; getting angry.

Josh was purposefully building up the anger in his tone. He was starting to play a hand that would hopefully bluff Sofia into revealing hers. He knew anger could play a big part in getting someone to blurt out truths; truths that they knowingly or unknowingly have suppressed. He knew that by attacking someone's beliefs would usually put them on the defensive—causing them to want to attack back. This was the usual reaction. By getting someone emotionally worked up enough could produce a desired result; one that would get them to accidentally reveal more than they would really want to.

Josh grew his anger further. "Can't you see you're wasting your time? People want to stay ignorant; they choose to stay ignorant! All they wanna do is make money, drive their shiny car, live in their crappy house, and let T.V. brainwash them. That's their fucking reality! Give them a little freedom from their 'prison', so they can drink themselves stupid, and they'll be happy enough. They don't want to face truth; most people can't handle truth! Talk to them about your Time-folds, other dimensions, and secret organisations, and at best you will be laughed at, and at worst, spend the rest of your days drugged up in a psych hospital! Your father's death was a wasted life! Wasted on people who wouldn't give a shit!"

It didn't work.

Surprisingly, Sofia remained calm. She didn't fall for Josh's trick and didn't reveal her hand. She was either playing the game more skilfully than him, or was simply unlike a "normal" person. She just looked at Josh with that smile in her eyes again.

"These men will show you the way out," said Sofia, unaffected by Josh's rant, and nodded to the two bodyguards to take over.

Stepping closer, the bodyguards gestured to Josh, showing him the direction of the exit. Accepting that this was the end of his stay, he knew he had other avenues to explore.

"Sure," replied Josh, then turned his back on Sofia.

Following the bodyguards' direction, Josh walked to a set of stairs at the other side of the underground complex. It was larger than he had first thought, with doorways leading to other doorways. Ascending the stairs to the top, the leading bodyguard unlocked and opened the steel door, allowing Josh to leave.

At that moment, Josh remembered when the stranger—his former older self—was killed whilst exiting the bunker complex, so paused just inside the doorway. He uncovered his submachine gun from under his jacket, sharply pulled on the cocking lever—pushing a round in the chamber—and placed the butt in his shoulder ready for firing. He changed persona; flicking back into the dangerous government operative he was trained to be.

Josh looked at the bodyguards who said nothing. He was looking for signs they knew of an impending ambush, but they appeared ignorant to any such trap. Josh turned his attention outside, raising his weapon to look through the telescopic sight. He began scanning the fields and trees outside the bunker, starting with the foreground then moving backwards into the distance. He checked for likely firing positions of hidden hostile forces and scanned for sniper hides. It appeared he had a clear path.

Looking at the bodyguards again, Josh gave them a quick nod of farewell before racing from the complex doorway. He zig-zagged left and right for the first twenty metres or so—to make himself a difficult target to shoot, in case he hadn't identified an enemy firing point. He was safe.

He continued running straight, in the direction of his SQRV, reaching the dirt track he was familiar with that led back to the underground bunker complex. Walking down the track, he could see his car, positioned as he had left it. Stopping short and as a precautionary measure, he scanned the area around the vehicle for hidden threats—looking underneath for attached devices. He was satisfied it was safe.

He walked up to the car and opened the boot, removed his rifle and equipment; placing them inside. While closing the boot, he couldn't help but think about the time when he was the boy, with his older self—the facsimile. Or was he the facsimile of the other? Either way, to Josh, it was strange to think that the boy he was with was no longer alive: in his time. It was even stranger, but a relief to him, to think that where he was now standing, his former self had never made it—but was killed. It was all still difficult to fully reconcile.

Josh had to now decide on what benefit it would be to investigate further, or why he should even stick his neck out to get involved in something that was beyond him. He wasn't a hero. He didn't really care much about others. So why should he bother? He just wanted an exciting life away from the ordinary rut of life. That was all he ever wanted.

Sitting in his car, Josh tossed the thoughts around in his head; thoughts of all the happenings he had had since meeting up with himself—the so-called 'stranger'—those many years ago as a boy. He couldn't figure out why him. Why was it him, and were there others like him? Questions begetting questions was all he could come up with.

"Why should I be concerned? What has this got to do with me now? I'm okay." he thought selfishly.

These troubling thoughts were going over and over in his mind. But something was wrong, something was gnawing at him, gnawing at his conscience. He now knew, and knowing what he knew bore the responsibility of taking action. His conscience wouldn't let him get away with doing nothing. HE—wouldn't let himself get away with doing nothing. It was a conscious decision—a dangerous path he was now putting himself on—one of finding out the ultimate truth, one of taking decisive action: whatever it takes!

Grab Book Two

I hope you enjoyed **THE FUTURE IS SET** as much as I enjoyed writing it. The second book—**GEMINOS**—in the Josh Brannon series continues the plot, and so I hope you will continue with me. There are more thrilling twists and deadly turns; revealing deeper hidden truths.

Get Book Two ~ GEMINOS

Find out more at: www.nigelbillington.com

About the Author

I'm a self-published British author who grew up in the county of Dorset, in the South of England. If you want to know more about me or my books, please visit my website **www.nigelbillington.com**

If you enjoyed this book, you can help me out by leaving an honest review...

As a self-published author, reviews are an essential way of getting more attention for my books. Honest reviews of my books help to support the continuation of my writing. So, if you enjoyed this book, I would be deeply grateful if you could take a few moments of your time to leave a review, wherever you obtained this book. It can be short and sweet, or as long as you want.

Thank you so much!

Join My Readers Club

Join The Others in My Readers Club

When you join my Readers Club you'll be first to get the LATEST on what I'm up to, my SPECIAL book promotions, and news of my future NEW book releases. PLUS, you will get my EXCLUSIVE novellas and short stories for FREE. I look forward to hearing from you!

Join my Readers Club here: www.nigelbillington.com